A DEAD GIVEAWAY

A DEAD GIVEAWAY

Clare Curzon
Gillian Linscott
Peter Lovesey
Dorothy Simpson
Margaret Yorke

WARNER FUTURA

A *Warner Futura* Book

First published in Great Britain in 1995
by Warner Futura

Collection copyright © Little, Brown and Company 1995

The stories are copyright respectively:
What's in a Name? © Clare Curzon 1995
In at the Death © Gillian Linscott 1995
Wayzgoose © Peter Lovesey 1995
Just Deserts © Dorothy Simpson 1995
A Taste of Freedom © Margaret Yorke 1995

The moral rights of the authors have been asserted.

A CIP catalogue record for this book
is available from the British Library.

ISBN 0 7515 1339 3

Photoset in North Wales by
Derek Doyle & Associates, Mold, Clwyd.
Printed and bound in Great Britain by
Clays Ltd, St. Ives plc

Warner Futura
A Division of
Little, Brown and Company (UK)
Brettenham House
Lancaster Place
London WC2E 7EN

Contents

What's in a Name?

Clare Curzon

What's in a Name?

WDC Rosemary Zyczynski settled with her Joanna Trollope paperback on a dumpy wall edging the mass of tangled weeds which was once a rockery. Already, at a little after eight, the morning sun was heating the stones through. Voluptuously she soaked up the warmth through her cotton shorts, and raised her face to the sky.

Perfect, with only the occasional fleecy puff of cloud. A scent of wallflowers wafted in from the real gardens on either side. Too often here there was only the sad, sour scent of cats or a whiff of other residents' exhausted frying fat.

She sat savouring the difference. It matched the glory of a free weekend after a fortnight of grinding inquiries which had driven the Thames Valley team into unaccustomed backbiting. And then when it seemed the case had gone irretrievably pear-shaped, the Boss had been inspired to send DI Mott off to Rotterdam where he hunted up and brought back an unshakeable eye-witness. So the supposed wild goose, which top brass had thought unchasable, was suddenly a regal eagle. Transformation scene, as in the Christmas pantos which Auntie had taken her to as a child: Fairy Queen's wave of magic wand; magnesium flash; and all was instant glittering sweetness. Except,

3

in the present instance, for oppressive paperwork to follow.

Not that Angus Mott was anything of a fairy queen, with his powerful water polo shoulders and his totally male outlook. Almost disastrously male until Zyczynski applied head to heart on that one barely bridled occasion, backing off mindful of team repercussions and of his too-long-absent fiancée Paula.

Her coffee finished, she pushed her paperback into shadow and stretched out along the wall, dozing until grit persistently biting through her tank top, plus the sawing conversation of muffled voices, recalled her to the present.

She sat up, her head coming level with the rear basement ceiling of Beattie's kitchen. The sash window was slightly raised and she looked down into a room flooded with morning sunshine.

Aware that the intrusive voices came from there, she leaned forward and made out a dumpy figure seated at the kitchen table. This was her landlady, her unruly mop of pepper and salt hair streaked with faded red, her fingers – splayed to grip the table edge – denoting tension. The words were indistinguishable but her voice rose in protest, wobbling with passion: Beattie, normally the most bubbling and friendly of women. The recipient of her protests remained concealed beyond the window's edge.

So who was baiting her? It couldn't do much good, Z considered. Unless the argument ceased soon she'd be knocking on the door to discharge the heat with some mundane request, then make sure Beattie had her heart pills handy.

Her sudden movement had made her visible. Beattie glanced up and the voices broke off. As Z rose to brush off the wall's fine grit, there came the clash of brass rings on curtain rod. The sunlit interior was blanked off.

Right, she could take such a pile-driven hint. Seated

again with her back to the house, she picked up her paperback and cut herself off. The drawn curtains absorbed the now lowered voices.

Almost an hour later the phone began ringing in the hall and continued unanswered. Eventually she gave in, raced indoors and snatched up the receiver. 'Zyczynski,' she panted, convinced it was a CID summons.

'Rosebud, you're out of condition,' a droll male voice accused.

'I was in the garden. Afraid you might give up before I got here.'

'You should know by now: I never give up. With which in mind, I thought perhaps a picnic – ?'

'Taking Granny's wicker hamper?'

'That's the only attraction? My own charm lags behind?'

She could see him, head cocked, the intelligent eyes – which could be intimidating – screwed up by his quirky smile, one forefinger pushing back the centre of his glasses as they slid down the bridge of his tip-tilted nose. Max Harris, columnist for the *Courier*, first known to her as the mysterious 'man in the fishing-hat', wanted for questioning in a labyrinthine murder case.* And one of the few who didn't believe that her soft exterior concealed a hardened steel automaton.

'The combined lure's overwhelming. What do I wear?'

'How typically a woman! Not too many buttons, please.'

'I meant—'

'Country garden, stately home stuff. I'll pick you up in half an hour.'

Max dropped her off after midnight. They had said

---

* See *Past Mischief* (1994).

goodnight thoroughly in the car. Diplomatically he never came indoors when there were no lights showing in the house. It was in total darkness then, although Beattie, a poor sleeper, often sat up to watch the late night movie on TV.

And no CID demand was waiting on the upstairs answerphone. So Sunday was blissfully free too. A pity Max was booked to go abroad. Z dumped in the bath the boxes of bedding plants which she'd brought back for the garden, went straight to bed and slept warmed through with the recollected events of the day.

At a little after ten next morning she went out to clear and dig over a small patch of soil for planting. Kneeling with her back to the house she again heard the brass rings clash as curtains were opened in the basement kitchen. She waved her trowel at the little woman peering out. A few minutes later there came the shuffling of Beattie's moccasins up the outer steps. She looked strained and rather confused, her nose questing like some small rodent on an indeterminate scent.

'Watcha doing, then?'

Z explained, indicating the boxes.

'Oh, nice. Anti-whatsits. Bunny faces we useda call them.'

'With alyssum and lobelia to go in front. We went to a Garden Party yesterday and they had bedding plants for sale.'

'That'll make a nice splash of colour I can see from me kitchen.' Despite the words she sounded anything but bright.

'Time I had something to cheer the place up. Let things go a bit, haven't I? That's what *she* said.'

The last was pronounced with such gloom that Rosemary smiled and asked, 'Who said?'

'Me sister. Long-lost sister. Not seen each other for over thirty years, wouldja believe?'

'You never told me you had a sister, Beattie.'

'Had two. One died way back. This one married money second time round. Got some very uppity ideas.'

'That doesn't mean you have to share them. Better be cosy than smart: you've said so yourself.'

'Got sloppy,' Beattie condemned herself. 'Let me standards slip. Mental laziness, she says. Well, I guess she's right. Can't see the point meself in chasing round fussing over details.'

Z laid down the trowel. 'Coffee time. Come indoors and I'll put some on. You're in the dumps.'

'A bit hungover's the truth. She came back last night with a Chinese takeaway and some bottles. I didn't really fancy the food.'

Poor old girl, and she'd been trying quite hard to master her craving for gin. 'What were you on?'

'Cape wines. She's into that sort of stuff, seeing that's where she's been living. I never knew they could hit yer head so.'

Z steered her back indoors and set her down at the table while she started up the percolator. 'Where's your sister staying?'

'In London. The Inn on the Park. Real snooty. Time was I'da liked that sort of thing meself. She just came slumming to see me. Now she's off touring. Back here in another three weeks. Checking up on me, most like.'

It wasn't just the hangover. This sister from South Africa had injured Beattie's self-esteem. Rosemary had never seen the dear old thing so depressed. Cheerful generosity and instant bubble were the essence of her admittedly bohemian lifestyle.

'Does it matter what your sister thinks, if you're comfortable in your own way?'

Beattie sighed. 'It's not what *she* thinks, but what *I* know,' she said with unaccustomed insight. 'I got to thinking about the past, the way we were, us girls all together. I bin looking out some snaps me old dad took. There's a studio portrait too, with us all three in.

Only black and white, because we never had colour in them days. I'll get 'em for you.'

They weren't far. She had stuffed them in a drawer of the Welsh dresser.

'Here we are. The Whizzo Weyman Girls, they called us. Beattie, Bertie and Bernie. Real names Beatrice, Roberta and Bernice. Bernie, the youngest, died just before Bertie went out to SA with her first hubby. Only twenty-nine, she was.'

She held out a glossy ten-by-eight. 'Pity it's not colour. Bertie and me we had the same red hair. Bernie's was different, nearer black, but she was the really pretty one.'

More than pretty; she'd been beautiful. The other two were less fine, rather jolly, cheerful girls in their early teens. Apparently since then Bertie had undergone some cultural engineering, gone upmarket, and wasn't beyond patronizing a sister she felt she'd outgrown.

She had threatened to return in three weeks, doubtless with a further dose of discouragement. Perhaps by then something could be done to repair Beattie's morale. Z pushed a cup of coffee along the table towards her, and considered rehabilitation.

'Not going out with your young man today, then?' Beattie cut across abruptly. 'You wanna take care of that chap. Don't go messing up yer chances like I done.'

'Did you, Beattie?' It seemed more useful to encourage the stream of reminiscence than to deny having any 'young man'.

'Didn't I just? Three times in all, got to the brink and then lost out. By then I'd sorta gone off the boil for marriage. Mighta risked another throw if a real Prince Charming had come along. But my frogs all seemda get worse once I'd kissed them.' She cackled gently.

'So you never married?'

'Nuh. Got engaged, though. Nineteen, I was.

Stanley, a lovely feller. Trouble was: once he set eyes on Bernie it was farewell-Annabel. Or retreatie-Beattie, I s'pose. Waited for her to hit eighteen and then they was off in a flash. Eloped. Never heard hide nor hair of them till he sent a note about her funeral, eleven years later. None of us went. Bertie was packing to go off to SA and I couldn't leave poor old Dad. He'd got Parkinson's by then. Had to give up me job as dresser at the Windmill to nurse him.'

Z smiled. 'The Windmill? Not much dressing done there, surely?'

'You wouldn't believe! Them aswstridge feather head-dresses was nearly as tall as the girls themselves. And all them spangles and the make-up! Gorgeous, they was. It was a luverly job. And wonderful people. Tommy Trinder, Maxie Miller. Useda meet them most days in the corridors, and sometimes we'd get invited to their parties. Best time of me life.'

But with one sister dead and the other living abroad, it had fallen to Beattie to take care of their ailing father. Which meant the 'best time of her life' was brought abruptly to a close.

'You were a good daughter,' Z said by way of comfort.

'I saw 'im out. Left me a nice little nest-egg as thankyou. I was thirty-three by then. That's when I took me beautician's course. I was good at it, had a natural talent. Spent seven years at Dickins and Jones as consultant for *Clovis de Paris*. Saved up and started on me own, taking a lotta clients with me. Rented a little salon off Wigmore Street. It was me posh days, you could say.'

She spread her hands, palm upwards. Her sad brown eyes said it all: And look at me now!

Z gave the old woman a hug. 'Don't allow your sister to get you down. You've probably had a far more interesting life than she has.'

'Still it's true what she said. I 'ave – *have* – let meself

go. I oughta make more effort. Gawd knows I can
afford it. And I know all the things I should be doing.'
She gently stroked her cheeks upwards with the tips of
her fingers. Despite her wrinkles the flesh was soft.
Her streaky hair was the real disaster.

'Your sister's coming back later, so surprise her. I bet
you could. Take a turn on the beautician's couch.'

'I still gotta better figure,' Beattie said with quiet
pride. 'A bit chubby maybe, but she's scrawny. D'you
know, you're right. I'll get meself done over. Only the
best. I'll treat meself to the whole works!'

Roberta Knol took a second turn round the shopping
precinct without finding anything she cared to waste
money on and made her way back to the Forte Crest
for afternoon tea. London had been more tolerable.
She regretted her impulse in driving north. Sitting in
the lounge here she could be anywhere in the world.
There was nothing specially Nottingham, nor especially English to be had. Even the local lace on sale was
factory-made. Was it the UK in general or some part of
herself that made the quest so disheartening? What
was the use of being so seriously rich when there was
nothing to buy and no one worth indulging any more?

Beattie had been her first big disappointment.
Perhaps she shouldn't have clung to the memory of
dynamic big sister full of zesty sparkle, bubbling with
fun stories about the showbiz people she moved
among. The present faded and jaded reality had
shocked her, spoke too frankly of mortality.

If only she'd kept in touch by writing, she would
have been better prepared. Some inkling of what time
could wreak must have filtered through. But,
unprepared, she had been stung to angry contempt for
her sister, that she should have crumpled under age's
onslaught, not bothering to fight back.

And her next visit, to this Midland city, had been a
total fiasco. The writer of those intriguing, witty letters

which had delighted her for almost two years now, had gone away two weeks back and no one had the new address. There again, she shouldn't have decided to spring a surprise, coming three months before she had said she would. But at least she'd discovered some new background, and it wasn't at all what she had been hoping for. The private investigator hired from Capetown hadn't turned up these details when he'd made the original trace.

And no one in this cold, uncaring country had welcomed her, either for herself or, as she was accustomed, for what they thought she could provide. It was galling: she'd do better to give up on nostalgia and take a holiday among strangers on the continent. She didn't know Europe, so it couldn't disappoint her. Yes, in a day or two she'd go back to London and see a travel agent about a coach tour down into Italy and Greece. And before leaving England she'd make sure her silly sister knew exactly what she'd missed.

Zyczynski saw only distant glimpses of Beattie over the next few days, because two cases erupted almost simultaneously. First a hostage situation, when a man with a shotgun held his common-law wife and their three children in a barricaded semi in Lower Earley. Then Dorothy Brazil, owner of a gaming club in Reading, reported a male staff member missing after irregularities at one of the roulette tables.

Superintendent Yeadings, senior Intelligence Support officer of the CID team known as the Four Jacks, elected to call in person on the formidable middle-aged lady. She was delighted.

'Mike Yeadings,' she welcomed him, leaning seductively in her office doorway. 'It's been long enough! Are you interested in my missing security man?'

She led him in, flicked a switch on her desk and murmured a few words into the mike. He observed she took care to switch off before they began their discussion.

'Combined with trouble at the tables, the disappearance suggests a whiff of intrigue,' he said, starting in at once. 'So I'd like to put one of my team in.'

'A sink of iniquity,' Dorothy said, sliding sinuously into an easy chair and waving her old acquaintance into another. 'A complete can of worms: that's what this place is. Thames Valley's a vast area, but policed so well that the villains are driven off the streets. And gaming clubs will always draw them. Doubtless your Plod would turn up God knows what hotch-potch of crime undreamt of by an innocent like me.'

Yeadings smiled at her ironic self-description. 'So we're agreed that much. I can't at present spare our manly Adonis, Inspector Mott, but DS Beaumont's available. You'll find him shrewd, with a rather special line in humour.'

'You're sure you'd find trouble here, aren't you? This is the very excuse you've been waiting for. As it happens, I've already appointed someone to the vacant post. A lounge lizard unexpectedly qualified in martial arts; to start later this week. But I could do with a trainee on the tables, if you have a bright female who's attractive.'

They fell silent while a waiter whisked in with a tray of coffee and liqueurs. Yeadings sniffed delicately at his glass as the man smoothly withdrew. 'Calvados? That brings back memories.'

'You see, I haven't forgotten your tastes. Nor all you did for my late lamented.' She raised her glass. 'To a good future.'

Yeadings sipped thoughtfully. 'There's WDC Zyczynski. I'd better write that out for you.'

'Don't trouble. We'll call her Gina. When can she start?'

*

So Z, in tight, sequinned mini-dress and her Cleopatra-style wig, went on loan that same night at Omphale's as trainee croupier from 10.00 p.m. until 2.00 a.m., to pick up the atmosphere and any significant gossip.

By 2.30 a.m. she was home to snatch some sleep. Then from 8.00 a.m., in track suit and trainers, she was on call in a radio van near the siege house, awaiting any decision by the gunman to release the woman and children.

On the morning of the fourth day his nerve broke. The police negotiator had patiently built up a relationship until the gunman seemed on the point of surrender. Then, without warning, a single shot was fired inside the house, followed by high-pitched screams.

In her flak-jacket, WDC Zyczynski burst from the waiting van and through the line of Tactical Support officers as two small children raced from the house followed by the woman stumbling out with a baby in her arms. Shepherding them, she had her hands full, while armed colleagues rushed the house and saw to the dying man.

From that point on she worked eight hours at a stretch – writing up her report after dealing with social services, Victim Support and the distracted little family – followed by the nightclub stint which no one had seen fit to cancel. Returning home at 2.25 a.m. she had barely the strength to get out of her car.

Yesterday's milk stood on the doorstep.

She lifted the pint bottle of semi-skimmed. It looked as though, newly mindful of body care, Beattie had settled to a diet. Her normal daily order had been full cream Channel Island. And now, disenchanted by the more Spartan taste, she'd not even bothered to take the low-fat stuff indoors!

The single refrigerator which the two women shared was in the scullery off the basement passage. Z went down quietly to put the bottle away and found its door compartment already full. In which case, this pint could be poured away, having stood all day unchilled.

The tin of ham she had put there two days back was at the front, reminding her she'd not eaten for some fourteen hours. She pulled it out and went into the kitchen for a can opener, crossing to where it was fixed to the wall. No need to turn on the light; enough came in from the clear sky outside. Her landlady hadn't bothered tonight to close the curtains.

It startled her, turning away with the opened can in one hand, to find Beattie seated there in the half-dark, at the table, and staring in her direction. 'Beattie, what's up?' she demanded.

The old woman said nothing, just sat unmoving.

'Beattie, you all right?' She went closer, fearfully reached for her hand, touched cold flesh on joints already stiffening. 'Oh God, no!'

Too late to do anything. She had seen enough bodies to know when life was past recall. But this was Beattie, warm, generous old Beattie, not a cadaver she'd been called to on duty.

It must have happened suddenly and she'd not had time to get her pills. Mercifully quick, but cruel all the same. Tired and hungry, the girl found her eyes brimming with tears.

Sudden death. You know what to do. Do it, she told herself. And touch nothing until the quack has certified death. No harm, though, in turning on the light.

Back at the door she switched on, and stood a second before turning round to face the truth. And found it obscene, incredible. The body was propped up like an effigy, crammed tight between chair-back and table edge, an arm to either side to balance it upright. The newly dyed hair had a quite different browny-black redness fitted over like a cap of coarse lace, veiling the once-homely features. And across the skull's crown and the brow three gaping crevasses, with terrible glimpses of crimson-jellied depths.

The first car to arrive discharged a pair of flat caps who were strangers to her, bringing a scent of greasy chips and sharp vinegar. They wanted to see the body but she refused them entry past the kitchen door, insisting on her CID rights. One stayed with her, seated on the third step up on the stairway that led to her floor, while the other reported back on the car radio.

She struggled to be rational but found herself repeatedly staring at her watch because she'd failed to register what it showed, so couldn't work out how long she'd been waiting for the scenes-of-crime team to assemble. And then DI Mott was suddenly there, filling the doorway, his Greek-god face taut under the crisp blond curls. He ordered the uniformed men out, smothering her briefly in a bear hug.

'God, girl, you've had a day of it!'

'Angus, it's Beattie.'

'Hang on, Z. I'll take a look. You needn't go back in.'

She leaned against the door jamb as he went through, hands in pockets, walking round by the walls until he came opposite the terrible face. She saw him look quickly away, turn and survey the rest of the room, then back at the body.

He came out stiff-featured. 'Sorry, Z, but it looks like number four.'

'The axe man.'

He hadn't struck for almost five months. They had begun to hope he'd given up or moved on. Meanwhile three earlier brutal murders remained unsolved.

'Same situation: pensioner living alone, similar wounds – three blows, no obvious signs of a break-in, no damage to the room. You'll need to check if anything's missing, but my guess is there's no robbery motive. We've got ourselves an obsessive killer.'

'But Beattie *didn't* live alone. There was me.'

Angus stared back. Z didn't need telling how feeble that protest was. She was always away on the job. There's never a policeman there when you want one.

2

In all the time that she had shared Beattie's house, Rosemary couldn't remember her using an axe. Nor had she ever come across one when rooting around for other tools. The heating was gas-fired, so there were no log baskets in the Victorian hearths, even for decorative purposes.

'Not even a meat cleaver,' she told Angus with distaste. 'Beattie's butcher trims and chines everything for her.'

'*Did*,' she corrected herself. It seemed impossible, Beattie not being any more. Such a cosily accepted part of Z's own life's framework.

She forced herself back into the police role: hard to achieve just then, but less painful than open grief. Means of access, associates, victim's daily routine, she reminded herself.

'Let's go upstairs,' Mott suggested. 'SOCO team's on its way. The man on the door can let them in.'

She led the way towards her own rooms on the top floor: a small bedroom above the entrance hall, a minute kitchen and a comfortable living-room with two long brocade-draped windows overlooking the street.

'Coffee?' Mott requested, giving her something to occupy her hands. She plugged in the machine, filled the water container, spooned ground beans generously into a fresh filter cone.

'There was some rigor,' she said, trying to beat down the horror of having touched the body. (Just a body, not an old friend brutally killed.)

'Warmish room,' Mott prompted gently.

Yes, grapple one's mind on to the problem, not the suffering. 'No very distinctive smell,' she said faintly.

'So rigor probably building, not leaving. Can we assume it happened last evening?'

'Must be.' She stared at the bone china cups and saucers. Normally it would have been pottery mugs for herself and anyone in the job. But Beattie had objected to that modern habit: it was one of the few standards she'd hung on to. And at this moment Z had unconsciously yielded to Beattie's prejudice.

'Whoever it was,' she said slowly, 'Beattie must have let him in. There are only three doorkeys: hers, mine and the spare kept with Mrs Carpenter next door. So it sounds like someone familiar to her. Someone she thought she'd no reason to fear.'

'Would Beattie have left her key in the door?'

'No; she's not forgetful. And never deliberately left the door unlocked, even for the doctor when she was in bed with bronchitis. Mrs Carpenter came in then as chaperon.'

'Lost her key and had another cut from the neighbour's?'

'I'm sure she would have mentioned it.' But admittedly Z hadn't been around lately for her to tell.

'So we'll check with Mrs Carpenter. How about entry from the rear?'

'The scullery door leads into a basement yard. It locks, with a bolt top and bottom. From there six steps go up to a narrow walled back garden. We're the middle house of five in the terrace, so there are two to each side. Six-foot solid brick walls. Scalable at a push, but I wouldn't come home that way myself.'

It was a feeble enough effort at humour but it won her a comradely thump on the shoulder.

'So let's start with a list of the people Beattie might let in. What family had she?'

Last week Z would have said none. But out of the blue this sister had reappeared. There'd been Beattie, Bernie who died young and – who was the third?

'Roberta,' Z remembered. 'She's the only remaining sister, here on holiday from South Africa. Touring somewhere, but I've no idea of her married surname nor of where she's likely to be. She'll have to be found and informed.'

'There'll probably be correspondence,' Mott said comfortably.

'I'll be surprised if there is.' And Z explained how Roberta had arrived unexpectedly after an absence of over thirty years.

'But I do know she's been staying in London at the Inn on the Park. They'll not have had many elderly women from South Africa in the past week or two, so we can probably get to her that way.'

'Good. Give me a description.'

'I never saw her. Overheard her once.' Or more properly she'd overheard Beattie protesting to her sister about something. 'I'm sorry, Angus; I can't help you there.'

'But Beattie would have spoken about her since?'

'I've barely seen Beattie either. Just the once to talk to, the Sunday morning after her sister's visit on the Saturday. She showed me some photographs. They're in a dresser drawer, but there's nothing recent. They all date from the forties and fifties.'

'I'll pick them up later. Did you get any impression at all of this sister from what Beattie told you?'

'That she'd married twice, the second time to money. I guess she's a widow, because there was no mention of the husband. Beattie considered her "uppity", and the poor old thing got a drubbing for not keeping up appearances.'

'Hostile, would you say?'

'Tactless is probably more like it. And overbearing.'

Mott drummed his fingers on the chair arm. 'M'm,

we can probably eliminate her. I'd take some persuading that Lizzie Borden treatment helps anyone "keep up appearances".'

'*Treatment*.' The word reminded Z: 'That's what Beattie had intended. She said she'd get herself "the whole works".' She shuddered at the more deadly meaning of the phrase.

Mott was waiting for an explanation.

'Her sister had needled her so much that she decided to do something drastic about her appearance. And I encouraged her. That's how she'll have spent this past week; with a round of the beauty salons. Maybe she met someone new when having a hairdo or facial, someone whom she took on trust, and unwisely brought back here.'

'You mean a *woman*? Who just happened to have an axe on her at the time?'

'You mentioned Lizzie Borden yourself. *She* was female. And Beattie could have invited someone back by appointment.'

'Possibly,' he granted. 'It's a line to follow. So where do we start looking?'

'She'd trained as a beautician herself once, so she'd go for the best. Let's look in *Yellow Pages*.'

Z had started listing salons when a shout from below announced the police surgeon arriving. 'I'll see to her,' Mott offered, from the window recognizing Sheila Hadfield's red racer drawn up at the kerb.

He hurried down. Less than five minutes later the SOCO team turned up and began donning their disposable white overalls. Z went down to join them and sat again at the foot of the stairs, watching through the open doorway.

A familiar scene, yet grotesquely alien because in place of the buzz of excitement at an opening inquiry there was the sick stupor of shock. Murder is different when it strikes close at home.

Without thinking she stood up and began to move

towards the rear of the basement, going for clean air. One of the white-clad civilians, a woman, called her back. 'We've not done the scullery yet. I'll tell you when we're ready.'

She sat again on a lower stair and put her head on her arms. 'OK,' she was told at last. 'The way's clear.'

In the garden the air was fresher, the sky starlit with a sickle moon, so that in the half-dark the annuals planted almost a week back glowed with a pale phosphorescence against the turned black earth.

The earlier heavy scent of wallflowers had given way to something more delicate: Albertine roses. Invisible from here, old Mr Blake's rambler next door had burst into flower since she was last in the garden.

She kept her back to the basement window and, slumped against the brick wall, dozed until startled awake by a hovering figure.

'Sorry, Z.' DS Beaumont hunkered beside her. 'Just picked up the call. Came as soon as I could. You OK?'

'Fine.'

He rolled his eyes comically, recognizing the lie as such. 'Daft question. Poor old doll. Who would ever have wanted to harm her?'

'No sane person.'

They both considered this. 'Unless,' Beaumont ventured, 'she walked in on an intruder.'

'What was she wearing?' Z asked. 'I saw her but I didn't see her, if you understand.'

'Day clothes. Quite a smart skirt and blouse. The matching jacket was folded over another chair. She'd had a hairdo and a half.'

'Yes. Dyed red, the colour it was naturally as a girl. She'd decided to smarten up.'

'For a man?'

'For a sister.' And again she explained about the unexpected visit of the previous Saturday.

'Poor old doll,' he said again. 'I'd better get back and see what Angus wants me to do.'

'I'm coming.' She had made up her mind. Being connected with the incident, she'd not be allowed into the main investigation, but there had to be some way in which she could help, information which only she could supply, facts which would need checking . . .

The duty police surgeon had left, the photographer was packing up and the experts were still going over the kitchen. Inspector Mott met them in the hall. 'We've got your dabs on record already, Z. Let's go back upstairs.'

In her sitting-room Beaumont removed the empty cups and started making tea. She left him to it.

'The back door,' Angus said, 'you told me it would be locked and bolted.'

'Always after dark.'

'And the kitchen curtains?'

'Closed every night. Beattie didn't have a set time to do it. Quite early if she'd started baking, but she'd spend most of her evenings watching TV in her sitting-room on the middle floor, and only go down last thing to make a hot drink. Which is when she'd pull the curtains. She always closed them as soon as she switched the light on. But last night they were left open, weren't they?'

'Which means either that she'd just come in from outdoors, and possibly the killer with her; or else she'd gone down for that final drink and caught an intruder there.'

'How could anyone have got in?' Z insisted.

'Maybe from the back garden. There was fine grit on the floor by the table. Could be soil. And the scullery door was locked but not bolted on the inside. Where was the key kept?'

'In the lock. Beattie insisted, because it's a solid wooden door and no one outside could see through. There's a spare key on a hook beside it.'

'That's the one we used to open the door. The one from the lock had been removed. Can't be found.'

Beaumont came and hung over a chair-back. 'So whether an intruder came in by the scullery or not, most likely he left that way, locking the door after him and pocketing the key?'

'Unless we're just meant to think that.'

Z started up. 'Beattie's front-door key! Have you looked in her handbag?'

'I wondered when you'd ask,' Mott said softly. 'That key's gone too. But the bag was there all right, containing bank cards, her bus pass and a purse with fifteen pounds and tenpence in it.'

Dawn wasn't far off when the experts sealed off the basement floor and left. DI Mott had gone half an hour earlier. Because she had refused to move out, Beaumont settled for finishing the night on Z's living-room settee. They were both due for the Boss's debriefing at 9.30 a.m.

When she knocked on the door marked Superintendent M. Yeadings CID, she felt red-eyed and crumpled, but had herself under control. She and Beaumont found DI Mott already there. The Boss didn't look up until he'd finished reading the papers on his desk, then he said drily, 'Business is getting brisk. Sit down, will you.'

The glance he gave the WDC took no longer than his acknowledging Beaumont's presence, but she wasn't fooled. He would treat her like any other officer until official discussion of the case was over, but he'd know how she felt.

'Right, Angus,' he invited, and Mott mapped out the possible lines of investigation. Local uniformed branch would be covering door-to-door inquiries in the neighbourhood and reporting through their Inspector. A mobile Incident Room was being set up at the end of the street. A recent snapshot of the dead woman – one Z had taken the previous summer on a river trip to see the Cutty Sark – was being photocopied and distributed. DS Beaumont was to trace and question the sister, with a first visit to the Inn on the Park. WDC Zyczynski was to make appointments with everyone supplying beauty treatment to the dead woman during the past week. (Good, Z approved; so he'd allotted her a part.)

'As a purely civilian client,' Yeadings amplified, 'however superfluous the treatment may be.'

'Sir,' she said modestly.

'Provided that she does nothing to alter herself too drastically?' Beaumont suggested.

They all looked at Z. 'Toning table, massage and facials,' she suggested. 'But what about the hair dye?'

'Fix it to have the same stylist who worked on the dead woman. And get her talking. What she does to you is your business.' There was an almost puckish expression on the Boss's face.

He knows damn well, she thought, that I can't grieve and be furious at the same time. Z was privately proud of her curly, home-shampooed crowning glory.

'Brighten it up a bit,' Beaumont said wickedly. 'Mouse is such a drab colour.'

Her hair was a warm brown. Enough red there to excuse any rise in temperature when someone deliberately needled her. She gave Beaumont a cool look which belied it.

Superintendent Yeadings cleared his throat, calling them to order. 'So what are the chances that this murder's another in the series?'

Angus enumerated the points discussed before. 'So unless the forensic experts come up with significant traces to the contrary, chances are rather more than fifty-fifty.'

'Five months interval since the last axe murder,' Yeadings mused. 'Could be a copy-cat killing. Too much detail on the other three cases was leaked by the national press. I think I'll join you at the post-mortem, Angus. Have we formal identification of the body yet?'

'No. Failing the absent sister,' Mott said, 'there's the neighbour who holds the spare key. Would you say she was the closest associate, Z?'

This was the point she'd been dreading, but she played cool. 'I guess I knew Beattie better than anyone. Mrs Carpenter is on the elderly side.'

'But not frail, nor blind?'

'I wouldn't say so, but . . .'

'Z, you're already involved; having discovered the body. It makes a better case to spread responsibility.'

In case the coroner questions my part in it? she asked herself. Thank God I was on public view elsewhere at the time Beattie must have been killed.

'I do have an alibi, sir,' she reminded him stiffly.

'Ah yes. Undercover at Omphale's. Better take you off that duty now, I suppose.'

'I could be getting warm there, sir. Maybe a couple more nights?'

He looked at her over the half-lenses he'd started affecting, and the black, bushy eyebrows went sky high. 'I hope you're not developing a taste for casino life?'

'Anything but, sir. But Estelle who's training me had just broken off an affair with the missing man. I think she's almost ready to confide.'

'Good. She was particularly tight-lipped when we had her in. All right: so you can have a few more nights' roulette. And beautification by day. It's a hard life for some!'

On that sardonic note he dismissed them, only calling Z back when they were half-way down the corridor. She returned and shut the door at his nod.

'Message from Nan for you,' he said, standing by the window and jingling keys in his trousers pocket. 'She'd – we'd both – be pleased to have you stay until you make new arrangements. I can't say how sorry I am about what's happened, Rosemary.'

'Thank you, sir. Actually I've arranged to stay with

the Beaumonts tonight. And when the locks have been changed I'll be going back. It's only the basement that's sealed off.'

He didn't care for the idea, but he didn't argue either. 'As you wish, but don't push yourself. Nobody expects that. Think about having someone in to stay with you for a while. And our offer stays open.'

Decent of him, she thought, but I'll fit in better at Beaumont's. On one of his cases he acquired a stray dog, so why not me? And the ménage is one that should keep me diverted.

She couldn't move on the murder case until the WPC checking on Beattie's beauty routine had identified the assistants who had worked on her. They didn't need *Yellow Pages* after all because appointment cards tucked in her dressing-table mirror provided addresses of three establishments Beattie had patronized; two local, one in London's Bond Street.

A phone call from the Met provided the name of a Miss Oliphant (Ask for Carrie) as the Bond Street cosmetics expert. Z rang the number given and asked for an urgent appointment with her. Nothing was available for two weeks. But surely, if there was a cancellation . . . ? A cool receptionist took her number but expressed doubts.

In the corridor she caught Dolly from the canteen and pulled her into the CID office. She was delighted to put on a fancy accent and phone the salon, cancelling Beattie's next appointment.

Z had half an hour to wait, imagining someone jumping the queue, or Miss Oliphant intending to use the heaven-sent free hour for a personal shopping jaunt. But the call came. Z was booked in at Bond Street for ten the next morning.

After that the two local appointments followed fast. Toning and aromatherapy the same afternoon. Hairdo two days later, on Monday. Considerable outlay on expenses; she had better collect some useful information to justify it.

Meanwhile 10 p.m. would see her back at the gaming tables observing how the affluent other half lived and exchanging girlish confidences over the shared mirror in the staff loo.

3

In the Bond Street salon, while Carrie's firm fingers smoothed cream from Z's clavicles to chin, to cheek, to brow, she lay trying not to think what Beattie's toe-tagged body currently endured on the cold, guttered slab of the autopsy table.

DI Mott would be present as investigating officer, with Beaumont as backup. The Boss had also opted to attend, as well as the Coroner's officer and the usual gallery of forensic ghouls. Not herself this time, thank God.

It was better to visualize the live Beattie here, enjoying Carrie's ministrations, stroked and petted into a glowing mood to match the cosmetic change. Would she have been lulled into half-sleep or stimulated into self-revealing chatter?

Carrie worked in silence and intently. 'You're very quiet,' Z commented, to get her started.

'Sorry,' she said, and tried to fix a smile where the frown had been. 'Had a bit of a shock this morning.'

'Are you sure you're all right to carry on?'

'I'm fine. Just something I saw in the *Mail*. I was reading it on the train. Upset me a bit.'

'Bad news?'

'A sudden death. Well, a murder, actually.'

'How awful. Not someone you knew?'

She sniffed, seeming genuinely affected. 'Not all that well. A new customer. Actually it's the lady whose appointment you took over. I can't believe it. She was so cheery and bright that one time, making plans to entertain a sister back from abroad. You'd never think anything nasty would happen to a friendly old lady like that. There are some terrible people about.'

It was incredible luck that Carrie had launched on the subject herself, but she could tell Z nothing she didn't know already. Once she had exhausted the subject Carrie confined herself to explaining what she was doing with her fingers and why.

'As this is a one-off treatment, I'll show you what preparations you ought to buy and the best way to carry on using them.'

Sales talk, but Z confessed to being as vain as the next woman, so she let herself run up a bill. Then, feeling made-over, she took a train back to Reading, expecting to startle the natives.

No one at the nick noticed the slightest difference. She hoped the make-up would last until her nightclub stint that evening, where clients could prove more responsive.

She arrived early and Estelle, duly impressed, took her aside for some poker-dealing practice in the back room. The cards were clean, from a sealed pack, but the other girl knew her way round them. Z was getting speed up at shuffling, yet she still couldn't feel the marked edges. Learn all the dodges, Estelle told her; and practise like mad. Slickness was what it was all about, if you wanted to get on in club life. That and versatility.

'There's a new security guy on tonight,' she warned Z as they undulated towards the wheels. 'Replacing my Pepe.'

It wasn't until almost an hour later that Z saw the new man making his way through the crowd. He was tall, hollow-cheeked, with an indoor pallor, a razor-slash mouth and slatey eyes. His straight, near-black hair was fine and worn rather long, centre-parted to fall forward over his temples. There was no warmth in his gaze as it fixed on Estelle. He's feral, Z thought, and she seemed to catch a snake-pit scent off him.

Estelle was magnetized. Z let his eyes pass over her without reacting. They went back to Estelle's swathed buttermilk hair. Z's Cleopatra-style wig had no pull: the gentleman clearly preferred blondes.

It was company policy for the croupiers not to be familiar with clients. They were there to rake in their chips. Nor might they communicate unduly with other staff. But there were sparky conversations going on between those two silently at eye level.

'What d'you think?' Estelle asked Z breathily when they shared a break.

'Interesting.'

'Hang in later. I think there's something on.'

'Something' was apparently a party after their stint was over. Z was ready for bed, but it wasn't to be. Estelle had fixed for a cab to be waiting outside. The driver was known to her; she didn't have to tell him the address. Things were becoming more interesting by the minute.

They were heading west into real country, the houses getting grander and more isolated all the way. Up a curving drive between giant rhododendrons the cab turned into a well-lit parking space before an impressive mansion. Edwardian italianate, complete with a campanile. Under the ornate portico, double doors stood open, guarded by two large men in tight dinner jackets.

Estelle slid past with a saucy flutter of the fingers. Z was stopped, with a shock aware that ahead the new, snake-pit man had materialized.

'Oy, oy,' one of the bruisers challenged her. 'Oo we got 'ere then?'

He stood back as the new man slid up alongside. The eyes were, if possible, even colder than before. 'I don't think we've met,' he challenged. His voice was silky, over-nice. Someone had once spent a lot of money on his education.

She jutted one hip. 'No?' she teased. 'What's this then? We're here, together.'

She saw a new awareness in his eyes as he registered her indifference to his brush-off. She leaned closer, the upward glance emphasizing her smallness against his height. 'What you really mean is that I'm gatecrashing.'

He tried looking inscrutable while he considered how to take it.

'Well, isn't it? Gatecrashing's what I do. Do you know your Gerard Manley Hopkins? He once wrote, "What I do is me. For this I came." Powerful stuff.'

There was just the hint of a twitch at the ends of the man's single-line mouth. 'I think perhaps we could legitimize you. Temporarily. Come in and meet my other guests. You do have a name, I imagine?'

'Imagine away,' she invited, since being outrageous seemed to work. 'I'm sure you can magic one out of thin air.'

'You might prefer me not to.'

'Surprise me.'

'Oh, I will. Believe me. That is what *I* do. And I do it very well.'

He introduced her around as Zuleika, Estelle's partner, and some of the company picked up the reference, others were already beyond it, seeing merely another woman, brunette, available. For a moment Z's heart seemed to miss a beat as she thought he must have known her real name. But it was sheer coincidence that he'd happened on one that began with the same letter.

The party was warming up: there was an air of barely suppressed expectation, only partly due to the hectic compulsion of the music's rhythm pulsating out of the silk-swathed walls. Strobe lights distorted reality. The dancing was becoming obscene.

It was all about drugs, of course. She knew she'd not get out of there undamaged unless she played along. And that at a price.

In the job they learnt to recognize the goods; bone up

on the effects, and get to pick up the dealers' language. Z stayed at first with the soft stuff, taking convincingly long pulls, but with the reefer's end tightly nipped between thumb and fingers, keeping it alight in between with short, uninhaled draws. The flickering of coloured lights helped to camouflage the deceit.

She danced herself round the company, eluding the pawings, smiling her way back to the man who'd claimed he was good at surprises. When he teased her with a little plastic envelope she smiled sphinx-like until he dangled it too close and then she pounced greedily, slipping it down her cleavage, mocking him back. No money passed. A few minutes later, as he was occupied with Estelle, Z made for the ground floor cloakroom, ostensibly for her fix. She felt his gaze follow her.

But there was no way out there. Behind the taffeta-swagged drapes the windows had locked steel shutters. She emptied most of the crack down the loo, screwed the envelope shut again and tucked it in the waistband of her briefs, reserved as evidence. Then she staged some wild whoopee for the benefit of the female onlookers before subsiding in a corner and, judged stoned insensible, actually snatched about ninety minutes' needed sleep on the cool tiles.

Someone came later – a man, to judge from his shoes and trouser ends – and threw whisky over her, more as scent to account for her supposed groggy state than as a reviver. Then she was loaded into a large, purring car with her emptied purse thrown in after. She lolled on the back seat with Estelle's dead-weight head on her shoulder and the ravaged buttermilk hair tangled over her face. At an all-night taxi shelter they were decanted from the limo, transferred, and the cabbie directed to Estelle's address.

Once they were clear Z sat drunkenly up and countermanded the order. They'd get better 24-hour service at Area Headquarters. But as a precaution they changed cabs again en route.

It was too late to make any move against the dealers then, but there would be other opportunities, provided that Estelle kept her mouth shut. With all Z had on her and her friends, she guessed the girl could be persuaded to help out later with details.

On another occasion Z might have felt some secret pleasure that the Boss gave priority to the inquiry she was currently on and tackling alone. But the alternative was Beattie's murder, and it seemed intolerable that it shouldn't override everything else, just because of who she'd been.

They had gathered for team conference in the CID office later that Sunday morning while outside the sun shone and the cracked tenor bell at St Botolph's made an attractive nonsense of the change-ringers' efforts.

The murder investigation was continuing ploddingly in several directions but with little to show for it as yet, Beaumont reported. The South African sister had left no forwarding address with the Inn on the Park because, affluently, she'd retained the suite for the three weeks of her intended absence, leaving some of her luggage in it. An appeal was to be made through the media for Roberta Knol, née Weyman, to contact Thames Valley police. It seemed likely she was touring to look up friends from her early days in England, but it wasn't known where the family hailed from. All Beattie's stories originated from her arrival in London to work at the Windmill.

Weyman wasn't a common name but, unrelated to any locality, was of little help. And with her own family extinct, Roberta might be contacting her two husbands' relatives – always supposing that they had any in the UK.

Uniform branch's house-to-house inquiries had concentrated on sightings of visitors in the neighbourhood over the previous week, and progress on follow-up had been slow. Since this case hung fire, and in view of Z's exploits overnight, attention switched to planning a raid on the country-house drug scene.

After de-tox treatment in Casualty, Estelle wasn't talking freely yet, but she'd admitted that Pepe had introduced her to the pay parties, which he'd run until he disappeared. She'd always felt safe with him there: he'd never let her go so far. She was sufficiently scared of the new man to cry off duty at Omphale's for the following night, which made Z's presence there doubly necessary. She too, despite putting a bold face on it, wasn't feeling happy about her next encounter with Snake-eyes.

DI Mott had better luck with the cabbie who had picked the girls up at the casino. He provided the name of the country house they had been taken to, but claimed his instructions and cash pre-payment always arrived anonymously by post. He was to ferry passengers from Omphale's as required, identifying them through the password 'Cotopaxi', and later return to the cab rank to pick them up as dumped by private car. Pressed further he thought this could have been a light-coloured Mercedes, but he'd not noted the registration number. No, he wasn't the only cabbie on the scheme. Two other owner-drivers followed similar instructions. He swore he had no part in anything illegal, and had always assumed that unconscious passengers were simply drunks to be transported home.

The Boss hadn't pressed for more at that point, content to leave the man believing that he'd talked himself out of complicity, and scared enough not to contact those more closely involved. But with two minor participants already pulled in for questioning, it was vital to move quickly before word could spread. A raid was being set up with Drugs Squad for the next date when the cabbie was to operate, which was Tuesday, two nights ahead.

Meanwhile Z's next casino stint passed without

incident, with Snake-eyes – now known to her as Aristide – making no attempt at communication. Dorothy, the proprietress, descended in person since Estelle had defected, and took over in her place.

Z spent the remains of a second night under Beaumont's roof, but sensed some relief on suggesting a return to her own place. Cathy and he still slept in separate rooms although her abashed return from a mid-life bid at singles self-discovery was now several months old. This left only young Stuart's cramped quarters with its disturbing teenage décor on offer for Z, while he humped his bedroll downstairs to share the kitchen with the elderly basset hound.

Returning to Beattie's house in Monday's early hours Z found relaxation impossible before the sun was up, and then slept on until almost the time for her hair appointment.

To date her retracing of Beattie's beauty quest had yielded nothing new, so she was not expecting exciting revelations as she hung backwards over the basin and permitted Edna's over-long nails to dig into her scalp. But her torturer was a local girl interested in everything that went on around her.

'You're a lady copper, aren't you?' she demanded, blowing Z's cover straight off. Z grunted.

'Awful business, that murder. You lived there, didn't you? Can't say I'd care to go back meself.'

She was generous with the lather, flicking it energetically on to Z's face, who kept her eyes closed.

'Me mum's flat's nearly opposite. Upstairs, luckily, so she's not bothered with people coming to the door. Peeps through the curtains when she hears a knock, and stays quiet till they've gone away. A real old aspidistra face, I tell her.'

Z reared her head. 'Did she come down to speak to the police?'

'Not her. Says you can't tell if they're genuine. Could be anyone with a fake uniform and a card they'd printed themselves. Your old Miss Weyman, she was more trusting, and look where it got her.'

Z tried to sit up and was pushed firmly back against the basin's rim. 'How do you mean, "trusting"?'

'Well, she'd got a chain on the door and all that. Only, if she had to fetch change or keep anyone waiting she'd ask them in. Seen her meself when I've been calling on Mum. Sally Army, Blue Cross, Alexandra Rose Day, all that.'

'Did she? I never knew.' Beattie had sworn she always used the door chain. Hadn't bothered to explain she then took it off for charity callers.

'Do you suppose your mother saw anyone call at number 31 that Thursday evening?'

'Could be. Depends how rotten the TV programmes were that night. Yeah, she could've.'

'I'd like to go and talk to her.'

'No good ringing her bell. She'll not let you up.'

'But she allows you in.'

'I phone first, to warn her. Then I give a special knock.'

'So would you take me to see her?'

The last rinsing water gushed down the drain. A fluffy towel was wrapped round the WDC's head and she was spun in the chair through one-eighty degrees.

'Now, have you thought any more about those highlights?' Edna demanded in merchandizing tones.

It struck Z that this was reciprocal bargaining, so she gave in without protest. And that was how she learned of the strange behaviour of the blind lady's guide dog three days before the murder.

'Well they're supposed to train them properly,' Edna's mother protested. 'Nobody'd be safe with a beast like that, sighted or not. He just got one glimpse of number 25's cat and he was off chasing her, pulling the poor woman after him. Could've broken both her legs if she hadn't bundled her skirts up and run like a good'un.

Real comic, it was. Only she didn't ought to have kicked the poor thing like that afterwards. I mean, fair's fair. It didn't mean any harm. It was just big and powerful.'

'And untrained,' Z reminded her. 'So what was the blind lady like?'

She passed the description to Angus who went with her to the Boss. Two houses on Beattie's side of the road – numbers 27 and 29 – had reported being visited by a woman collecting for the blind; none on the opposite side. That had been on the previous Monday evening, three days before Beattie was thought to have been killed. She was described as tall, middle-aged, with shoulder-length greying hair. She had worn dark glasses, a long fawn summer coat and a wide-brimmed drab straw hat.

'She wasn't seen going into number 31?'

'No. Mrs Sawyer watched her visit the first two, but her daughter phoned just then. When she got back to the window she saw the business with the dog, and the collector shutting it in a car parked round the corner.'

'Don't tell me she saw the blind woman driving off!'

'No. There must have been a sighted driver sitting inside.'

'What do you think?' the Boss asked doubtfully.

'There was nothing similar reported with the earlier axe cases,' Beaumont reminded the team.

They looked at the enlarged street map on the wall. A low side gate to number 27 showed a couple of centimetres from where the car was now pencilled in.

'Two six-foot walls between it and the back door of number 31,' Mott reflected. 'But according to Mrs Sawyer, Beattie would have opened up the front door to a charity collector anyway.'

'And it all happened three days *before* the killing.'

'Which doesn't rule out the collector coming back on

the Thursday night, or sending someone else.'

'Maybe I've made too much of this,' Z apologized. 'All we're basing suspicion on is the behaviour of a dog.'

Superintendent Yeadings rose heavily from his perch on the corner of a desk. 'Not just an ordinary dog: a guide dog. I've seen the training they get. A cat chaser would have been eliminated before the start. Temperament is the first test, and then discipline is drilled into them. This blind lady smells like a phoney. But it could be just another charity fraud.

'However, wildly assuming that behind the dark glasses was a killer casing the neighbourhood, we'd need to discover where the dog came from. And its harness. Try Dog Rescue, Blue Cross, RSPCA, and the animal sales ads in all local papers. Also check with RNIB for any dog-owner who's given up lately and would have a spare harness. Read the obits if you have to, but get a connection somehow.'

At the door he turned back. 'A good possible lead, Z. A charity collector who visits only two or three houses: we should have picked it up before this.'

He stared hard at her highlighted hair. 'Then we could have spared you the dappled effect.'

4

At a little after eight on Tuesday morning two uniformed constables arrived on Z's doorstep. One was carrying a metal detector, the other something long wrapped in sacking. They informed her they had orders to dig in the garden.

'For what?' she asked muzzily, still in her pyjamas.

They didn't need to answer. Since nothing was obviously missing from the house, it must be an object brought there by the killer and abandoned. The axe perhaps? She wasted no time getting to the Superintendent's briefing.

His decision sprang from findings at the post-mortem. A sharp blade had been confirmed as the murder weapon. The three blows had been delivered heavily at much the same angle as in the previous murders, but the wounds were of different depth and width, made by a slimmer instrument having a concave, not convex, edge: a billhook or sickle, rather than a full-sized felling axe.

'Light enough for a woman to use,' Mott murmured.

'Small enough to be easily concealed,' Z said at the same moment.

'But most importantly,' Yeadings pointed out, 'the change of weapon sets this murder apart from the others. And, if it was a one-off, then the killer would probably discard the weapon afterwards. So we look for it first in the vicinity.'

And in no time the men digging unearthed it, because in only one part of the garden had the soil been recently disturbed. Z hadn't much hope of her bedding plants' survival after a second uprooting. Not that they mattered much now, with no Beattie to give pleasure to.

'A billhook,' Yeadings confirmed. 'And digging there wasn't a wild shot in the dark. Fine soil on the kitchen floor set me wondering, and the samples analyzed had come from the garden.

'If no outsider could gain entry by the back door because of its bolts, then the grit was tramped back in by someone already in the house with some reason to visit the garden.'

'Why not Beattie herself?' Z asked. 'Or me, when I put the plants in earlier? Beattie was never too prompt about sweeping up.'

'But in with the soil were some shreds of dried petals. The lab confirmed what I thought: they were from roses. Albertines in fact. I checked with your neighbour at number 29. His rambler is the only one of that variety in the terrace. He's rightly proud of it,

sprays it daily because otherwise the blooms don't last
long. The first lot dropped on Thursday evening when
there was a force five wind blowing up. Westerly,
towards number 31.'

'So we could be wrong assuming the killer left by the
rear. He just went out to bury the billhook under my
plants. Then absently slipped the key in his pocket
after he'd locked himself back in,' Z said.

'And the petal pieces stuck to his shoe soles, or on
his trousers as he knelt to dig, dropping off later in the
kitchen.' The Boss nodded.

'*He, Him*self?' Mott queried. 'I thought we'd got the
phoney blind woman in the frame for the murder?'

Yeadings smiled. 'Sex equality in all things. Right,
Z?'

'Right, sir.'

'So – he/she. Let's wait and see.' The Boss was giving
nothing more away.

'Has anything come in yet on the sister?' Z asked.

'No. Do you fancy her as a suspect, because you
overheard the quarrel?'

'Not really. It seems too petty. But there's no other
close connection, and the murder happened right after
Roberta suddenly reappeared.'

'Nearly a week later,' Mott corrected her.

'And we've only a vague record from the London
hotel of what she did during that time,' Beaumont put
in. He flipped open his notebook and recapped for
their general benefit.

'Arrived by air the previous Tuesday, having booked
flight and hotel three weeks back. Rested on
Wednesday. Went sightseeing and shopped in
Knightsbridge for the next two days. Descended on
her sister, apparently without warning, on the
Saturday morning. Returned to the hotel 3 p.m. but
out all evening. Left next morning in a cab with only
two of her suitcases, having arranged to keep on the
suite for the next month. Told her sister she'd be

touring for three weeks, but didn't say where. Vanished without trace.

'I've requested recent photographs from the South African police *asap*. There's been no reply to yesterday's media requests for her to get in touch. The hotel register had given us her name: Mrs Roberta Knol.'

Yeadings fanned out over his desk the monochrome photographs from Beattie's kitchen drawer, sad little mementoes of lost childhood. But Z noticed the studio portrait wasn't there, the one with all three sisters together. Perhaps Beattie had sent it to be framed or removed it to her bedroom.

'Which is which?' Yeadings asked, examining the girls' individual faces. Z pointed them out.

'Beattie was eldest, then Roberta. This little dark one was Bernice.'

'Pretty name,' he said. 'And a lovely child.' His voice had briefly softened. His own little daughter's looks were blunter, puppy-like, just missing conventional beauty because of Down's Syndrome. The painful experience had made a vulnerable father out of a shrewd toughie.

'How old would Bernice be now?'

'Sixtyish, but she died young, at twenty-nine.'

He glanced up, still enchanted by the child's face. 'How?'

Z had no idea, and told him so.

'Hardly relevant anyway,' Mott said with some impatience.

The Boss shrugged lightly, but Z was left wondering: a second sister dead when the last one suddenly returned from afar. It would be interesting to know whether Bernice too had died from violence.

'We haven't a surname for Bernice,' Z told the Boss, 'nor her husband's address when she died. Our best hope is for Roberta to tell us when she returns.'

'It looks that way.' He pushed his chair back and

rose to dismiss them. 'Are you all right at home on your own, Z?'

'Fine, sir, thanks.'

'If you're in at about 8 p.m. I might drop by.'

'Coffee on the house, sir.' This was the night of the next Cotopaxi party, after her casino stint. And the raid would be laid on for some point after 2.45 a.m. Perhaps he had some final instructions for her. She only hoped he hadn't decided to ban her from a part in it.

'Good. That's the lot, then.'

Out in the corridor Mott was tight-lipped. 'Playing Jack Horner again,' he muttered. It was true that the Boss slipped his leash from time to time, abandoning his desk for a spot of the action. His possession of the ancient photos had surprised them all. It meant that he'd already been out to Beattie's house turning things over, and he'd even visited next door getting chatty about roses.

'You have to admit,' Z reminded her guv, 'that when Mr Yeadings does put in his thumb they are real plums he produces.'

Beaumont made a choking sound and rolled his eyes. Meaning, *that's exactly what gripes him!*

The Boss arrived at 7.35 p.m., almost half an hour early, apologizing a second time when he reached Z's sitting-room to find Max Harris installed. The two men had met over an earlier case and held a high opinion of each other, with the grudging addenda 'for a journalist', and 'for a copper', respectively.

'Dropped in with condolences,' Max explained himself. 'I'd have been here earlier but they sent me to Lithuania for a few days. I got back this morning.'

'Don't disturb yourselves,' the Boss said easily. 'I just want to poke around some more. No letters or diary have turned up so far to connect with Beattie's address book. And most of the names in that are crossed through: the cost of outliving your friends.'

'I doubt if she kept a diary,' Z admitted. 'Anything personal would have been in her handbag. She toted a lot around with her. It's all listed at the nick.'

After twelve fruitless minutes of burrowing among Beattie's things in her bedroom the Boss returned, drank two cups of coffee, conversed amiably a while and took his leave. At the door he turned to Max.

'Persuade Z to invite you for a few days. I've a feeling we could hear more from this killer.'

'There,' said Max, preening himself when the Boss had left, 'cohabitation prescribed with a constabular blessing. What more urging do you need?'

None, actually, because Z had been hoping Max had an overnight bag outside in the car. Not that she could benefit long from his warming presence. With the raid scheduled for 2.50 a.m., she'd not get home before dawn.

'I'll stay on one condition,' Max stipulated. 'That we halt that grandfather clock in the hall. It would stalk me all night.'

Z had rewound it, just as Beattie used to, on Sunday morning. Now she opened the case for Max to lift off the chain with the weight on it. It subsided on the floor with a dull thud.

Then she had to explain about her overnight absence.

After her stint at Omphale's the raid went off almost perfectly to plan. Angus Mott's car tailed Z's cab from half-way to the Cotopaxi party and as she approached the entrance steps he called to her from its open window. He got out and they kissed like old friends meeting. Chatting animatedly, they went up the steps, aiming between the two bouncers. And a pair of Drugs Squaddies fell in behind.

Taken by surprise the doormen were cuffed with minimum fuss. One went for his pocket transmitter but Z chopped his wrist and he lost it.

Then, 'Go, go, go!' came the call and blue lights were racing up the drive, peeling off to surround the house.

They made a sizeable haul: a wide selection of banned substances and a number of familiar faces among those lined up against the walls. But Aristide wasn't among them.

He had been at Omphale's earlier and Z had checked that he'd left in advance of her. As she called for play and raked in the chips she'd been conscious of him prowling close at times, watching every movement of her hands.

When he hissed, 'Outside!' she thought he suspected her of fiddling. A male colleague slid in to take her place as she followed Aristide into the staff corridor.

He swung to face her. He was electric, his eyes feverish, the usual reptilian manner quite gone. She thought he must already be high on something. He was staring at her black wig. 'Take it off,' he spat.

Scared stiff, she managed to shrug. He couldn't wait, grasping the black fringe and tearing it back. Her short curls were exposed, dark red-brown with their new gold highlights.

He sneered. 'G.M. Hopkins again. "God help all dappled things",' he misquoted viciously.

What he would have done next wasn't clear, but Dorothy's door opened and she stood looking out. 'What's wrong?' she demanded sharply.

'This girl,' Aristide snapped, 'was rude to a client.'

Z avoided Dorothy's questioning glance, praying she'd not be given away. 'Right,' the casino owner said sharply. 'I'll deal with it.' She stood aside for Z to enter her office.

'What's biting him?' Dorothy asked, once the door between was closed.

Z explained he'd taken exception to the wig. It must have been more obvious than she'd supposed.

'No,' Dorothy decided. 'It's completely convincing.

And even if it wasn't—' She shrugged. 'Is there any chance he recognized you from somewhere else?'

That had to be the explanation. If he'd somehow discovered that she was in the job, he could have taken fright. How he acted now could threaten tonight's operation.

'I'll have to warn the Boss,' Z said.

'No. Put your wig on, go back and carry on as normal. I'll ring Mr Yeadings.'

So Z had returned to duty at the wheel, looking suitably resentful for Aristide's benefit. After a few minutes' tense scrutiny he left her alone. She hadn't seen him again inside Omphale's, and the doorman told her he had left.

Z's part in the raid was completed. Mott dropped her off with instructions not to check in until after lunch. She felt fit to sleep on the banister rail, but had trailed half-way up the stairs when the doorbell gave a loud ping: Angus come back to revise his instructions. Wearily she unchained and opened.

The door crashed back and she staggered against the wall. A tall figure loomed in the opening: greying hair from under a wide-brimmed straw hat reached to her shoulders; long fawn coat. No dark glasses, but Z recognized at once the description of the blind woman.

She used one hand to close the door behind her. The other held a small pistol. A Derringer, Z noted; but no toy. She'd never used one but knew the theory: the smaller the gun, the louder the report.

Could she rely on the woman not wanting to raise the neighbourhood? Finding the answer could cost her her life, so she gave way as signalled and retreated down the passage. Backwards she stumbled into Beattie's sitting-room, and the woman followed. 'Who are you?' Z demanded.

With the free hand she/he dragged off the hat, and the hair came with it. As a few hours before he had torn off Z's own wig.

'*Aristide?*'

'What's in a name?' he said brutally. 'I promised you I was imaginative. Admit it: I have surprised you.'

'I'll say so,' Z admitted. She was still retreating, blindly making for the table where Beattie had her knick-knacks on display, wildly trying to plot in her memory their positions, their relative weights, their usefulness as missiles.

He sensed her intention, stepped forward and savagely whipped her with the gun. For a second she saw blackness, swaying on her feet. Then the pain caught up and a warm trickle of blood ran down one cheek from her temple. She had staggered clear of the table and had her back to the wall. She fought vainly to stay upright, but was slowly slithering down it.

'You killed – my friend.' She couldn't utter her name. There was a continuous buzzing in her ears, and she thought he said, 'Not yet.'

Not what yet? Was he putting off killing her?

'Her time will come. A traffic accident. Driving too fast. Unaccustomed to English motorways.'

The nightmare was getting ridiculous. Beattie had never in her life driven a car. Z made some attempt to say so and the man bent closer to catch the words.

He laughed softly. 'But she isn't Beattie any more. She's Roberta now. We can all change names when we have to.'

Z had a brief sense of half understanding, then it all became irrelevant. Only one reality was left: the small black hole growing ever larger as he slowly brought the gun up towards her eyes.

The smaller the gun, the louder the report. Would she actually hear it?

Just a sharp crack, and in a split second she knew she had died.

Then Max was standing over her in his convict-stripe pyjama trousers, a chain still swinging from one hand. The heavy weight from the grandfather clock had come off with the force of the blow. It lay daubed with crimson in the bright blood of Aristide's crushed skull.

Not really Aristide, the Boss explained next day; but Harold Batts. Hardly surprising that he'd fancied a change of name, someone so imaginative. Aristide, which suited his appearance well enough, was his pseudonym at Omphale's, as Z's had been Gina.

His true identity was turned up from two sources almost simultaneously. One through the job application to Omphale's from a sometime repertory actor with Magic Circle connections. DS Beaumont had tracked down the other, first through the marriage certificate of Bernice Weyman, and subsequently from a birth certificate issued to Stanley and Bernice Batts of Nottingham.

Z remembered then: Stanley had been the name of the 'lovely feller' who jilted Beattie to elope with her younger sister. And Bernice had died eleven years later. Perhaps in childbirth?

In any case, Harold was her son. Stanley, unable to raise him alone and still too ashamed of his betrayal to appeal to the child's two aunts, had agreed to his adoption by a wealthy couple who could provide all material comforts.

And it seemed they'd indulged him outrageously, made a heartless scrounger of him. Expelled from boarding school for supplying LSD and cocaine, he had appeared twice in court on charges of Actual Bodily Harm to his adoptive father, and was subsequently convicted of living off immoral earnings.

It seemed he'd had equally high hopes of living off his Aunt Roberta's fortune, inheriting as sole blood relative once Beattie had predeceased her.

Unlike Beattie he had been forewarned of Roberta's visit, though not of the changed date. The private investigator she had paid to hunt up the widower of her younger sister had revealed to him his client's identity. Harold swiftly recognized his opportunity and wrote to her, determined to become her sole beneficiary.

But when Roberta grew impatient and brought forward her visit, Harold was already in the South refining his plans. His first move was to contact an ex-Notts drug dealer operating in Thames Valley.

Accompanied by a golden labrador borrowed for the occasion, he walked in on his one-time cell-mate Pepe at Reading (conveniently close to Maidenhead Area), and demanded lodgings. During a marathon drinking jag he had boasted of his coming fortune. He'd shown off the dog's harness from the repertory company's props chest which had suggested the blind disguise. And in unwrapping the clothes stolen from the same rep wardrobe, the keenly sharpened billhook had fallen out.

In the cold and blinding light of the subsequent hangover, Pepe had disturbing recall. Batts' clear intention to eliminate the old aunt convinced him that he could end convicted as an accessory. Already he smelled trouble coming over crooked dealings at Omphale's threatening his job there and his profitable drug connection with the Cotopaxi pay parties for middle-aged, middle-income ravers. Leaving a note to suggest Batts took both over, he opted for sudden disappearance.

Harold Batts' first visit to survey the house and road where Beattie lived assured him that his plan would work. He had been accepted by the old trout in his blind-woman role and given a pound coin for the collecting box. He had only to make a second visit after dusk, gaining entry with some pathetic story of a fall or having the money stolen. A doddle. Meanwhile, he was making valuable contacts in his casino job and the Cotopaxi spin-off. Life had never looked more promising.

**Sell your books at
sellbackyourBook.com!**

Go to sellbackyourBook.com
and get an instant price quote.
We even pay the shipping - see
what your old books are worth
today!

0028365136

Sell your books at
sellbackyourBook.com!
Go to sellbackyourBook.com
and get an instant price quote.
We even pay the shipping - see
what your old books are worth
today!

Inspected By:Jose_martinez

00028365136

But the unforeseen caught him out on his vital return visit. His unsuspecting victim led him into her kitchen and there he was confronted by the other aunt. In the bright strip-lighting he had panicked and given himself away. Beattie had flopped, helplessly calling for her heart pills, but Roberta was a tough nut who didn't take to being fooled, though she hadn't full realization of his intentions until too late. The sharpened edge of the billhook, intended for one sister, was used to subdue the other. The killing was on automatic pilot, perfectly to plan and mimicking the murders the papers had been full of.

It was just the wrong victim.

And then, while Beattie slobbered and gasped, unaware fully of what had occurred, he suddenly saw the way out, because apart from their weight the two of them were now so alike, Beattie having smartened herself up and had her hair dyed the same red as her sister's since he'd called three days before.

In his head he tried exchanging their names. Why not? One old lady was the same as another. Their clothes weren't so different. He'd be really smart about the handbags. The expensive ostrich-skin one – Roberta's – he'd take away. The bulging one must stay and help identify the new Beattie.

He wedged the body upright between chair-back and table edge. When he had cleaned off his hands and got rid of the billhook he came back to take a critical look. No one could properly say now who the disgusting old object was with the blood all spilled down her face on to the table.

The fatter one was still gasping, hanging on to her pill bottle. That would have to go back in the handbag, but he took a loose handful out to keep her going. Until convenient. She had to live a while longer, because she was Roberta now, the rich one.

Since then he had been holding her at Pepe's, tied down in her bed, and she'd be all right until he could drive her a long way off and crash a car with her inside. Only it hadn't to burn right out, because everyone must know who she was, so they could trace her nephew, the only one left to inherit.

Beattie was making a splendid recovery. When she left hospital her tablets were exchanged for an inhaler, to be used only in emergencies. She had lost weight and that in itself seemed to help her breathlessness. Z was privately amazed how philosophically she had learned to accept her sister's murder.

'It was so quick,' she explained. 'Horrible, yes. But – you see, she was dying anyway, painfully. That's what made her so sharp. If she'd told me that the first time she came, I'd have understood. I wouldn't have taken it so badly when she lammed into me for being sloppy.

'She'd been given just eight months. Which was why she was so desperate to find someone to leave her money to. It'd always meant a lot to her, you see? And then that way, rushing about making arrangements and sorting out people, she felt she was still a bit in control of things. Bertie always had to be boss. I was more of a drifter.'

Z hugged her, while she blinked away the tears.

'Still, I'm glad we had that last little chat together when she came back. And she was real chuffed I'd took – taken – her advice about me appearance. Especially after finding all that out about her precious Harold, who'd been buttering her up in letters ever since she discovered he existed.'

'How did she discover him? I thought that when Bernie died you lost contact altogether.'

'She contacted a private detective in the Midlands somewhere, to see what had happened to Bernie's husband. And this man wrote back that Bernie had died in childbirth. The baby was a boy, now in his early thirties.

'But Harold must have got wise to him somehow

and got her address off him. And he started writing loving letters to his rich old auntie. Musta sniffed her money all those thousands of miles away. Maybe he paid the detective not to let on to her about his prison record. But she found out herself when she went up to Nottingham and inquired around, after she'd dropped in on me.

'Well, me sister had barely told me all this and the doorbell rang. When I went to open up he pushed his way in, all dressed up like the blind lady. Silly-like I'd left the chain off when I let Bertie in.

'It real knocked him back to find the two of us there, but it was Bertie that went fighting mad when she guessed who it was. Spitting and scratching and screaming at him, calling him a cheat and a wastrel. I think I flopped out then. When I came to he was hustling me out of the front door, half carried me into a car a coupla doors away. And then I passed out again and woke up in that house where they found me.'

'So you never actually saw what he did to your sister?'

'No, thank God. But I knew, because of the blood on his coat. It got on my clothes too. And he'd gone weird. Whenever he came to give me my meals he'd call me Roberta, said I'd better get used to my name because I was his rich auntie now and I was going to leave all my money to him after – after I'd had my sad accident.'

'Did he say how – ?'

'Driving a hire car.' She was silent a moment then cackled, a real crone's laugh. 'I never did say the joke'd be on him: that I'd never driven in me life! 'E was a real nutter, that one. Musta got it from 'is father. Nobody in our fam'ly ever went crazy before.'

It was doubtful he'd be found fit to plead, Yeadings said sombrely. Last interviewed, Batts had been trying to persuade the doctor how vital it was to get every last detail right. He must help him look after Roberta until he had a car hired in her name. Then he could complete his mission.

'I was scared Max had killed him,' Z confessed. 'Did you find out why he came back to the scene of the crime?'

'He'd tailed you home after you left Omphale's on the Monday night, because he sensed danger in you. It must have been the last thing needed to send him over the edge: to discover that the girl who made him uneasy at work was actually living in the murder house! He was going to deal with you after he'd got you fired by Dorothy next night, but it didn't work out that way.

'He was concealed in the grounds to watch for your arrival at Cotopaxi, saw the raid from a safe distance, and avoided being rounded up. He waited and followed Mott's car when he dropped you off at home. At the place he'd been forced into killing the wrong sister! He saw you as the manipulator foiling everything he'd so carefully set up. By then he must barely have known what he was doing.

'He didn't need to decide to kill you: it would have seemed predetermined, just a further extension of his original plan.'

Z shook her head, appalled at how near death had come.

'He was obsessed with the double murder,' Mott marvelled. 'He thought he was so clever, planning the perfect crime.'

'But it never struck him Beattie could die from natural causes while in his hands and save him the bother. Thank God she's pulling through all right.'

'Now we have to take another look at the corpse,' Yeadings reminded them sombrely. 'Z, I'm afraid it must be you this time, to annul the previous identification. Then we'll need dental records from South Africa for a positive on Roberta Knol.'

'I guess Mrs Carpenter didn't take a good look at the body,' Z said wretchedly. 'The sisters were still quite alike, but I would have known the difference at once after she'd been cleaned up.'

Beaumont sighed. 'Beattie, Bertie, Bernie – they were always bound to be confused. And then poor Harold. *Batts*, eh? What's in a name?'

Superintendent
Mike Yeadings

Mike Yeadings is in both senses the heart of the Thames Valley investigative team known as the Four Jacks. Big and bearlike, he skives from desk duties, claiming horror of shine on the seat of his office suits. But personal involvement in the chase is what draws him, exasperated by the prevalence of paperwork over people. Leaving matters of law to the younger and personable DI Angus Mott, he provides a background presence, perambulating like a benevolent sheepdog, accessible to both victim and criminal, all senses open to any hint of something 'off '.

Playing the ham performer when he finds it pays, he reminds DC Rosemary Zyczynski of a famous Welsh baritone, with gleaming eye under bushy black brows that give out storm signals or significant in-team semaphore. Following occasional bursts of inspiration, his bouts of ponderous silence have magnetic power over confidences and confessions alike. As each case draws to an end there is a sense of comfortable security about him which is deceptive, for he is a man deeply moved by viciousness.

Despite more than twenty years of closeness to the criminal mind, first in London's Met and later in Thames Valley force, he is not cynical, finding compassion for unfortunates pushed too far who take justice into their own hands. He owes much of his understanding to the stability of his marriage to Nan, one-time Nursing Sister at the old Westminster Hospital, who shares his agonizing care for their eleven-year-old daughter with Down's Syndrome. Helping in her simple struggle to account for a trick of 'magic', he realized how he had misread a complex murder in *Cat's Cradle*. In a later case, *Past Mischief*, his insight into DC Zyczynski's childhood abuse led him to untangle along with her a long history of malice and vengeance.

Human and occasionally bumbling in his paternal attitude to his team, he is, quite simply, the Good Cop.

Clare Curzon

Clare Curzon has several identities. She began her literary career in 1962 writing crime fiction under the pseudonym Rhona Petrie. Then in 1972, after her first ten novels were published, she wrote *Greenshards*, a paranormal psychology novel, and for this and the four historical novels steeped in witchcraft she became Marie Buchanan. Finally, having 'gone straight' for eight years, she returned to her life of crime, this time as Clare Curzon. Her most recent novel is *Past Mischief* which, like most of her mysteries, features the highly successful Superintendent Mike Yeadings and his Thames Valley team.

Clare Curzon was born in St Leonards-on-Sea, Sussex, worked extensively in Europe before her marriage, and now lives in Gerrards Cross, Buckinghamshire.

Also by Clare Curzon

Nice People
Past Mischief

In at the Death

Gillian Linscott

In at the Death

At eight o'clock on the first morning of 1912 Bobbie Fieldfare and I were on a Metropolitan Line train, just leaving Finchley Road station. We were the only people in the compartment not wearing riding clothes. Bobbie and I were dressed in the kind of thing you wear for a winter walk, tweed skirts, thick jackets, felt hats that had seen better days. As the only women in the compartment we'd attracted a few curious glances, but no more than that. If we chose to spend New Year's Day hiking on the Chiltern Hills that was no concern of the grooms in their boots and gaiters or the hunting gentry balancing top hats on their knees. They'd have had to give us more than a passing glance to note something odd about us – that even allowing for winter clothes, both Bobbie and I were unusually thick about the waist.

An unaccustomed feeling for both of us. Bobbie, in her mid-twenties, was as slim as a greyhound and twice as active, what with regular fencing classes, ju-jitsu and occasional bursts of outpacing the Metropolitan Police. I run to height rather than width and was also not short of exercise. The reason for our bulges was not Christmas indulgence – although I'd had my fair share of that – but what we were taking with us for our day in the country. Folded round Bobbie's waist, under her jacket, was a flag the size of a large tablecloth in our suffragette colours of purple,

white and green. Coiled round mine was a length of
hemp rope acquired hastily from one of my
mountain-climbing friends, late the previous night.
Bobbie and I were going climbing and as a result were
quite likely to be spending the first night of the new
year back in prison. Her idea, my fault. Her idea
because Bobbie comes from an eccentric family and is
as wild as a hare. My fault because I'm older and wiser
and should have known better. I did know better. As
the train carried us northwards into the grey winter
daylight of Kilburn, Wembley and Harrow on the Hill
on our way to damp green hills and copses of
Buckinghamshire, I knew that this was an unwise
expedition but there was no way of backing out
without being a little shamed in Bobbie's eyes and the
eyes of the friends who had found it such a hilariously
good idea at my New Year's Eve party.

It's become a tradition, that party. I hold it every
year in my narrow house in Hampstead. It spills out of
the living-room, into the kitchen and up the stairs as
more friends arrive bearing bottles, Dundee cakes and
Cheshire cheese, musical instruments. At midnight, as
every year, we drank a toast: 'This year, Votes for
Women'. So far we'd been wrong every time. The toast
was in champagne that year, because one of our richer
barrister friends had brought half a dozen bottles with
him. After it we sat in the firelight, on chairs, on stairs,
on the floor and a competition developed as to who
could quote the most stupid thing said by any of our
opponents in the past year. There were strong
contenders from both Commons and Lords but the
winner had been a dark horse from Buckinghamshire,
General Sir Robert Bringold, former Lord Lieutenant of
the county, Master of Fox Hounds. He was also
chairman of his local Conservative Association and in a
speech at its Christmas dinner expressed his opinion
that women were not morally entitled to have the vote
'because they will always be dependent on the

stronger nerves, greater physical strength and capacity for strenuous action of the male of the species'.

At that stage of the party the remark caused general hilarity. Some people even made an impromptu canon out of it and sang it. But Bobbie had gone uncharacteristically silent. When the singing died away in laughter, she got to her feet.

'Well, are we just going to laugh about it? Why don't we show him?'

And she made her proposal. She knew something about the Bringold family, which wasn't surprising as her family are well-connected as well as eccentric. One of the things she knew was that on New Year's Day the general played host to a large part of the county, at a meeting of his pack of fox hounds, starting outside the ancestral home and finishing there for drinks and dinner.

'It's a great barrack of a place up on a hill, you can see it from miles away. The point is, it might have been made for climbing, all gothic canopies and gargoyles and what have you.'

Somebody asked, unwisely, what climbing had to do with it.

'While they're all out hunting, two or three of us could swarm up the outside and hoist our colours on the flagpole on his roof so when they look round from wherever they are, he'll see them and with any luck drop dead out of the saddle from sheer humiliation. That'll show him who's got strong nerves and a capacity for strenuous action.'

It seemed like a good idea at the time. After two or three glasses of champagne practically anything seems like a good idea. We began to discuss the practicalities of it, as if we were seriously going to do it. Somebody asked how the team would get out to rural Buckinghamshire in time, but Bobby had an answer for that. Didn't we know the Metropolitan underground line ran a special service for London sportsmen wishing to hunt with the Chiltern packs? General incredulity.

'Honestly. They load their horses on at Finchley Road, where it comes out from underground, then off they go to Chalfont or Amersham or wherever, in time to hack to the meets. Nothing to stop us getting the same train.'

For some reason, that seemed to settle it. The question arose as to who should join Bobbie. One more person was enough, she thought. Several of the men volunteered, offering wide experience of climbing college buildings, but Bobbie said the whole point was that the thing must be done by women.

Somebody said, 'What about you, Nell? You've been up Mont Blanc.'*

I could have pointed out the difference between Alpine mountaineering and climbing buildings, however gothic. I could have said, which was true, that the whole thing was a mad idea, guaranteed to bring the movement into disrepute and, incidentally, confirm Emmeline Pankhurst's expressed view that Nell has a tendency towards the troublesome. Instead I caught Bobbie's eye, issuing a challenge.

'Very well,' I said.

From then on it was a whirlwind. The rope and flag were collected from separate lodgings, along with a small brass telescope that somebody thought might come in useful. We were several hours into the new year before my guests departed, all except Bobbie who lay down in the spare room among piles of books and papers so as to be on hand for the morning. We got, I suppose, about two hours' sleep before it was time to make our way to Baker Street and the hunting train – not enough for rest, more than enough to blot out the cheering effect of the company and the wine. But by then I was committed.

* See *Widow's Peak* (1994).

After we'd passed through Pinner I began to recover enough to look round at our fellow passengers. They mostly had the strained heartiness of people who hadn't bothered to go to bed after parties the night before. Hip flasks were already appearing and I assumed they were counting on the first gallop to sober them up enough to get through the rest of the day. The grooms, in their dull jackets and workman-like boots, were quieter than their masters, sitting in a block at the end of the compartment. When the doors opened at stations the smell of horse and a few neighs and whinnies floated in from the boxes at the back of the train, along with wisps of straw. Bobbie sniffed and said it made her wish we were riding.

'Did you ever hunt, Nell?'

'A few times, when I was twelve, then I rather blotted my copybook.'

'How?'

'I rescued the fox.'

'You *what*?'

'Came across it by accident. It was exhausted, poor thing, all muddy with its tongue hanging out. So I bundled it in my jacket and took it to the other side of a road while the hounds were otherwise engaged. It got away, but somebody saw me and told the Master.'

'Nell, your parents must have been so ashamed.'

I'd never seen Bobbie shocked before. This was a young woman who, to my certain knowledge, had committed burglary and attempted blackmail, all for the cause, of course.* Now she was staring at me as if I came from another world.

'My father was delighted. He hadn't wanted me to hunt in the first place, but he said people were responsible for their own moral decisions.'

'Even at twelve?'

'Yes. Anyway, that was the end of my hunting career.'

* See *Sister Beneath the Sheet* (1991).

She glanced at the huntsmen sitting nearest to us, clearly hoping they hadn't heard, but she needn't have worried because they were competing in accounts of fields galloped and fences jumped. They were promising themselves a good day's sport with the general. I gathered that he was a man who liked to lead from the front and set a cracking pace. Some of them were obviously officers from the London cavalry barracks, in immaculate civilian array of hunting pink jackets.

There was one man I noticed sitting a little apart from the rest. He was, if anything, even more carefully dressed than most, if less colourful in a plain black jacket. His black leather boots with mahogany coloured tops gleamed like leaping purpoises, his white stock and buff breeches were miracles of cleanliness and he cherished on his knees a sleek bowler hat. He seemed to me nervous, glancing out of the window, then fixing his eyes on the far end of the carriage, fingers drumming impatiently whenever the train stopped. A good-looking man with a small moustache and a white, set face. I thought he might be nervous of hunting and pitied him a little.

At one stop he stood up and walked towards the men sitting closest to us. They seemed to know him, but I thought their greetings were a little guarded.

'Morning, Jack. Hunting with the general, then?'

Yes, he said. He'd come to ask them what time the train was supposed to arrive. They talked a little about the weather and if the scent would be good and as he leaned against the seat the ash from somebody's cigar got onto his breeches.

'Watch out what you're doing, old chap.'

He brushed it fastidiously from his immaculate knees and thighs, whisked an invisible spot from his boot top. The owner of the cigar apologized offhandedly and the man they called Jack went back to his lonely seat. The others went on talking about him in low tones.

'Jack Marcle not sporting his pink jacket today, then? He's usually one for putting on the dog.'

'Probably doesn't want to attract the general's attention.'

'No, but he'll be hoping to attract somebody else's attention, won't he?'

That was followed by a collective male snigger, *hrrr hrrr*, like the sound a horse makes when it hears feed buckets rattling.

'Not much difficulty there, from what I hear.'

'Maybe not with the filly, but plenty with the sire.'

Hrrr, hrrr.

Bobbie stirred in her seat beside me. 'Oh, that's the man, is it?'

'What man?'

I was rapidly taking a dislike to the over-confident group in front of us. The carriage was becoming misty with cigar smoke, hazed with brandy fumes.

'Jack Marcle, the one who's supposed to be courting Verity Bringold. I've heard about him, only I haven't seen him before.'

She glanced at the well-dressed man sitting on his own.

'Verity being General Bringold's daughter?'

'Yes. We're not interested in social gossip, are we?'

'Why not? It's a long journey. I take it Father doesn't approve.'

Bobbie grinned and sank her voice to a whisper, not that she need to have worried with the increasing heartiness of the compartment. We were out in the country by now, passing fields and hedges, and some of our fellow passengers were pretending to ride over them, whooping at five-bar gates, flinging their arms in the air.

'No, her father doesn't approve. Jack Marcle's a cavalry captain with practically no money of his own and the general thinks he's fortune hunting. He wants her to marry a major from his own regiment, Toby somebody, heir to a baronetcy and heaps of money.'

'Has the daughter indicated any preference?'

'I gather she prefers Jack, not that she actually dislikes this Toby man, but everybody says Jack has a lot more dash.'

I pointed out that he seemed nervy and aired my theory that he was apprehensive about the day's hunting. Bobbie was practically indignant on his behalf.

'Not possibly. He won the regimental point to point twice running. He must be one of the best riders in the home counties.'

'He's nervous all the same.'

Bobbie took another glance at him.

'I think you're right, Nell.' She laughed. 'Do you suppose this is the day he's going to chance it?'

'Chance what?'

'Ask Verity to marry him. It's been done that way often enough, riding home side by side in the dusk after a good day in the saddle. Most men look better on horseback.'

'Which would be all very well if you could spend an entire married life in the saddle. Or is that Verity's ambition?'

'Shouldn't think so. She hunts quite a lot, but that's probably because riding habit suits her.'

'You dislike her?'

Bobbie shrugged.

'Don't know her well enough to like or dislike. Just one of those womenly women.'

'And what will she say to him, yes or no?'

Against my will, I was becoming interested in Jack Marcle and his wooing. There was such a contrast between his tense silence and the behaviour of the rest of the men.

'Yes, I should think. It's getting Father's consent that won't be easy. He's a widower and Verity's his only child.'

The train wound on through the countryside with its cargo of horses and riders. A pale sun was breaking through the mist, over copses of bare trees. By the time we'd reached our destination, a halt with a wide station yard and a few cottages round it, it was a clear day.

As soon as the train came to a standstill the grooms were out and the yard became a cross between a gymkhana and a military operation. Horses were led onto the platform, swathed in their travelling rugs, snorting in the cold air. The riders lingered by the carriage doors, lighting fresh cigars, while their horses were prepared for them. Bobbie and I took ourselves to the far end of the platform, away from all the excitement, sat on a bench and studied our map like earnest walkers. We'd decided that we'd wait until the huntsmen were on their way, then cut unobtrusively across country to General Bringold's residence, Grackle Hall, about three miles from the station. We were in no hurry because the hunt wouldn't move off until about eleven and we had to wait until it was well clear of the house before we could go into action.

Away they went, in twos and threes, walking their horses towards the grey house on its hilltop above a belt of trees. Soon the road between the station and the house was threaded with moving blobs of black and red, standing out against the damp greens and greys of the winter landscape.

Bobbie said, looking up at the house, 'If we get our colours up there, they'll see them over half the county.'

I could feel in her, as in myself, a combination of nervousness and excitement. Now we were here, the question of whether it was a good idea or not had ceased to matter. The thing was to get on with it and do it properly. I was impatient with the riders who were lingering, delaying us. Most of the grooms, who were riding the spare horses for their employers to change onto in the middle of the day, were now also

mounted, following the huntsmen up the road. Only a
few were left by the horse boxes, and those few
included Jack Marcle.

It looked as if he'd been having an argument with
his groom, who was going about his business in the
emphatic, dogged way of a man who knows he's in the
right.

'What are they doing? He's taking the saddle off
again.'

Bobbie sounded as impatient as I felt. Now that most
of the others had gone, we could hear what Jack was
saying to the groom.

'I told you to use the other saddle-cloth today. He'll
be getting saddle galls if you don't watch out.'

The groom put the saddle carefully on the ground,
took a navy blue saddle-cloth from the back of the tall
black horse, went into the box and came out with a
larger version. Jack snatched it from him.

'There you are, doubled over, like this.'

He folded it, put it on the horse's back. The groom,
resentment in every movement, put back the saddle,
buckled the girth then went round to the other side to
hold the stirrup while his employer mounted with ease
and lightness that suggested Bobbie was right about
his riding skills. There was no spare horse for the
groom to ride, but then Jack Marcle wasn't rich.

I'd expected him to follow the other riders up the
road, but as soon as he was out of the station yard he
turned left along a stony lane and broke into a trot.
Then, after a hundred yards or so he must have turned
uphill onto a bridleway because all we could see were
occasional glimpses of his black coat and bowler
through the hedges, accompanied by the rhythm of his
horse's hooves, cantering. The groom, who was
leaning on a fence watching him, spat disgustedly into
the grass and I could see why. When a horse has been
cramped into a travelling van for hours and has a hard
day's work ahead, the last thing you do is start him

uphill at a canter.

Bobbie said, 'Perhaps he wants to pop the question to her before they start.'

We'd worked out a way to Grackle Hall by footpaths that should keep us clear of the riders on the road, and for the next half-hour or so we simply enjoyed the walk. We scrambled over a keeper's stile in a post and rail fence into the woodland circling the general's estate. A pheasant flew from under our feet, making a noise like a wooden rattle, but there were plenty of disturbed pheasants around that morning. It was mostly hazel coppice at first, moist leaf mould underfoot and small twisting paths that might have been made by deer or badgers. We followed them uphill then paused where the hazels gave way to a thinner plantation of ash trees for a look at the house through the telescope. Bobbie had been right about its possibilities. Its most recent architect, high Victorian rather than medieval, had been generous with hand and footholds for climbers. A rhododendron shrubbery provided good cover for us to get up close to the wall of what looked like an old tithe barn that had probably been there longer than the house. Its narrow windows sprouted wisps of hay and from the other side we could hear the clatter of hooves on paving stones and confident voices giving instructions to the grooms.

'If we get in there we can watch them go.'

There was a narrow doorway on our side, half-blocked by hay, but we managed to shoulder a way through it into the dim, sweet-smelling cavern of the old barn. A wooden ladder led to an upper gallery stacked with more hay and we shinned up it to find that we'd done even better than expected. By standing on stacks of hay we could look out of a window slit at the stable yard below. There must have been at least twenty horses, either out in the yard with grooms holding them or looking over the doors of their boxes. Some of the general's house party were already mounted, fussing with gloves or stirrup leathers. Only one woman was there so far. She was young and slim with swags of fair hair caught up in a net under her black bowler, dressed for riding side-saddle in a waist-hugging jacket and full navy blue skirt. The dark colours emphasized the paleness of her face and the shadowed half circles under her eyes. She stood quite close to our barn and we watched as a groom led out a bright chestnut mare, good-looking but light-boned.

'No, not Sonnet. I said I'd ride Apple today. Didn't they tell you?'

Without a word, the groom gave the chestnut's reins to a stable lad and disappeared from view. Apple's box must have been just below us because we could hear the sounds of grooming, the swish of a brush, the steady hissing of the groom. The woman walked restlessly up and down, swinging her riding crop.

I whispered, 'Is that Verity Bringold?'

Bobbie nodded. Another man appeared in the yard, a tall young man dressed for hunting and in a hurry. He came over to where Verity was pacing and although she must have seen him she gave no sign of it until he spoke to her.

'You weren't at breakfast.'

'No.'

He held his top hat in his hand and the sun shone on his fair hair. His nose was Wellingtonian and his chin conceded victory to it.

'I wanted to talk to you.'

She tried to turn aside, towards the stable door, but he blocked her way.

'I think I have a right to an explanation.'

'What about?'

With the clatter going on in the stable yard they weren't bothering to speak quietly and their voices came clearly up to us.

'You know what about. Are we still engaged, or aren't we?'

'We never were engaged.'

'I thought we had an understanding. Didn't we?'

A mixture of petulance and appeal in his voice. Bobbie made a face at me. I suppose we should have moved away, but it would have been difficult to do that without alerting the groom down in the box.

'Well, didn't we?'

No answer.

'What's changed? Is it Jack Marcle?'

She turned her back on him.

'Haven't I got the right to know that, at least?'

Her bowler hat tipped at an angle, rose again.

'So it is him. That squalid little fortune hunter.'

Bobbie drew in her breath sharply. Although Verity hadn't moved after that nod her whole figure radiated anger. The air was full of it like a fox's smell, hers and his. He took a step towards her. She drew aside.

'So I can't even touch you now, and he . . . ' He stopped on the edge of something unforgivable, tried one last appeal. 'Don't make your father unhappy.'

She still didn't turn and he stared at her back for long seconds.

'I'm not leaving it like this. Don't think I'm leaving it like this.'

He jammed his top hat on his head, went striding across the stable yard and grabbed the reins of a big showy bay from a waiting groom. When he clattered out of the yard she still hadn't moved.

A grey-haired man with a red face arrived carrying hat and hunting horn and the grooms snapped into an even greater state of activity.

Bobbie hissed, 'General Bringold.'

Ready for a day of strong nerves and strenuous action, the bald crown of his head shone in the sun, his cheery voice carried all over the yard.

'Morning, Verity. Thought you'd be mounted by now.'

She turned to him, no trace in voice or expression of what had happened.

'They're just plaiting Apple's mane.'

The old man was pleased.

'Decided not to ride that chestnut maniac of yours, then? Good job too.'

'I know you worry when I ride Sonnet, Father.'

Bobbie glanced at me. Verity's voice was honeyed, submissive, quite unlike the tones she'd used to Toby. A broad grey cob was led out of the box underneath us, a groom applying a final polish to its dappled hindquarters as it came. Verity mounted. As she turned the cob to follow her father and the rest of the house party, something happened visible only to Bobbie and me in our hiding place. When she thought nobody could see her face, her head came up and a smile gleamed out like a vein of quartz in wet rock. Then they all rode off to the front of the house where the stirrup cup would be circulating, leaving the yard quiet apart from the swish of brooms and scrape of shovels.

Bobbie was annoyed.

'Doesn't the woman know she's living in the twentieth century – changing onto a quieter horse just to please her father? I suppose she'll go on deferring to Daddy until she finds a husband to order her around.'

I said I wasn't so sure about that.

'You heard her.'

'Yes, but I saw too.'

'That simper?'

'More than a simper. I have the impression she's just where she wants to be.'

It had been there for only a second, and yet it had struck me as the smile of a someone who'd just done something difficult and dangerous, like a trapeze artiste completing one mad loop before spinning off on another. Perhaps it was fellow feeling because Bobbie and I were about to do something like that as well.

'What, riding a duller horse?'

'It put the general in a good mood with her, didn't it? It might suit her very well to please him by giving way in a small thing, if she wants to get her way on a much bigger thing later.'

'Jack Marcle, you mean?'

'Yes. We'd already guessed that today's the day he puts the question. I'd say Verity's thinking one step ahead.'

'Heaven defend me from ever having to manipulate a man like that.'

'Amen.'

And yet, in her own way and with her own weapons, Verity was fighting too. I thought about it until the grooms had cleaned the yard and gone and it was time to make our dash for it.

When the history of mountaineering on the mansions of the home counties comes to be written, our New Year's Day climb up the east face of Grackle Hall may have a part in it. In spite of all the balconies, ledges and fanciful stonework it was harder than it looked. At one point I was holding Bobbie by the wrist as she slithered and kicked for a foothold, hoping she'd find it before I was dragged off my narrow ledge. At another my wretched skirt hooked itself round the head of a griffin and she had to lean out at a giddy angle to free me. A housemaid opening a window at the wrong time would have wrecked us, but our gamble that they'd be at the front of the house to watch the hunt move off was justified. Breathless, shaking but unobserved we rested for a few minutes in the wide lead gutter behind a line of gargoyles, then negotiated the gently sloping tiled roof between us and the flagpole.

Bobbie took off her jacket, flaked with lichen, and unwound the flag from her waist.

'Such sharp fingernails you've got, Nell. My wrist may be scarred for life.'

'If you'd wanted me to let go, you should have said so.'

We laughed, half-drunk with triumph and relief. It took some time to get our flag hoisted, because it was so much larger than the conventional kind, but we managed a lash-up job with some string I had in my pocket and there was the purple, white and green flying over the Chiltern Hills. It caught the breeze, flapped then streamed out just as we'd wanted. General Bringold and his guests would see it from miles away.

We began to wonder what the hunt was doing and how long it would be before anybody noticed it. From where we were, on the highest point of one of the highest houses in the area, we had a view for miles around but at first we could see no sign of horses and hounds, even with the telescope. Then Bobbie pointed to a copse about half a mile from the house, in the middle of pasture-land.

'They haven't got far. They must be drawing that covert there.'

I looked and could just make out glints of horses and red coats among the bare bushes. Bobbie had an expert eye to the telescope.

'I'll be surprised if there's not a fox in there somewhere, Nell, but by the look of it hounds haven't picked up a scent yet.'

We waited for the hounds to give tongue, for the horses to burst out of the woodland and across the pasture, but there was silence apart from the flapping of our flag in the wind.

'I can see Verity, at any rate, no mistaking that fat grey. Looks as if she's keeping out of the way of the others. No sign of Jack Marcle yet. Wonder where he's . . . Oh ho.'

'Oh ho what?'

I wanted to get down and be done with it, but Bobbie was absorbed.

'Toby's having another try. He's moving over to her. Look, by the hedge there.'

She handed me the telescope. Even with it I couldn't make out faces, but I could see the man in the red coat on the big bay moving towards the figure on the grey horse, on its own at the edge of the covert. But the rider of the grey saw him coming too, and made the horse walk away. Over the next few minutes we watched a sort of slow motion minuet on horseback, with the rider of the bay determined to come alongside and the rider of the grey equally determined to keep a distance between them. All this while the rest of the hunt were intent on the efforts of the general and his hounds to pick up a scent.

Interesting in its way, but not what we were there for. I handed the telescope back to Bobbie and pointed out that nobody seemed to have noticed the flag yet.

'Might take them hours. Can we trail them? I'd love to see the general's face when he notices.'

We argued about it gently for a while. Bobbie thought the job was only half done unless we could take news of his reaction back with us. I couldn't see how, even with telescope, we could get close enough. In the end we agreed to compromise, spend a couple of hours trailing the hunt like any other followers on foot, then give up and go back to London.

Bobbie took a last look towards the hunt.

'Looks as if they're moving off to try somewhere else.'

Horses and riders were filing at a walk out of the copse and into a lane. Then a gasp from Bobbie.

'I think he's seen it. There's somebody coming back. It looks like Verity.'

As the hunt went in one direction a single rider on a grey horse was coming in the other, at a full gallop across the pasture-land. The rider was unmistakably side-saddle, in dark habit.

'He's sent her back to see what's happening. He must be furious.'

I pointed out that her return might have nothing to do with our flag, that she'd simply had enough of trying to avoid Toby in slow motion and had decided to make her escape while he wasn't looking. Bobbie wasn't convinced, but at least agreed that it was time to move. We went down the side of the house faster than we'd gone up. For the last awkward forty feet or so we tied the rope to a balcony and slid down it, skinning our hands. It meant we had to leave the rope where it was, but by then it didn't matter. I picked myself up off the gravel and we sped across the lawn, expecting at any minute to hear shouts from the windows.

If Verity had been sent back because of our flag she should have reached the house by now. I imagined her clattering into the stable yard, raising the alarm, sending servants rushing. There was no question of going back the way we'd come. Instead we bolted into a shrubbery and found a deep ha-ha on the other side, separating garden from fields. In and out of that, across a wire fence and we were comparatively safe in the ash wood. A little scrambling brought us back onto the path we'd taken on our way up. Following it in one direction would lead back to the safety of the Metropolitan Railway line, in the other to the area where the general was still looking for his fox – or any acceptable substitute. We turned as agreed towards the place where we'd last seen the hunt, going carefully until we were well out of sight of the house. Soon we came across a broad ride, much trampled by fresh hoof prints, that showed we were on the track of them. Bobbie, cautious for once, said we'd better keep an ear open in case the general himself came galloping back.

'He'd never abandon his hunt, would he?'

'Depends how angry he is. After all, we've stormed

his headquarters. I'd like to hide behind a bush and yell ''strenuous action'' at him.'

'You'll do nothing of the kind. We're taking enough risks already. I'm just humouring you with a closer look, then it's back to the train. Understood?'

'Understood.'

We walked on along the muddy path, with the barking of hounds in the distance. It was further to the copse than it had looked from the roof, with the going very muddy, but at least our immediate surroundings were quiet with no sound of a general's avenging hooves.

Then we heard it – a noise both familiar and alarming. Familiar because it was no more than a horse whinnying, alarming because it was close. We stopped and looked round, expecting to see vengeful horsemen converging on us. Bobbie grabbed my arm.

'Sounds as if the hunt is up.'

'I know how that fox felt.'

I was trying to think like a fox too, weighing up the spaces between the ash trees where horses couldn't follow us. The whinnying again.

'It's down there, below us.'

There was a narrow path leading off the main ride into the bushes and the sound was coming from down there, but there was still no sign of anybody or anything. I told Bobbie to stay where she was, not trusting her to keep quiet if it really was the general, and went a few steps down the bank, sliding from tree to tree, until I could see another path below us. There was no man or horse on it, but the whinnying went on. After a few more cautious steps I found myself looking at the roof of a small building with a trampled space in front of it. The noise was coming from there.

'Somebody's left a horse in there.'

I slid down a chalky bank to the open space in front of the building and Bobbie followed. It looked like a disused lime kiln, used to store farm implements. The door was shut and bolted. As I looked at it a hoof rattled against it from the inside. I looked in through a crack and saw, dark against the half darkness, a big black horse with a white blaze. Its eye was rolling and it whinnied like the whistle of a steam train.

'It's all right, fellow. All right.'

Jack Marcle's big black horse. No sign of Jack Marcle. Bobbie was behind me.

'What's going on?'

She spoke soothingly to the horse and put her eye to the crack in the door.

'In a muck sweat, but so should I be if I were tied up in here with the rest out hunting. What in the world is the man doing?'

'A different sort of hunting.' Light was beginning to dawn. 'I thought Verity might be trying to get away from Toby, but there was more to it than that. She's on her way to meet Jack Marcle.'

Bobbie stared at me.

'They're going to all this trouble just to meet?'

'More than meet, I'd say. I think they're eloping. They probably arranged that she'd slip away from the others as soon as she got the chance, and he'd be waiting for her. They'll ride off to the station and hope to be in London or on the boat train for the Continent before her father knows what's happening.'

'Well, good for little Verity.'

'I thought there was more to her than there looked. She was so pleased with herself when they rode out of the stable yard.'

'It would explain why Jack was so nervous.'

'Another thing – you remember the men on the train? One of them was surprised because Jack Marcle was in his black coat today, not his hunting pink. Less conspicuous if you're eloping.'

My detective reputation had not been of my seeking in the first place, but since it was a label my friends seemed determined to pin on me, I might as well live up to it.

'At least it means there's no point in tracking the hunt. If the general didn't even notice his daughter sneaking away, he won't have seen our flag.'

Bobbie was starting to say something when the black horse began whinnying again and throwing his head around.

'Nell, I think there's somebody coming.'

Another horse was coming up the path, brushing through dead leaves and nettle stalks. Jack's horse, delighted at company, yelled to it again and again so that Bobbie had to put her mouth close to my ear to be heard.

'This will be Verity arriving. What do we do?'

'Wish them *bon voyage*.'

I was becoming tired of skulking. The horse wasn't in sight yet, but a man's voice called from that direction.

'Verity. Verity, are you there?'

'Oh dear, he is going to be disappointed to find us instead.'

'That isn't Jack Marcle's voice. That's Toby.'

'Toby, oh God. Poor Verity.'

'Perhaps we should try to draw him off for her.'

Unjustifiable. Quite unjustifiable. It was no business of ours which man she married and at that point I knew very little about either Jack or Toby. But an elopement is like a hunt itself. Whether you're directly involved or not, something makes your heart go out to one side or the other, fox or hounds, eloping couple or angry father. Just as, twenty years or so ago, I'd had to help the fox, now we had to help Verity. We stayed where we were.

Toby, arriving, goggled at us from the back of his big bay.

'What are you doing here?'

I said, 'We were looking for the hunt.'

It made no impression on him. His face was red with effort or exasperation. His ears stuck out from under his top hat.

'There's a horse in there.'

He slid off his own animal and, trailing it by the reins, went and opened the door of the building. He stared from us to the big black horse and back again.

'It's not her horse. Is it yours?'

'No.'

'Have you seen a girl on a grey cob?'

'Half an hour ago, galloping towards the house.'

This had the merit of being strictly truthful but misleading at the same time. I was certain her real destination was here in the woods, to meet Jack. Whether we'd have succeeded in sending Toby in the wrong direction I don't know, because at this point there were footsteps in the dead leaves, then another voice, loud and strained.

'Verity, what's happening?'

Jack Marcle strode round the side of the shed. He took in the horse and the other man, hardly noticed us.

He said to Toby, 'What the hell do you think you're doing here?'

He was less tidy than in the train, face red and flecked with mud, black horse hairs clinging to his buff thighs. There was a bunched up anger about him. Bobbie had moved towards him, I think with some idea of trying to warn him, but he held out a hand to keep her aside. Even the palm of his hand was mud smeared.

'I don't think that's any business of yours. What are you doing, for that matter?'

Toby had the advantage of being cooler and made the best of it.

'As it happens, I'm looking for Miss Bringold.'

'What makes you think Miss Bringold wants to see you?'

'Her horse bolted off with her.'

'Miss Bringold does not get bolted off with. She knows how to manage a horse.'

Toby drawled, 'Well then, perhaps she'll give you some lessons.'

Jack looked at him as if he couldn't believe what had been said.

'Meaning?'

'If a man has to hide his horse in a lime kiln because he's scared to risk his neck over fences, he might need a lesson or two from a girl.'

Unfair, of course. By Bobbie's account Jack was not over-careful of his neck. But if Toby hadn't guessed about the elopement it would look very much to him as if he'd caught Jack shirking. Jack stared at the other man and his face, from red, turned pale so that the mud smear stood out. I was amazed at the effect of the sneer, but I should have remembered that Jack Marcle was a cavalry officer, and in his code the charge of cowardice on a horse was probably the worst thing that could be said about a man. Even Toby looked taken aback by his own effectiveness and when Jack took a step towards him he held up his hunting crop, as if warding him off. But Jack simply walked past him and opened the door of the old kiln.

The black horse nuzzled his shoulder but he didn't acknowledge it. He'd been carrying his saddle-cloth over his left arm. Now he unfolded it, put it over the horse's back, then took the saddle from an old trestle where it had been resting. He did everything methodically, but so quickly that the horse was tacked up and out in the open before Toby knew what was happening. Then he swung himself into the saddle and started into a canter from a standstill, charging Toby and his horse aside. The canter became a gallop as he went straight up the slope, dodging between the trees. By then, Toby was on his horse and following. As they disappeared we heard, from several fields away, the barking of hounds and the sound of hunting horns.

Bobbie picked herself out of the undergrowth where she'd been flung by Jack Marcle's charge.

'Sounds as if they're going to get a chance to break

their stupid necks, if that's what they want. I just hope
they don't break the horses' as well.'

As we picked the worst of the thorns and burrs out
of her jacket we discussed the effect this would have
on the elopement. Bobbie thought it might have to be
postponed.

'It's a good horse he's got, but if he and Toby are
going to be riding like maniacs, it won't have the
energy left to take him to the station.'

'In Verity's place, I'd be angry with Jack.'

'Well, he didn't have much choice after what Toby
said to him, did he?'

Privately, I thought he'd had all the choice in the
world between behaving like a rational human being
or a demented centaur but since Bobbie's code was
probably much the same as a cavalryman's – apart
from an injection of brains – I decided not to argue the
point.

'The question is, was Toby lucky or is he more
intelligent than he looks?'

She stared. 'Does he strike you as intelligent?'

'No, but that could be deceptive. Suppose he'd
found out about the elopement and went to the
rendezvous to stop it.'

'In that case, why didn't he say so?'

'That would put some of the blame on Verity – and
he wants to marry her.'

Bobbie thought about it.

'You know, Nell, you could just be right. So that
challenge to Jack was to ruin his plans without
bandying a woman's name. And Jack fell for it.'

'You said he had no choice. Anyway, if I'm right the
question is whether Jack can do anything about it.
What would you do in his place?'

She didn't even need to think about it.

'I'd gallop the legs off him, lead him over the nastiest
places I could find then come back here to meet Verity
while he's floundering in a ditch.'

'I take it that's what Jack will try to do. The question is, whether Verity will be here waiting for him.'

'We shall just have to make sure that she is.'

Sporting instinct had thoroughly taken hold of Bobbie. She said she had no intention of going back to London until she'd seen the game through. Even though sporting instinct was less highly developed in me, my incurable vice of curiosity had the same effect. There were already two things that bothered me about that meeting between Jack and Toby. Small things only, but if we bolted for London now the puzzle would stay unsolved. We argued a little, but the upshot was that we settled down inside the lime kiln and waited for Verity.

It was about ten minutes before she arrived, riding up to the door on her grey cob.

'Jack?'

We came out quietly so as not to frighten her horse. Like Jack, she'd lost some of her hunting morning gloss. There were bits of dried bracken clinging to the hem of her skirt, mud and leaves caked on the sole of the boot visible underneath it. She blinked when she saw us.

I said, 'If you're looking for Jack Marcle, he's been here. We think he'll be back.'

She had self-possession. Instead of coming out in a splutter of questions, she sat there and absorbed it. Then, 'How do you know?'

We gave an account of ourselves, without mentioning the flag, or that we'd guessed about the elopement. We were walkers who'd stumbled on this, regretted if we were trespassing.

'Did he give you a message for me?'

'I don't think he had time.'

I decided I'd leave the explaining to Bobbie, as she took a more tolerant view of Jack's madness.

'What Nell means is that he went rampaging off like the hounds of hell with the man called Toby.'

'Toby?' She stared at us, eyes huge through the hunting veil. 'Jack went off with Toby?'

'I'm afraid so. Toby found him here and accused him of being scared to take his fences.'

She stared from one to the other of us. Her grey cob bent its weary neck and nibbled grass blades.

'Toby accused Jack of being scared and they've gone off together?'

'I'm afraid so.'

I expected anger or even tears. What we got instead was a sudden peal of laughter.

'If Toby's trying to out-jump Jack, then he's got a surprise coming.'

The joke, whatever joke it was, seemed to matter more than the hitch in their elopement plans. I wondered whether I'd got it wrong after all, then I looked at her boot and skirt and knew I hadn't. It struck me that Verity, like me, believed Toby was deliberately trying to divert Jack away from her. Her eyes sparkled and she looked fizzing with the thrill of it. A century ago men might have fought duels for women like Verity – and women like Verity probably found it the most exciting thing that ever happened to them. That was very reprehensible of them, of course, but better than fainting.

'We'll go and watch them, somewhere they won't see us.'

Without questioning our right to be there, she was letting us in on the joke. Perhaps she'd caught a whiff of lawlessness about us and – on this day when she was making a run for her kind of freedom – shared it. The wildness of the moment was increased by the sounds of the hunt from not far away, hounds and horns in full cry. She snatched at the reins and the cob raised its head, weary but obedient.

'You'd need Pegasus to catch those two,' I said. 'Don't you think you'd better wait here for him, as you planned?'

'I want to watch.'

Bobbie was practical.

'If you've got any plans for that mare later, you'd better give her a rest now.'

Verity saw the force of that.

'We can get there just as well on foot. I know a short cut, and they're less likely to see us.'

She slid off the grey and led it into the lime kiln. We helped her take off the saddle and hitch up the reins. While we did it, I thought about the new puzzle that had been added to my existing set. Verity said she knew a short cut. It was obvious that Toby and Jack were going to rejoin the hunt and compete with each other over the stiffest places. The hunt, from the sound of it, was now moving fast and the only creature that could know where they were all heading was the object of it all: the fox. So how could Verity possibly guess where they were going?

I wished I had a chance to discuss it with Bobbie but by then the three of us were climbing the bank, approximately in the direction the two horsemen had gone. Verity, in her full riding skirt and thin boots, had a hard time of it among the bracken and brambles and I had to give her a hand up several times. We eventually found ourselves out on a broad ride, with the sounds of the hunt somewhere up ahead of us. I expected Verity to lead us in the same direction but she cut straight across the ride through a grove of young beeches.

'They'll turn soon. We can save a mile on them this way.'

She hurried on, slipping and sliding. Behind her back, I mouthed one word at Bobbie.

'Drag?'

She nodded.

'There. We can wait here and watch.'

Verity, panting and with a hand pressed to her side, halted at the top of the bank under a beech. We were looking down on a kind of shallow valley, no more than a broad scoop in the hillside with muddy banks on either side, carpeted with dead beech leaves. At one end was an open gate, at the other an unkempt hedge about four foot high with a little ditch in front of it. There was a gap in the middle of the hedge filled by a low post and rails. I looked up the valley to the open gate and the meadow beyond it and realized that we were in the beech copse where the grey horse and rider must have galloped as we watched from the roof. Sure enough, a deep line of hoofprints went along the valley, the fresh crescents of mud gleaming from the leaf covering.

'I suppose that was your horse galloping,' I said.

She looked at me and nodded, biting her lip. I still had the feeling of a joke half-shared.

Bobbie said, 'You did well to get him to gallop away from the others. Not easy when you're hunting.'

'Shhh.'

Verity held up her gloved hand. Now that we weren't crashing through undergrowth we could hear the sounds of the hunt again, distant but coming closer.

I said, 'I hope the hounds don't smell the aniseed on your glove.'

I could even smell it faintly on my own fingers, where I'd given her a hand to help her up the bank. For hounds it would be a scent so seductive that they'd follow it anywhere. She gave me an alarmed look.

'What do you mean?'

'That's not a fox they're following. You must have been up very early this morning to lay a false trail.'

She hadn't got back in time for breakfast. The conversation we overheard with Toby made that clear.

'I suppose the idea was to keep your father and the rest of the hunt busy and out of the way up here while you and Jack made for the train.'

Her eyes went from me to Bobbie and back.

'Don't worry about Nell,' Bobbie said. 'She can't help doing it. The point is we're on your side.'

She didn't waste time asking why, or even thanking us but that smile broke out again, a smile of pleasure in her own cleverness, innocent as a young otter playing on a riverbank. I smiled back – I couldn't help it – and Bobbie was laughing outright.

'Poor Toby didn't know what he was up against, did he? We watched him trying to get close to you in that first covert.'

That seemed to puzzle Verity, as well it might, since she couldn't know we'd been watching through a telescope from the roof. She looked as if she wanted to ask a question, even alarmed for a moment, but Bobbie was chattering on happily.

'Now I suppose it all depends on whether Jack can outride him.'

'Jack can outride Toby any day.'

She said it with total confidence, but you could tell that some of her attention was on the sounds of the hunt coming closer.

'You and Jack weren't leaving anything to chance, were you?'

'No,' she said. 'Except the biggest chance of all.'

She was sure they were winning, and yet I still worried about Toby. If, as I suspected, he'd somehow guessed what they were doing, he'd tell her father as a last resort. I asked her if Toby might have found out about the drag trail, but she shook her head. By then the noise of the hounds was so loud that it blotted out everything and the hunt was coming into the little valley below us.

The hounds, going strongly, filled it from side to side, a river of white and black and tan. Their leaders made for the gap in the hedge and as they scrambled under the rail the first of the red coats came into view at the other end of the valley. There were three or four of them, with the portly figure of the general immediately recognizable, leading from the front as they said he always did, yelling on the hounds. I felt a hand gripping mine. Verity's.

'He's not there.'

But as she said it, the thing happened. Two riders came bursting through the gateway into the valley and galloped past the general, one to his right and one to his left. Even I could see that it was a shocking breach of hunting field protocol. His horse swung its hindquarters, kicked the air. The riders with him yelled their indignation. There were angry cries of 'Hounds. Hounds, sir.'

Bobbie gasped, 'Surely they're not . . .'

But they were. The two wild riders, one in red coat and top hat, the other in black jacket and bowler, were committing the unforgivable hunting-field sin of riding down hounds. The back markers of the pack scattered yelping from under their galloping hooves and the curses of the general and the men round him rose like a battle chant.

Toby and Jack were riding like jockeys, standing up in their stirrups, whipping on their horses. Toby was leading by a short head. I expected him to make for the obvious place to jump, the gap with the rails, but he was hauling his horse's head to the left to put it at the four foot hedge. No matter what happened to the rest of the field, his duel with Jack was still going on. Verity's hand tightened on mine. As Toby's horse took off in a mighty jump over the hedge, Jack was pulling at his reins to turn aside from the easy place and follow him. He'd have managed it except for one thing. The general lashed out at him with his hunting whip. He'd clearly intended the blow for Jack but he was going too fast. Instead the very end of the lash flicked the hindquarters of Jack's horse as it galloped past. The horse kicked out and the best rider on earth couldn't have prevented it from swerving. In those last two strides Jack, still sawing at the reins, was carried away from the dangerous hedge his rival had jumped to the easy gap. Verity gave a shaky laugh and her grip on my hand relaxed. Jack was going to save his neck for their elopement.

For a horse as good as Jack's the low rails should have been easy, even from a gallop. It jumped a good six inches clear of the top rail, then it seemed to falter in mid-leap and – while Verity's laugh of relief was still hanging in the air – checked and somersaulted onto the far side. The hounds, the hooves, the cursing must have been going on all the time it was happening, and yet it stays in my mind as a moment of silence, just the leafless branches, the grey sky and the black horse tumbling.

Verity dragged her hand away from me and rushed down the bank. Men, horses and hounds shouted, whinnied and yelped in a swirling mass on our side of the post and rails. They were all trying to get over but there was no room for a horse to take off. As we ran one of the men jumped clean out of his saddle and landed on foot on the other side.

There was a shout of 'Wire!'

An answering bellow from the general: 'No wire in my fences, sir.'

By then Verity was pushing her way through the scrum, oblivious of plunging horses or the men who tried to stop her.

'Keep back, my dear. No place for ladies.'

She went and we followed, among hooves and sweating horseflesh, between top and middle rails. On the other side a man in buff breeches was lying on the leaves, the man who'd jumped from the saddle bending over him, hiding his face. The black horse was back on his feet, reins broken, shivering and snorting but apparently not seriously injured. His rider was another matter. Verity ran to him.

'Jack.'

More men were over the fence on foot now, running

towards the fallen rider. They stopped in a collective panic when they heard the way she said his name. The same fear of her grief was on the face of the man who'd got to him first when he looked up. It was that fear, even more than the way the fallen man was lying, that showed Jack was dead. After that momentary check, they all came forward again, lifted Verity up from her knees beside him and pushed her into my arms and Bobbie's, as if we were somehow more equipped to handle this raw business than they were.

While he was still on the ground and they were ranging up and down the hedge looking for branches strong enough for a stretcher, Toby came back. He came trotting along on his big bay, apparently puzzled that neither Jack nor the hunt had followed him. By then Jack's head was covered by somebody's jacket but he only had to look at Verity, leaning on my shoulder, to know who it was. He said nothing. His face went red then, very slowly, he took off his top hat.

Verity didn't need us long. There were other women at the house, aunts, cousins, friends, with better right to act as comforters. Her father too. The general was ill at ease and clumsy, but at least he showed some tenderness for her when he abandoned his horse to a groom and walked back to the house with his arm round her waist. After that first cry of Jack's name she'd said nothing, to us or to anybody. They went in at the front door and, arriving after a decent interval, the men carrying Jack's body went in at the back. Bobbie and I simply walked away in the dusk down the road to the station. A few riders passed us, saying nothing, their horses pacing heavy-legged. Even those who hadn't been up with the hounds knew what had happened by now. In the yard by the railway line even the grooms seemed subdued, cigarettes glowing in the failing light. Cold air nipped through our gloves.

Bobbie dragged me to the far end of the platform

where nobody could hear us.

'Well, are we going to leave it like this?'

'Leave what?'

'Leave Toby to get away with it. We heard it. We saw it. He tells her, "I'm not leaving it like this." Then he finds Jack Marcle, deliberately insults him and leads him into a trap.'

'You think that was how it happened?'

'Oh for goodness sake, even I can see it. Toby had stretched wire across the top of that gap. A man going at it full gallop like Jack was almost guaranteed to break his neck. Toby challenged him so that he could take the hedge to the side instead, while Jack . . .'

'Jack tried to take the hedge too, tried very hard.'

I remembered the desperate pull on the rein, his whole body straining.

'And didn't make it. You'd have to be an exceptionally good rider to make a horse jump that great hedge when there was what looked like a perfectly good low fence to the side.'

'But Jack was an exceptionally good rider. And he'd have managed it if the general hadn't hit his horse.'

'Nell, you're hiding something. What is it?'

'I'm hiding nothing. You saw everything I saw.'

'Are you trying to tell me Toby didn't kill him?'

'Yes, I am.'

A train arrived. I suggested we should go inside while they were loading the horses in at the back. Bobby refused.

'I'm not leaving Toby to get away with it.'

'Just think about it for a moment. Remember up on the roof, looking down at that rider galloping away from the hunt.'

'Verity on Apple. Of course.'

'Which way were they going?'

'Along that little valley in the beechwood. The same way as the hunt came on the drag . . . oh.'

She stopped.

'Exactly. The same way the hunt came along the aniseed trail that Verity had set earlier. She knew that valley. The easiest way to get out of it on a horse is to do that little jump over the rails. You saw it. Yes?'

'Yes, but . . .'

'So how would a rider get Apple out of that valley to the place where they had their rendezvous? It was either a four-foot hedge, side-saddle on a tired old cob, or over the little rails. The rails where somebody put the wire that killed Jack Marcle.'

'Toby.'

'Bobbie, he couldn't know the hunt was going that way. Only somebody who knew about the aniseed trail could predict that, and Verity certainly didn't tell Toby.'

There was still just enough light to see the look of horror coming over her face.

'Nell, I think we will go and sit down after all.'

I followed her into the train and waited while she worked it out.

'Verity knew the hunt would be coming along that valley because she'd laid the drag trail. She must have jumped that rail, so the wire wasn't there when she . . . oh God. But she was eloping with the man. She loved him. For heaven's sake, why should she want to kill him?'

'Who says she did?'

'You've just said so. She and Jack were the only ones who knew about the drag. She must have jumped those rails, then turned round and put the wire across and gone to meet Jack, cool as you please. We even helped the woman.'

'She didn't do it.'

'But you've just proved that she did. We even watched her galloping off to do it.'

'We didn't. We saw a horse and rider galloping.'

'Her horse. She said so when you noticed the hoofprints.'

'Her horse, but another rider. It was Jack Marcle on that horse.'

'It was a woman, riding side-saddle.'

'Anyone can ride side-saddle, and the point about riding clothes is that they're quite similar for men and women, bowler hat and dark jacket.'

'Skirt. That person on the grey cob was wearing a dark skirt, like any woman hunting. In case you've forgotten, Jack was wearing buff breeches.'

As if I could forget. It was less than two hours since we'd seen them on legs flopped lifeless on the beech leaves.

'Did you notice anything about those breeches? Black horse hairs on the thighs.'

I thought how careful he'd been about them in the train that morning, brushing off cigar ash.

'Nell, his horse is black.'

'Can you think of any way a man rides a horse with the front of his thighs in contact? Outside a circus, that is.'

She shook her head, defeated. I noticed that the urge to rush off and do something had left her.

'Think back to this morning. We watched him make his groom take off a perfectly good saddle-cloth and put on a larger one. Navy blue. He takes off that saddle-cloth later and wraps it round his waist over his breeches to look like a skirt. It has black horse hairs on it by then. Naturally some of them will cling.'

'That means they'd planned it.'

'The elopement? Of course they did. It depended on Verity riding away from her father and the hunt. But as you pointed out yourself, that's not easy to do once they've started, unless you're a very strong rider. My guess is that Verity met Jack in a shrubbery near the house very soon after they'd ridden off and he took her place then. If her father or anybody else happened to look for her she'd be there at the back of the field, in correct ladies' riding gear on her grey cob – provided you didn't look too closely.'

'Was that why she was so determined that Toby shouldn't talk to her in the covert?'

'Yes, except by that point "she" was Jack. No wonder he didn't want a heart-to-heart with Toby. Once he knew the general's attention was distracted he made his break, met Verity as arranged and helped her back up on her cob. Remember the mud on his palm when we met him at the lime kiln?'

I cupped my hands, to remind her of the way a man makes a step for a woman to get back into a side-saddle.

'It was obvious she'd spent some time on foot, from the mud on her boot and the bracken on the bottom of her skirt.'

There was the noise from the back of the train of doors being bolted. Riders, muddy and subdued, began to join us in the carriage, considerably more sober than when we'd left London.

Bobbie said, quietly, 'So he jumped those rails on Apple then put the wire there?'

'Yes.'

'Then galloped right into it?'

'That was exactly what he intended not to do. You saw how desperately he was trying to get his horse to jump the hedge instead. We thought it was because he was competing with Toby, but he had a much more compelling reason than that.'

'So was Jack trying to kill Toby?'

'Not Toby. Think. Suppose Jack and Toby weren't having their duel and the hunt had come galloping through normally.'

'The first rider would have gone over the rails and hit the wire instead.'

'And who would that first rider have been? Who has a reputation for always leading from the front?'

'Oh . . . the general.' She closed her eyes and thought about it for a while, then echoed what Toby had said in the stable yard.

'Well, the squalid little fortune hunter.'

'Yes. Jack didn't only want Verity. He wanted Verity as heiress to her father's money. He'd rush her away to Paris or somewhere before the sad news of her father's death in the hunting field came through – and nothing to prove that Jack had been anywhere near that post and rails.'

The grooms came in, rubbing their hands against the cold. More doors slammed.

'Did Verity know what he was doing?'

'I'm sure she didn't. She was relieved when Jack was riding towards the easy place rather than the hedge. She wouldn't have been if she knew what he was riding into.'

Once we were on the way back to town the riders began to recover their spirits a little and hushed voices rose again.

'How did the old boy take it?'

'Shouldn't think the general will lose much sleep for the likes of Marcle. It was the other thing that really bothered him.'

'Other thing?'

'Didn't you hear? No sooner he's back inside than somebody tells him there's a bloody great banner flying from his flagpole and platoons of suffragettes rioting all over the roof.'

'How would they get up there?'

'How would I know? Rode there on their broomsticks probably. The bloody women get everywhere.'

Bobbie's face broke into a great grin.

She whispered, 'Platoons. Just you and me, Nell.'

Soon after that she slumped against my shoulder and slept. She woke around Harrow.

'Do you think Verity knows what Jack did now?'

'I think she guessed almost at once. She's really no fool.'

It had been a double shock that hit her by the fence – her lover's death and the realization of how he'd tried to use her.

'What on earth will she do?'

'She'll recover. In fact, it wouldn't surprise me if by midsummer you see an announcement in *The Times* that she's going to marry Toby.'

'You don't suppose I read that sort of thing, do you?'

She was silent almost until Finchley Road then, 'I wonder if you're right.'

'I usually am,' I said.

Nell Bray

Nell Bray writes: *I have been asked to give some account of myself for people who know me mainly by my chance and unsought reputation as a solver of mysteries. Here it is:*

I was born in Liverpool in 1877. My father, Charles Bray, a doctor, was working there at the time. I have a brother, Stuart, my senior by three years. My mother Ida (née Kellman-McCloud) came from Edinburgh. When I was a child we moved around frequently because my father combined a strong sense of duty with tactlessness on a grand scale – a quality some people say I inherited. He was a rebellious younger son from a family of minor landed gentry and twice stood unsuccessfully for Parliament as a radical. He'd recover from his political disappointments by going climbing in the Alps. My mother loved amateur theatricals and caused some scandal by taking part in early productions of Ibsen.

As a child, I wanted to be an actress, later a barrister. It was planned that I should follow my brother to Oxford. The death of my father in a diphtheria epidemic when I was 17 prevented this. My mother took to travelling and for several years I had to look after her while we wandered around Europe, usually on unfounded rumours that meals and a roof over our heads would be cheaper in the next country. At least during this period I had a chance to develop my interest in languages.

When I was 20, we went to Athens, where my mother met and married a German professor of classical archaeology. This meant I was free at last to go up to Oxford. I attended Somerville College for three years. While I was growing up, we'd always assumed that by the time I reached voting age, the suffrage would have been extended to women. When it became obvious that this was not going to happen I knew that any career or personal ambitions must give way to this struggle. I set myself up as a freelance translator to get enough money to live on and joined the most militant and effective of the groups fighting for the Vote, the Women's Social and Political Union, soon after it was founded by Mrs Emmeline Pankhurst in 1903.

Gillian Linscott

Gillian Linscott's journalistic career has ranged from reporting chip-pan fires in Bootle to street riots in Belfast. Her previous jobs include civil servant, market gardener, playwright and parliamentary radio reporter.

She lives in a cottage in Herefordshire with her husband – also a writer – and enjoys skiing, riding and hill-walking. Exotic locations and off-beat, first-hand research are characteristic of her books, the first of which was set in a French nudist colony.

Her eleventh whodunnit, *Crown Witness*, is the fifth to feature the suffragette sleuth Nell Bray, a detective heroine who has already acquired a large and loyal following.

Also by Gillian Linscott

Sister Beneath the Sheet
Hanging on the Wire
Stage Fright
Widow's Peak

Wayzgoose

Peter Lovesey

Wayzgoose

A slight, worried woman in a leather jacket walked into Bath police station.

The desk sergeant eyed her through the protective glass. 'Yes, ma'am?'

'Can I speak to someone?'

'You're speaking to me, ma'am.'

'Someone senior.'

The sergeant had been dealing with the public across this desk for twelve years. 'I'm the best on offer.'

Unamused, the woman waited. Her hair was dark and short, shaped to her head. She wore no make-up.

The sergeant coaxed her, 'Why don't you give me some idea what it's about?'

'I just killed my husband.'

The sergeant bent closer to the glass. 'You *what*?'

'I came in to confess.'

'Hang about, ma'am. Where did this happen?'

'At home. 32, Collinson Road.'

'He's there now?'

'His body is.'

'Collinson Road. I ought to know it.'

'Twerton.'

The sergeant gestured to a woman police officer behind him and told her to get a response car out to Twerton. Then he asked the woman, 'What's your name, ma'am?'

'Trish Noble.'

'Trish for Patricia?'

'Yes.'

'And your husband's name?'

'Glenn.'

'What happened, Mrs Noble?'

'He was in a drunken stupor at four in the afternoon when I came in from work, so I was that mad that I threw a teapot at him. Cracked him on the head. It killed him. Is that murder? Will I go to prison?'

'A china teapot?'

'Half full of tea. I've always had this wicked temper.'

'Are you sure he's dead? Maybe you only stunned him.'

She shook her head. 'He's gone all right. I'm a ward sister, and I know.'

'A *nurse*?'

'Shocking, isn't it?'

'You'd better come in and sit down,' said the sergeant. 'Go to the door on your right. Someone will see you right away.'

The someone was Superintendent Peter Diamond, the senior detective on duty that afternoon. Diamond was head of the murder squad and this looked like a domestic incident, but as homicide had apparently occurred, he was in duty bound to take an interest. He made quite a courtesy of pulling forward a low, upholstered chair for the woman, then spoilt the effect by seating himself in another with a bump as his knees refused his buttocks a dignified descent. He had a low centre of gravity. A rugby forward in years past, he was better built now for anchorman in a tug-of-war team. 'You're a nurse, I understand, Mrs Noble?'

'Sister on one of the orthopaedic wards.'

'Locally?'

'The Royal United.'

'So . . . ?'

'I came off duty and when I got home Glenn – that's

my husband – was the worse for liquor.'

'You mean drunk?'

'Whatever you want to call it.' She closed her eyes, as if that might shut out the memory.

Mild as milk, Diamond said, 'You came in from work and saw him where?'

'In the kitchen.'

'Did you have words?'

'He wasn't capable of words. I saw red. That's the way I am. I picked up the teapot—'

'You'd made tea?'

'No. I'd only just come in.'

'So he'd made tea?'

'No, it was still on the table from breakfast, half-full, really heavy. It's a family sized pot. I picked it up and swung it at him. Hit him smack on the forehead. The pot smashed. There was tea all over his face and chest. He collapsed. First, I thought it was the drink. I couldn't believe I'd hit him that hard. He'd stopped breathing. I could get nothing from his pulse. I lay him out on the floor and tried mouth-to-mouth, but it was no good.'

She conveyed a vivid picture, the more spectacular considering what a scrap she was. She spoke calmly, her pale blue eyes scarcely blinking. I wouldn't mind mouth-to-mouth from you, sister, Diamond incorrectly thought.

The door behind him opened and someone looked in, a sergeant. 'A word in your ear, sir.'

Diamond wasn't getting out of that chair. He put a thumb and forefinger to the lobe of his right ear.

The sergeant bent over and muttered, 'Report just in from the house, sir. Body in the kitchen confirmed.'

Diamond nodded and asked Mrs Noble, 'You said this happened at four in the afternoon?'

'Yes.'

'It's twenty to six now.'

'Is it?'

'Quite a long time since it happened.'

'I've been walking the streets, getting a grip on myself.'

'You're doing OK,' Diamond told her, and meant it. She was a nurse and used to containing her feelings, but this was a stern test. He admired her self-control and he was inclined to believe her story, even if it had strange features. 'You didn't think of phoning us?'

'I'm here, aren't I?'

'Earlier, I mean. When it happened.'

'No point. He was beyond help.'

He offered her a hot drink for the shock – and just stopped short of mentioning tea.

She declined.

'You said you saw red at finding him drunk,' he recapped.

Her face tensed. 'I disapprove of drink.'

'Was he in work?'

She shook her head. 'He was one of those printers laid off from Regency Press a year ago.'

'Was he still unemployed?'

'Yes.'

'Depressed?'

'Certainly not.'

'It must have been difficult managing after he lost his job,' Diamond said, giving her the chance to say *something* in favour of her dead husband.

'Not at all. He got good redundancy terms. And I'm earning as well.'

'I meant perhaps he was drowning his sorrows?'

'What sorrows?'

'This afternoon bout was exceptional?'

'Very.'

'Which was what upset you?'

She gave a nod. 'It's against my religion.'

Diamond treated the statement as if she were one of those earnest people in suits who knock on doors and ask whether you agree that God's message has relevance in today's world. He ignored it. 'You're a nurse, Mrs Noble, and I imagine you're trained to spot the symptoms of heavy drinking, so I don't want you to be insulted by this question. What made you decide that your husband was drunk?'

'The state of him. He was slumped in a chair, his eyes were glazed, he couldn't put two words together. And the brandy bottle was on the table in front of him. The brandy he was given as a leaving present. He promised me he'd got rid of it.'

'Didn't he like brandy?'

'It's of the devil.'

'Had he drunk from the bottle?'

'Isn't that obvious?'

'Had he ever used drugs in any form?'

She frowned. 'Alcohol is a drug.'

'You know what I mean, Mrs Noble.'

'And I've seen plenty of drug-users,' she riposted. 'I know what to look for.'

'No question of drugs?'

'No question.'

'Did he look for another position after the printing came to a stop?'

'There wasn't much point. All the local firms were laying people off.'

'So how did he spend the days?'

'Don't ask me. Walks in the park. Television. Have you ever been out of work?'

He nodded. 'And my wife couldn't find a job either.'

'Then you ought to know.'

'Unemployment hits people in different ways. I'm trying to understand how it affected your husband.'

'You're not,' she said bluntly. 'You're trying to find out if I murdered him. That's your job.'

Diamond didn't deny it.

'It wasn't deliberate.' She raised her chin defiantly. 'I wouldn't dream of killing him. Glenn and I were married eleven years. We had fights. Of course we had fights, with my temper. That's my personal demon – my temper. I threw things. Mostly I missed. He could duck when he was sober.' Her lips twitched into a sad smile. 'We always made up. Some of the best times we had were making up after a fight.'

Trish Noble's candour was touching. Diamond sympathized with her. There was little more he could achieve. 'We'll need a statement, Mrs Noble, a written one, I mean. Then you can go. Do you have someone you can stay with? Family, a friend?'

'Can't I go home?'

'Our people are going to be in the house for some time. You'd be better off somewhere else.'

She told him she had a sister in Trowbridge. Diamond offered to make the call, but Trish Noble said she'd rather break the news herself.

2

To most of the staff at Manvers Street police station this room on the top floor was known as the eagle's nest. John Farr-Jones, the Chief Constable, greeted Diamond, who had arrived for a meeting of the high fliers. 'You're looking fit, Peter.'

'I used the lift.'

'What's it like to be back in harness?'

The big detective gave him a pained look and said, 'I gave up wearing harness when I was two years old.' He took his place in a leather armchair and nodded to a chief inspector he scarcely knew. The wholesale changes of personnel in the couple of years he had been away had to be symptomatic of something.

'Mr Diamond's problem is that we haven't had a juicy murder since he was reinstated,' Farr-Jones told the rest of the room. Since it was thanks to Farr-Jones's recommendation that Diamond had got his job back, he may have felt entitled to rib the man a little. But really the recommendation had been little more than a rubber stamp. In October 1994, a dire emergency had poleaxed Avon and Somerset Constabulary. The daughter of the Assistant Chief Constable had been taken hostage and her captor had insisted on dealing only with Diamond. The old rogue elephant, boisterous as ever, was now back among the herd.

'What about this teapot killing?' Farr-Jones persisted. 'Can't you get anything out of that?'

There were smiles all round.

John Wigfull unwisely joked, 'A teabag?' There was a history of bad feeling between Wigfull and Diamond. Many a time Diamond had seriously contemplated grabbing the two ends of Wigfull's ridiculously overgrown moustache and seeing if he could knot them under his chin. Now that Diamond was back, Wigfull had been ousted as head of the murder squad and handed a less glamorous portfolio as head of CID operations. He would use every chance to point to Diamond's failings.

Tom Ray, the Chief Constable's staff officer, hadn't heard about the teapot killing, so Diamond, wholly against his inclination, was obliged to give a summary of the incident.

When he had finished, it was rather like being in a staff college seminar. Someone had to suggest how the law should deal with it.

'Manslaughter?' Ray ventured, more in politeness than anything else.

'No chance,' growled Diamond.

Wigfull, who knew *Butterworth's Police Law* like some people know the Bible, seized the moment to shine. 'Hold on. As I remember, there are four elements necessary to secure a manslaughter conviction. First, there must be an unlawful act. That's beyond doubt.'

'Assault with a teapot,' contributed Ray.

'Right. A half-full teapot. Second, the act has to be dangerous, in that any sober and reasonable person would recognize it could do harm.'

'Clocking a fellow with a teapot is dangerous,' Ray agreed, filling a role as chorus to Wigfull.

'Third, the act must be a cause of the death.'

'Well, he didn't die of old age.'

'And finally, it must be intentional. There's no question she meant to strike him.'

'No question,' Ray echoed him.

Diamond said flatly, 'It was a sudden death.'

'We can't argue with that, Peter,' said Wigfull, and got a laugh.

'I'm reporting it to the coroner. It's going in as an occurrence report.'

Wigfull said, 'I think you should do a process report to the CPS.'

'Bollocks.'

'It would be up to them whether to prosecute,' Wigfull pointed out.

Diamond's patience was short at the best of times and it was even shorter when he was on shaky ground. He stabbed a finger at Wigfull. 'Don't you lecture me on the CPS. I refuse to dump on this woman. She's a nurse, for pity's sake. She walked all the way here from Twerton and reported what she'd done. If the coroner wants to refer it, so be it. He won't have my support.'

Ray asked, 'Have you been out to Twerton yourself?'

'I haven't had a chance, have I?' said Diamond. 'I'm attending a meeting, in case anyone hadn't noticed. Julie is out there.'

'Inspector Hargreaves?' said Farr-Jones. 'Is that wise? She isn't so experienced as some of your other people.'

'She was my choice for this, sir.' He didn't want to get into an argument over Julie's capability, or his right to delegate duties, but if necessary he would.

He was first out of the meeting, muttering sulphurous things about John Wigfull, Farr-Jones and the whole boiling lot of them. He stomped downstairs to his office to collect his raincoat and trilby. He'd had more than enough of the job for that day.

Someone got up as he entered the room, a stocky, middle-aged man with black-framed bifocals. Dr Jack Merlin, the forensic pathologist. 'What's up?' Merlin said. 'You're looking even more stroppy than usual.'

'Don't ask.'

'Have you got a few minutes?'

'I was about to leave,' said Diamond.

'Before you do, old friend, I'd like a quiet word. Why don't you shut that door?'

The 'old friend' alerted Diamond like nothing else. His dealings with Merlin – over upwards of a dozen corpses in various states of decomposition – were based on mutual respect. Jack was the best reader of human remains in Britain. But he rarely, if ever, expressed much in the way of sentiment. Diamond grabbed the door-handle and pulled it shut.

'This one at Collinson Road, Twerton,' said Merlin. 'The man hit with a teapot.'

'Yes?'

'You don't mind me asking, I hope. Did you visit the scene yourself?'

Diamond shrugged. 'I was tied up here. I sent one of my younger inspectors out.'

'Good,' said Merlin. 'I didn't think you had.'

'Something wrong?'

'You interviewed the wife, I believe?'

'Yes.'

'She claimed to have topped him with a teapot?'

He nodded. 'She's a ward sister at the RUH. Bit uptight, got religion rather badly, I think, which makes it harder for her.'

Merlin fingered the lobe of his left ear. 'The thing is, matey, I thought I should have a quiet word with you at this stage. Shan't know the cause of death until I've done the PM, of course, but . . .'

'Give it to me, Jack.'

' . . . a first inspection suggests that the victim suffered a couple of deep stab wounds.'

'*Stab* wounds?'

'In the back.'

Diamond swore.

'Not a lot of blood about,' the pathologist added, 'and he was lying face up, so I wouldn't be too critical of that young inspector, but it does have the signs of a suspicious death.'

3

Collinson Road, Twerton, backs on to Brunel's Great Western Railway a mile or so west of the centre of Bath. Diamond drove into a narrow street of Victorian terraced housing, the brickwork blackened by all those locomotives steaming by in years past. Several of the façades had since been cleaned up and gentrified with plastic guttering, picture windows and varnished oak front doors with brass fittings, but Number 32 was resolutely unaltered, sooty and unobtrusive behind an overgrown privet hedge and a small, neglected strip of garden. The door stood open. The Scenes of Crime Officers had received Diamond's urgent instruction to step up the scale of their work and were still inside. Most of them knew him from years back and as he went in he had to put up with some good-natured chaffing over his intentions. It was well known that he'd been moodily waiting for a murder to fall in his lap.

The team had finished its work downstairs, so he went through the hallway with the senior man, Derek Bignal, and looked inside the kitchen. Almost everything portable had been removed for inspection by the lab. Strips of adhesive tape marked the positions of the table and chairs and the outline of the body.

Diamond asked if the murder weapon had been found.

'Who knows?' said Bignal with a shrug, practically causing paranoia in Peter Diamond so soon after his conversation with Merlin, the laid-back pathologist. 'We made a collection of kitchen knives. See the magnetic strip attached to the wall over the draining-board? They were all lined up there, ready to grab. Some of them had blades that could have done the business.'

'No other knife in the sink, or lying on the floor?'

'With blood and prints all over it? You want it easy, Mr Diamond.'

He tried visualizing the scene, which was no simple task with the furniture missing. According to her story, Trish Noble had returned from the hospital at four in the afternoon. If she was speaking the truth she must have let herself in at the front door, stepped through the hallway and found her husband seated facing her at the small table against the wall to her left as she entered the kitchen. In a fit of anger, believing him to be drunk, rather than mortally injured, she would have taken a couple of steps towards the table, where the teapot was, snatched it up and hit him with it. He had fallen off to the right of the chair – her right – and lay on his back on the floor, where she had tried resuscitation. That, anyway, was her version. The taped outline of the body didn't conflict with what she had stated.

To Diamond's left was a fridge-freezer. The doors were decorated with postcards and photos. The shiny surfaces bore traces of powder, where they had been dusted for prints. Holiday snaps of Glenn Noble, deeply tanned, in shorts and sandals, his arms around the shoulders of his pretty, bikini-clad wife. More of Trish Noble in her nurse's uniform, giggling with friends. A sneaky shot of her taken in a bathroom, eyes wide in surprise, holding a towel against her breasts, evidently unaware that her right nipple wasn't covered. Surprising that a woman who claimed to be religious kept such a picture on her fridge door, Diamond mused, then decided that nurses must have a different perception of embarrassment. Another that took his attention was clearly taken on some seaside promenade. Glenn and an older, stocky man were giving piggyback rides to two women in swimsuits, one of them Trish – but it wasn't Glenn's back she was riding.

Diamond sighed. To study people's private snaps systematically like this was an invasion of privacy, an odious but necessary part of the job. He wasn't in the house to look for evidence. Others had already been through for that. He was getting a sense of how the couple had lived and what their relationship had been. Having thought what a liberty it was, he stripped every photo off the fridge door.

'What's a wayzgoose when it's at home?' he asked Bignal.

'Come again.'

'A wayzgoose. This picture of the two couples horsing about on the seafront has a note on the back. Wayzgoose, 1993, Minehead.'

'Is it a place?'

'Minehead is.'

'Could it be the name of some game, do you think?'

'I doubt it.'

He looked into the other rooms downstairs. One was clearly the living-room, with two armchairs, a TV and video, a music centre and a low table stacked with newspapers. The Nobles read the *Daily Mirror* and possessed just about every recording Freddie Mercury had made. On the wall were a bullfight poster and an antique map of Somerset. He picked an expensive-looking art book from a shelf otherwise stacked with nursing magazines. 'Who's Eugène Delacroix?'

'A French romantic painter,' Bignal informed him.

Diamond flicked the pages over. 'Doesn't seem to go with Freddie Mercury and the *Mirror*.'

'There were also two coffee mugs on the table,' Bignal told him. 'By the look of them, they were left over from last night. They're going to the lab.'

It was not vastly different from his own living-room. He moved on. The front room was used as a workroom by the couple, for sewing, typing and storing household bills and bank statements. They had a joint account and seemed to be steadily in credit, which was better than the Diamonds managed.

In another ten minutes the team finished upstairs. No signs of violence there, they informed Diamond. The aggro seemed to have been confined to the kitchen.

He went to see for himself.

The Nobles favoured a rather lurid pink for their bedroom, slept in a standard size double bed and had a portable TV on the chest of drawers Glenn used for most of his clothes. Trish Noble had a wardrobe and a dressing table to herself. She was reading Catherine Cookson and the Bible and Glenn had been into one of the Flashman books. If the quantity and variety of condoms in Glenn's bedside cabinet was any guide, their sex life hadn't been subdued by Trish's religion.

The second bedroom contained a folding bed, an ironing board and various items the couple must have acquired and been unwilling to throw away, ranging from an old record-player to a dartboard with the wire half detached.

He glanced into the bathroom. Nothing caught his attention.

'What's in the back garden?' he asked Bignal.

'Plants, mostly.'

'Don't push me, Derek. Have you been out there?'

'Personally, no.'

'Has anyone thought of looking for a murder weapon, footprints, a means of escape?'

'Not systematically,' Bignal admitted. 'It was already dark when we got here.'

'Not systematically,' muttered Diamond with heavy sarcasm. 'It backs onto the railway, doesn't it?'

'Yes.'

'Tomorrow, early, I want a proper search made. In particular, I want to know if there are signs that anyone got in or out by way of the railway embankment.'

Bignal's eyebrows peaked in surprise. 'You think someone else is involved, as well as the wife?'

'That's the way they would have escaped.'

'*They*?'

'He, she, they or nobody at all. Let's keep an open mind, shall we?'

4

Julie Hargreaves may have expected a roasting for having failed to notice the stab wounds, but she need not have troubled. Diamond was more interested in roasting Trish Noble.

'She had the kid-glove treatment from me yesterday,' he summed up as they drove out to Trowbridge. 'Today she's got to be given a workover.'

'Do you see her as the killer?'

'Do you?'

She paused for thought. 'It would be unusual, a woman using a knife as a weapon. The teapot, I can believe – but why would she hit him with the teapot if she'd already stuck a knife in his back?'

'To finish him off.'

'Ah.'

'However, there could be a second person involved.' Diamond casually tossed in some information he'd received that morning from the SOCOs combing the back garden at Twerton. 'There's evidence that someone climbed over the fence to the railway embankment. Two slats are freshly splintered at the top.'

'An intruder? Nothing was stolen.'

'Yes, but if she had an admirer, for instance . . .'

Julie didn't buy the idea. 'That's pretty unlikely, isn't it?'

'You mean with her religious convictions? I said "admirer," not "lover".'

'No, I mean he wouldn't need to climb over the fence. She'd let him in. And they would have to be real thickos to stab the husband and then go down to the nick and report it.'

He responded huffily, 'I didn't say it was a conspiracy. Unrequited love, Julie. The admirer is obsessed with Trish. She's unattainable while her husband is alive, so this nutter breaks into the house and knifes him. Trish comes home and finds Glenn dying, but mistakenly thinks he's drunk.'

'And bashes him with the teapot?'

'Exactly. I think she told the truth yesterday. By now she may have something else to tell us.'

'I wonder,' said Julie. 'I find it difficult to believe in this crazy admirer.'

Diamond said loftily, 'You may understand better when you meet Trish Noble. She's on the side of the angels and bloody attractive. Dangerous combination.'

'That would explain everything,' murmured Julie in a bland tone. 'Shall I organize house-to-house to find out if anyone was spotted on the railway embankment yesterday afternoon?'

'It's under way,' he told her. 'Two teams.'

Trish Noble's sister lived in a semi-detached on a council estate north of Trowbridge. But it was the bloody attractive young widow herself who answered their knock. In jeans and a white tee-shirt, with the height and figure of a pre-teen schoolgirl, she looked too frail to use a knife on a chocolate cake, let alone on a man. The hours since the killing had taken a toll. Her big eyes were red-lidded and they seemed to have sunk deeper into her skull. Julie must have wondered at Diamond's ideas of attractiveness.

He introduced her and said there were things he needed to ask. Trish calmly invited them in, explaining that she had the house to herself because her sister was at work. In a narrow sitting-room, watched by two unwelcoming spaniels, Diamond took the best armchair and launched straight into the workover. 'You didn't kill your husband with the teapot, Mrs Noble. He was stabbed in the back.'

She frowned and stared.

Julie said, 'Why don't you sit down?' She stood behind the second armchair until Trish Noble acted on the advice.

'Did you stab him?' Diamond asked.

Trish seemed to have difficulty taking in what she had just been told – or she was making a convincing show of being stunned by the news. She shook her head.

Diamond said, 'If you'd like to explain how it happened, we're ready to listen.'

She said, 'Stabbed?'

'Twice, in the back.'

'That's impossible. He was sitting in the kitchen.'

'Your story.'

'It's true! He was at the table when I got in. I've told you this.'

'You didn't stab him yourself?'

'That's insulting.'

'We'd like a clear answer, Mrs Noble.'

She said vehemently, 'No, I did not stab my own husband.'

'That's clear, then.' Diamond glanced across at Julie, who had found an upright chair by the sideboard. 'Got that? She denies it.'

Julie opened her notebook.

'If you didn't stab him yourself,' Diamond plunged in again, 'we've obviously got to look for someone who did. Was there anyone else in the house when you got home from the hospital?'

The tired eyes widened. 'No one.'

'You're sure? You can't be sure, can you? Let's take this in stages. Did you see anyone?'

'No. This is unbelievable.'

'Or hear them?'

'No.'

'Is there anyone else living in the house?'

'What do you mean – a lodger? No.'

'Does anyone have a key?'

'What?'

'Some friend, perhaps?'

'We don't give keys to our friends.'

'I'll tell you what I have in mind,' Diamond offered. 'If someone let himself into the house unknown to your husband, he could have taken him by surprise and stabbed him shortly before you came in.'

'Who would do that?' she said, and there was a note of scorn in the voice. She was getting over the shock.

'Do you have a lover?'

She reddened, but that wasn't necessarily an admission. Almost anyone would have blushed at the question. She told him with a glare, 'You should wash out your mouth.'

'Would you like it rephrased?' Diamond said. 'A boyfriend? A fancy man? A bit on the side? Come on, Mrs Noble, you work in a hospital. Life in the raw. I don't have to pick my words with you, do I?'

'I am a married woman – or was,' she answered primly. 'I took vows before the Lord.'

'No need for a boyfriend?'

The look she gave him was her response and he was convinced by it. Moreover, he'd seen inside her husband's bedside drawer.

'In that case, we have to consider what used to be

called unrequited love. To put it crudely, some nutter who fancies you. You see what I'm driving at, don't you? This man obsessed by you murders your husband to have you to himself.'

She sighed like a scythe and said, 'I can't listen to these serpent-words.'

'No secret admirer you're aware of? Let's look at another possibility. Did your husband have any enemies?'

The change of tack brought a more measured response. 'Glenn didn't have enemies.'

'Then did he have friends? Encouraging him in bad habits, perhaps?'

She said, 'I can do without your sarcasm.'

'These are friends, presumably?' He took from his pocket the photo taken at Minehead, the piggyback picture. 'Were these people in the printing trade?'

She snatched it possessively. 'You were the one who stole them, then. My photos are personal.'

'Who are the people?'

The resentment remained in her voice. 'The Porterfields. Friends of ours. We had a day out with them.'

'Is Mr Porterfield a printer?'

'No. Basil is a businessman. He sells car-parts.'

'And the lady?'

'His wife Serena. She's an art teacher.'

'That's Serena mounted on your husband's back?'

She gave him a cold stare. 'That was for a silly photograph.'

'At Minehead?'

'Yes.'

'For a wayzgoose?'

She frowned. 'I beg your pardon.'

'Look on the back. My dictionary says that a wayzgoose is a works outing for those in a printing house. A silly photo at a wayzgoose makes sense to me.'

She glanced at the words on the back of the photo and shrugged. 'It doesn't make any to me. Basil and Serena had nothing to do with Glenn's job. Besides, he was already redundant when we went to Minehead. He'd been out of work for over a year.'

'I noticed an art book in your living-room. French painter.'

'Delacroix?'

'Yes. Was that a gift from Mrs Porterfield?'

'No. Glenn bought it himself.'

'So he was interested in art?'

'Only in Delacroix.'

'Are the Porterfields local?'

'They live up by the golf course.'

'What's the address?'

'I don't want them troubled. They've got nothing to do with this. They're decent people.'

'In that case, they'll want to help me find your husband's killer.'

She said openly, 'I can't believe this is happening. I thought I killed him. I was sure of it.'

If she is playing the innocent, Diamond thought, she's doing it with style. He tried to resist making up his mind. First impressions were so misleading. In his time he'd made more mistakes over women than King Henry the Eighth. And this one with her martyred eyes was taking the steam out of his workover.

'After you hit him with the teapot and he fell off the chair, what did you do? Tell me precisely.'

'I went to him at once. I could tell from the way he fell that he was out cold when he hit the floor. I found he'd stopped breathing, so I tried to revive him. Tilted back his head and drew the chin upwards. I don't have to go through the drill, do I?'

'Mouth-to-mouth?'

'Of course.'

'Think carefully. While you were doing it, did you hear any extraneous sounds?'

'What do you mean?'

'If anyone else was in the house, in that kitchen, even, they may have picked this moment to run out.' It was a wily suggestion. He couldn't have handed her a better opportunity of shifting the suspicion to some mythical intruder.

She hesitated, then said, 'I didn't notice a thing.'

Innocent, or refusing to be drawn? He couldn't tell. 'After the resuscitation had no result, what did you do?'

She bit her lip. 'It's difficult to remember. It's just a blur. I was deeply shocked.'

'Did you stay in the kitchen?'

'For a bit, I think.'

'You didn't go upstairs, or in the other rooms?'

'I don't think so. I was horrified by what I'd done. I got the shakes. I think I ran out of the front door and wandered up the street asking the Lord to forgive me. It took Him a long time to calm my troubled spirit. In the end I walked all the way to Bath to confess to you.'

'Did you speak to anyone between leaving the house and coming to us?'

'No.'

'See anyone you knew?'

'I wasn't noticing other people.' She made it all sound plausible.

'If there was anyone,' said Diamond, becoming reasonable in spite of his best efforts to be tough, 'it would help us to account for your movements.'

'I've told you my movements.'

'And we only have your word for them.'

'That was after he died. Why do you want to know what I was doing after he died?'

He declined to answer. 'Is there anyone you can think of who ever threatened your husband?'

'No.'

Julie looked up from her notes and said unexpectedly, 'Was he seeing a woman?'

Trish Noble blinked twice and flicked nervously at her hair. 'If he was . . .' she started to say, then stopped. 'If he was, I'd be very surprised.'

'The wife usually is,' Diamond added, privately wishing he'd remembered to ask. Smart thinking on Julie's part. 'Anyone you can think of who may have fancied him?'

'How would I know? Look, you're talking about the man I loved and married. He isn't in his grave yet. Do you have to be so cruel?'

Julie said, 'You want us to find the person who stabbed him, don't you?'

She nodded.

'There is someone, isn't there?' said Julie.

'I don't know.'

'But you had your suspicions?'

She looked down and fingered her wedding ring. Speaking in a low, scarcely audible voice, she said, 'Sometimes he came home really late. I mean about two in the morning, or later. He was exhausted. Too tired for anything.'

'Drunk?'

'No. I would have noticed.'

'How long was this going on?'

'When it started, it was once every two months or so. Lately, it was about every ten days.'

'Did you question him about it?'

'He snapped my head off when I did. Really told me to mind my own business. It made me think there might be someone, but I had no way of finding out. He didn't smell of scent, or anything.'

Diamond told her to collect her coat.

She looked seriously worried. 'Where are you taking me?'

'Home. Julie will take you home. I want you to look at the scene and tell Julie everything you remember.'

'Aren't you going to be there?' A question that might have conveyed disappointment was actually spoken on a rising note of relief.

'I may come later.' He turned to Julie. 'On the way,
you can drop me off at the hospital.'

Trish's anxiety flooded in again. 'The hospital? Do
you mean the RUH? You don't have to talk to them.
They can't tell you anything.'

'It isn't about you,' said Diamond. 'It's another
matter.'

And it wasn't about his weight problem either.

5

'Believe it or not, I didn't come here to admire your
sewing,' Diamond told Jack Merlin.

There was no reaction from the pathologist.

'May I see the other side?'

'Not *my* sewing. My assistant Rodney does the
stitchwork.' In the post-mortem room at the Royal
United Hospital, Merlin had the advantage of familiar
territory. No visitor was entirely comfortable in the
mortuary. Attendance at autopsies is routinely
expected of detectives on murder cases. Diamond
ducked out whenever he could think up a plausible
excuse. On this visit he arrived late. The gory stuff had
already been got over. With only a sewn-up corpse to
view, he was putting on a good show of self-
composure, but it didn't run to treating these places
like a second home.

The assistant Rodney stepped forward and helped
Merlin turn the body of Glenn Noble. Two eye-shaped
stab wounds were revealed.

Diamond's hands tightened behind his back. 'Not
much doubt about those.'

Merlin watched him and said nothing.

'They don't look superficial, either.'

Still nothing.

'I reckon they tell a story.'

There was a long interval of silence before Diamond spoke again. 'You're a helpful bugger, aren't you? You know I'm pig-ignorant, yet you're not going to help me out.'

Merlin shot an amused look across the corpse and then relented. 'This one to the right of the spine did the main damage. Penetrated the lung two inches above its basal margin.'

Diamond bent closer to the body to examine the wounds. 'Obviously you've cleaned him up.'

'You don't get much external bleeding from stab wounds. There was a pint or so in the right pleural cavity.'

'So was that what killed him?'

'It was a potentially fatal injury.'

'The cause of death, in other words.'

'The potential cause of death.'

Diamond straightened up, frowning. 'Am I missing something here?'

'I can't be specific as to the cause.'

'With a couple of stab wounds like this and massive internal bleeding? Come on, Jack. Give me a break.'

Merlin said, 'As I understand it, the wife admitted to you that she cracked him on the head with a teapot.'

'I believe her. Somebody certainly smashed a teapot. His shirt-front was stained with tea, as I'm sure forensic will tell us in their own good time. Probably tell us if it was Brooke Bond or Tetley's and whether she warmed the pot.'

'There's bruising here on the head, just above the hairline,' Merlin confirmed.

'Look, what is this about the teapot? The man has two deep stab wounds.'

'And a bruised cranium.'

Diamond screwed his face into an anguished expression. 'Are you telling me it's possible that the teapot actually finished him off?'

'It's an interesting question. I can't exclude the

possibility of a fatal brain injury. Of course I'll examine the brain.'

'Haven't you done that?'

'It has to be fixed and cut in sections for microscopic examination.'

'How long will that take?'

'Three to four weeks.'

'God help us.' He complained because of his own frustration. He knew Merlin would give him all the information he could as soon as it was available. He was the best.

'And even after I examine the brain, I may not have the answer.'

'Oh, come on, Jack!'

'I mean it. I've examined people who died after blows to the head and I could find no perceptible damage to the brain. We don't know why it happens. Maybe the shock wave passing through the brain stem was sufficient to kill them.'

'So even after four weeks, you may not have the answer?'

'I'm a pathologist, not an ace detective.'

There was an interval of silence.

'Let me get one thing clear in my mind,' said Diamond. 'Is it possible that what Mrs Noble told me is true – that he was still alive when she clobbered him?'

'Certainly.'

'With stab wounds like this?'

'A victim of stabbing may survive for some time.'

'How long?'

'How long is a piece of string?'

'Your middle name wouldn't be Prudence by any chance?'

Merlin smiled.

'A few seconds? A few minutes?'

'I couldn't possibly say.'

'And how would he have appeared? Unsteady, like a drunk?'

'Your guess is as good as mine.'

'A distressed drunk?'

'Distressed is probably right.'

'Unable to speak?'

'That's possible. The knife cut through some of the blood vessels and airways in the lung, so there was bleeding not only into the chest cavity but into the air passages. That would have affected his power of speech.'

'You see what I'm getting at?' said Diamond.

Merlin grinned. 'You're testing the woman's story. I was at the scene before you, remember,' he rubbed it in. 'I saw the brandy bottle on the table. But I'm not given to speculation, as you know.'

'Jack, I could be making an arrest very soon. Someone entered that house and stabbed him. Not the wife. I'm convinced she's telling the truth.'

'Do you have a suspect?'

'I'm getting close.'

'I wouldn't get too close. If you nab them for murder at this stage, you could be torn to shreds by a good defence counsel. Mrs Noble admits that she clobbered her husband with the teapot. She may have killed him, stabbing or no stabbing.'

6

It was a five minute drive, no more, from the hospital to the murder house in Collinson Road. Frustrated by his session with Jack Merlin, Diamond looked to Julie Hargreaves for some progress in the investigation. He had left her there with Trish Noble, ostensibly checking the contents to see if anything had been stolen. More importantly, she would have been working on drawing Trish out, putting her at her ease and gaining her confidence in the way that she did with women suspects almost without seeming to try. If there were secrets in the lives of the Nobles, Julie was best placed to unlock them.

When he looked in, the two women were waiting in that chintzy living-room with the bullfight poster and the map of Somerset. The television was on and coffee and biscuits were on the table. There must be something wrong with my methods, Diamond thought. While I look at a dead body, my sidekick puts her feet up and watches the box.

'Am I interrupting?' he asked.

Julie looked up. 'We were waiting for you.'

'What are you watching – a kids' programme?'

'Actually we were looking out of the window at the SOCOs in the back garden.' She reached for the remote control and switched off. 'They look as if they're about to pack up. Would you like coffee?'

'Had a hospital one, thanks.' In a paper cup from a machine and tasting of tomato soup, he might have added. He wouldn't want another drink for some time. He reached for the packet of chocolate digestives and helped himself. 'What's the report, then? Anything missing?'

'Most of the furniture from my kitchen,' Trish Noble said accusingly.

'That'll be the scenes of crime team,' Diamond told her. 'They must have left you a check-list somewhere. You'll get everything back eventually.'

'They weren't the ones who pinched the photos from my fridge door.'

He said smoothly, 'You'll get them back.' He reached for the art book he'd remarked on before and leafed through the pages. 'Is anything of value missing? Money? Jewellery?'

Julie answered for her. 'We checked. Everything seems to be there.'

'Speaking of money,' Diamond said to Trish as if she had brought up the subject herself, 'we'll need to look at the bank account and your credit card statements.

You do have a credit card? How are you placed financially? I'm not being nosy. We need to know.' He knew, but he wanted to question her on the details.

'We're solvent,' she answered without looking up.

He hadn't Julie's talent for easing out the information. 'Your husband must have been given a lump sum when he was made redundant.'

She only nodded, so he talked on.

'It seems generous at the time, but it soon goes, I dare say. Where do you keep the statements?'

'They should still be in the front room if your people haven't taken them away.'

'Would you mind?' he asked her.

In the short interval when Trish was out of the room, Diamond asked Julie what she had learned of importance.

'Glenn was up to something that she didn't care for,' said Julie. 'I think we touched a raw nerve asking if he had been two-timing her with some other woman.'

'You touched the nerve,' he said. 'That was your contribution.'

Julie flushed slightly. She wasn't used to credit from Peter Diamond. 'Anyway, she's suspicious, but she isn't sure.'

'She wouldn't have stuck a knife in his back unless she was damned sure.'

Trish returned and handed across the statements. He studied them. 'High standard of living. Shopping at the best boutiques. Meals out at Clos du Roy and the Priory. A holiday in the south of France.'

'That's the way we chose to spend our money.'

'But it doesn't seem to have hit your bank balance.'

'Glenn had his redundancy cheque.'

'What's this restaurant in Exeter that you visited twice in August?'

'The Lemon Tree? We often eat there after visiting his brother. Alec's home is a working paper mill, a lovely old place in the country near Torquay, but he forgets that people need to eat.'

'I can take a hint. We'll get you back to your sister's,' said Diamond.

Seated in the front, whilst Julie drove, he tried drawing out Trish by talking about the pressures that nurses had to work under. 'My own health is pretty good, thank God, but in this line of work you get to see the insides of hospitals all too often. The RUH is one of the better ones. I still wouldn't care to be a nurse.'

She didn't comment. Perhaps she found it hard to imagine the big policeman nursing anyone.

'How long have you worked there, Mrs Noble?'

'Three years.'

'And before that?'

'Frenchay.'

Another local hospital, in Bristol.

'It's a vocation, isn't it?' Diamond rambled on. 'Nursing isn't a job, it's a vocation. So is doctoring. Better paid, but still a vocation. I'm less sure about some of the others who work in hospitals. The administrators. It's out of proportion. All those managers.'

She didn't take his pause as an invitation to join in.

'They tell me the Health Service managers are the only lot who are on the increase,' he said. 'Oh, and counsellors. Counselling is the biggest growth industry of all. We need it for everything these days. Child care, education, careers, marriage, divorce, unemployment, alcoholism, bereavement. I don't know how we managed before. If there's a major disaster – a train crash or a flood – the first thing they announce after the number of deaths is that counsellors are with the families. We even have counsellors for the police. Something ugly comes our way, like a serial murder case, or child abuse, and half the murder squad are reckoned to need counselling. Watch out for the counsellors, Mrs Noble. If they haven't found you yet, you may be sure they're about to make a case study of you.'

She didn't respond. She was looking out of the window.

'Me, too, probably,' said Diamond.

7

'Give me the dope on the Porterfields,' Diamond asked as Julie steered the car out of the police station yard and headed for Widcombe Hill. On his instruction, she'd spent the last hour checking.

'They've lived in Bath for the last five years. Moved out of a terraced house in Bear Flat at the end of 1993 and into this mansion by the golf course. There must be good profits in car parts.'

He grunted his assent. 'You're talking to a man who just had to buy a set of new tyres.'

'She drives a Porsche and he has a Mercedes.'

'And people like me paid for them.'

'Oh, and her name isn't really Serena. It's plain Ann.'

'What's wrong with Ann?' he demanded. 'I once had a girlfriend called Ann. The last word in sophistication. Stilettos and hot pants. Don't suppose you know what hot pants are.'

'Were,' murmured Julie.

'Well, we can't arrest her for changing her name.' Diamond wrenched his thoughts back from his steamy past. 'Who's your money on, Julie? Do you still think Glenn Noble had a mistress?'

'Yes – and Trish believes it, too.'

'So who's the killer – an angry husband?'

'Or boyfriend.'

He didn't mention Jack Merlin's bombshell – that Trish might, after all, have struck the fatal blow. 'Any idea who? Basil Porterfield?'

She said, 'I'll have a better idea when I meet him.'

'You can spot a skirt-chaser at fifty paces, can you?'

'If you don't mind me saying,' Julie commented, 'that's a rather outdated expression.'

'Un-hip?'

'Yes.'

'Well,' he went on, unabashed, 'I have to agree with you that it was some visitor to the house.'

'But who?'

He spread his hands. 'Could be anyone. Could be the Bishop of Bath and Wells for all we know.'

'The Porterfields were friends, close friends,' Julie pointed out. 'How many of your women friends would you hoist on your back for a photo?'

'All at once?'

She said on a note of exasperation, 'Mr Diamond, *sir*, I'm trying to make a serious point. We know that Glenn was often out until the small hours. If we could confirm that he was sleeping with Serena . . .'

'Hold on, Julie. That's a large assumption, isn't it? Trish Noble doesn't seem to think he needed to go elsewhere for sex.'

'She had her suspicions, believe me. You have to understand a woman's thinking. She may have said the opposite, but he was getting home so late that something was obviously going on. She's too proud or too puritanical to admit it to you and me.'

'He could have been up to something entirely different.'

'Such as?'

'A poker school. He wouldn't tell her if he was playing cards into the small hours. God and gambling don't mix.'

Julie wasn't impressed by that suggestion. 'She said he was tired when he got in.'

'Well, it *was* late.'

'Too tired for anything.'

After a pause, he said, 'Was that what she meant? This God-fearing woman who keeps a Bible by her bed?'

'That doesn't mean she's under-sexed.'

'Fair point,' said Diamond after a moment's reflection. 'There's more bonking in the Bible than there is in Jilly Cooper and Jackie Collins together. So she interprets his reduced libido as evidence of infidelity? It's speculation, Julie, whether it's her speculation or yours.'

She was resolute. 'Maybe it is, but if she's right, Serena Porterfield is in real danger – if she isn't already murdered. We can't ignore the possibility, speculation or not.'

The Porterfields' mock-Tudor mansion was on the slopes of Bathampton Down, with all of the city as a gleaming backdrop of pale cream stone and blue slate roofs. The house stood among lawns as well trimmed as the greens of the Bath Golf Club nearby. A gardener was on a ladder pruning the Albertine rose that covered much of one side of the house. A white Mercedes was on the drive. The chances of anyone from here being involved in a stabbing in a small terraced house in Twerton seemed remote.

Basil Porterfield opened the front door before they knocked. There was no question that he was the man in the Minehead photo – a sturdy, smiling, sandy-haired embodiment of confidence, even after Diamond told him they were police officers.

'Perhaps you heard that Glenn Noble is dead, sir?'

'Saw it in the paper. Devastating.' Porterfield didn't look devastated, but out of respect he shook his head. 'It's a long time since I saw Glenn.'

'But you were friends?'

'He was the sort you couldn't help liking. Look, why don't you come in?'

The welcome was unstinting. In a room big enough for the golf club AGM, they were shown to leather armchairs and offered sherry.

Diamond glanced at the teak wall units laden with pottery and art books. 'This is a far cry from Bear Flat.'

'We worked hard to move up in the world,' said Porterfield evenly.

'You're in the motor trade, I understand.'

'Curiously enough, we prospered in the recession. I don't sell new cars, I sell parts, and people were doing up their old vehicles rather than replacing them. The business really took off. We have outlets in France and Spain now.'

'You visit these countries?'

'Regularly.'

'And your business is based in Bath?'

'You must have passed it often enough, down the hill, on the Warminster Road.'

'Glenn Noble – was he a business contact?'

'Purely social. Through my wife, actually. She took a school project to the printers he worked for. Serena teaches art, printmaking, that sort of thing. You can see her influence all around you.'

'Is Mrs Porterfield at home today?'

'No. She's, em, out of the country.'

Julie's eyes sought Diamond's and held them for a moment.

He remarked to Porterfield, 'She must be devastated, too.'

'She doesn't know anything about it.'

Diamond played a wild card. 'You said you haven't seen the Nobles for a long time. Perhaps your wife saw them more recently.'

Porterfield asked smoothly, 'Why do you say that?'

Julie, equally smoothly, invented an answer. 'Someone answering your wife's description was seen recently in the company of Glenn Noble.'

'Is that so? Funny she didn't mention it.' He was unfazed.

'Just for the record,' said Diamond, 'would you mind telling me where you were on Monday afternoon between three and five?'

'Monday between three and five.' Porterfield

frowned, as if he hadn't remotely considered that he might be asked. 'I would have been at the office. I'm sure my staff will confirm that, if you care to ask them.'

'And your wife?'

'She's in France, like I said, on a school trip.' He smiled. 'She left last week. Last Friday.'

'Where did you say she teaches?'

Cavendish College was a girls' public school on Lyncombe Hill. The Head informed Diamond that Mrs Porterfield was indeed on a sixth form trip to the south of France. She frequently led school parties to places of artistic interest in Europe. She was a loyal, talented teacher, and an asset to the school.

Diamond used a mobile phone to get this information. He and Julie were parked in North Road, with a good view of the Porterfield residence.

'Are you relieved?' he asked Julie. 'Serena survives, apparently.'

'I still say he murdered Glenn Noble.'

'And I say you're right.'

Her eyes widened. 'Am I?'

'But he had the decency to do it while his wife was away. We'll arrest her when she returns.'

'Whatever for?'

'Hold on a little and I'll show you, if *my* theory is right. Serena's talent may be an asset to the school, but it's a bigger asset to Basil Porterfield. What time is it?'

'Ten past six.'

'After our visit he's not stopping here much longer.'

Twenty minutes, as it turned out. The Mercedes glided into North Road and down the hill with Julie and Diamond in discreet pursuit. Porterfield turned right at the junction with the busy Warminster Road. Three-quarters of a mile on, he slowed and pulled in to the forecourt of a building with Porterfield Car Spares in large letters across the front.

'Drive past and park as near as you can.'

Julie found a layby a short walk away.

When they approached on foot the only cover available was the side wall of Porterfield's building. From it they had a view of the empty Mercedes parked on the forecourt. 'I should have called for some back-up, but we can handle this, can't we?' said Diamond.

Julie lifted one eyebrow and said nothing.

Diamond issued an order. 'When he comes out, you go across and nick him.'

She lifted the other eyebrow.

He told her, 'I'm the back-up.'

Five minutes passed. The traffic on the Warminster Road zoomed by steadily.

'He's coming.'

Julie tensed.

Porterfield emerged from the building trundling a hand trolley stacked with white cartons. He set the trolley upright, took some keys from his pocket, opened the boot of the car and leaned in.

Diamond pressed a hand against the small of Julie's back. She started forward.

Sending in Julie first may have looked like cowardice, but it was not. While her sudden arrival on the scene caught Porterfield's attention, Diamond ducked around the other side of the Mercedes. Just in time, because Porterfield produced a knife from the car boot and swung it at Julie.

She swayed out of range and narrowly escaped another lunge. Then Diamond charged in and grabbed Porterfield from behind and thrust him sideways against the car, pinioning his arms. Julie prised the knife from his fist. Diamond produced a set of handcuffs and between them they forced him over the boot and manacled him.

'Want to see what's in the cartons?' Diamond suggested to Julie over the groaning prisoner. 'Why don't you use the knife?'

She cut along the adhesive seal of the top carton and parted the flaps. Neatly stacked inside were wads of French one-hundred-franc banknotes.

'*Money?*'

'Funny money,' said Diamond. 'We'll find the offset litho machine and the plates hidden deep inside the building. What with Serena's artwork, Glenn Noble's printing expertise and these premises to work in, making counterfeit notes was a profitable scam. But just like you said, Trish got suspicious of all the late nights. Glenn hadn't dared tell her what he was up to, even though it helped their bank balance no end. She was too high principled to be in on the secret.'

'Why French money?' Julie asked.

'Easier to make. No metal strip. I don't know how good these forgeries are, but Glenn would have got his brother in Devon to make the paper with a passable watermark.' He picked one up and held it to the light. 'Not bad. A portrait of Glenn's favourite painter, Eugène Delacroix. This has a nice feel to it. They coat the printed notes with glycerine. He'll have hand-pressed the serial numbers.'

'And why was he killed?'

'Because of Trish. Unwisely he told Porterfield that she was asking about the late nights. She would have seen it as her moral duty to shop them all, and Porterfield couldn't risk her wheedling the truth out of Glenn.' He hauled Porterfield upright. 'You thought you could get rid of Glenn and do the printing yourself, didn't you, ratbag? Last Monday afternoon you called unexpectedly at the house. Glenn let you in, offered you a drink, and when his back was turned you drove a knife into him. You escaped through the back garden just as Trish was coming in through the front. Right?'

'How the hell did you get on to me?' Porterfield asked.

'Through something Glenn Noble wrote on a

photograph. Someone took a picture of your day out in Minehead in 1993. Glenn wrote "wayzgoose" on the back.'

'What's that?'

'A word for a printers' outing. When I looked at it first, I couldn't understand why he called it that, since he was the only printer in the picture. Then it dawned that you and possibly your wife were involved in some printing activity. When I saw how well you were doing, and how large his bank balance was, I reckoned you were printing money. Julie, would you call headquarters and ask them to send a car?'

Porterfield asked, 'What was that word?'

'Wayzgoose,' said Diamond. 'Funny old word. Worth remembering. It'll get you a large score in Scrabble. Where you're going, you may get the odd chance to play. You'll certainly have the time.'

Superintendent
Peter Diamond

A problem.

How old is he? In *The Last Detective*, forty-one; in *Diamond Solitaire*, which takes place the following year, forty-eight – or so he tells Harrods, his new employers. Can we believe his own statements?

Let's start with the indisputable fact that Peter Diamond is fat, although he thinks of himself as 'burly'. He needed no padding to play Santa Claus after he quit the police towards the end of *The Last Detective*. He once played rugby for the Metropolitan Police and can still hand off a tackle. There are suspicions that his considerable poundage is useful in eliciting confessions. Whilst serving with the Met he was involved in the case against a youth called Missendale who was put away for murder and later had to be pardoned when the real killer confessed. Diamond doesn't ever say much about his career.

He is called 'the Last Detective' because his sleuthing style is out of sympathy with modern policing. Suspicious of the increasing reliance on forensic science, he is at one with the trilby-hatted Scotland Yard men of the 1940s, and regularly buys books of their memoirs. He has no time for crime fiction and is amused by donnish television detectives who quote Shakespeare, write poetry or listen to

Wagner. He can't do crosswords either. The best he can manage is the occasional jigsaw puzzle, and then he loses pieces.

What of his personal life? He would be the first to tell you that his wife *does* understand him. With one failed marriage behind her, Stephanie needed to be strongly persuaded that another was worth the risk. She was devoting most of her energy to the Brownie movement when Diamond wooed her and the entire summer camp – by arriving unexpectedly with two donkeys. Steph rejoices in his capacity to surprise her and tolerates his clumsy ways, his cussedness, his lack of any handyman skills. It is a loving marriage. There are no children, which is a pity, because Diamond has a remarkable rapport with kids. His patient efforts to understand the autistic girl, Naomi, in *Diamond Solitaire*, eventually uncovered an international scam and a murder, yet it was his concern for the child that drove him.

Diamond's dilemma is that after he quit the police he found so uncongenial in *The Last Detective*, he was unable to function happily or even find regular work in civilian life. When the call came, in *The Summons*, to return to the city of Bath and direct a highly sensitive police operation, he was buoyant again. He may tell others, 'I've gone soft as a cider-apple since I came down here,' but one senses that this apple is a variety that will stay firm, round and shining for some time yet.

Peter Lovesey

Peter Lovesey began his writing career with *Wobble to Death* in 1970, introducing Sergeant Cribb, the Victorian detective who went on to feature in seven more books and two television series. His recent novels have alternated between two contrasting detectives: Peter Diamond, and the Victorian sleuth, Bertie. Peter Lovesey's mysteries and short stories have won him awards all over the world, including both Gold and Silver Daggers of the Crime Writers' Association.

After a career in teaching, he became a full-time author in 1975 and now lives near Bath.

Just Deserts

Dorothy Simpson

Just Deserts

When Thanet saw who was on the doorstep his first instinct was to slam the door in his face. He found it virtually impossible to forgive Alexander for the heartache he had caused Bridget. It had taken her a long time to recover and the last thing Thanet wanted was for the affair to start up all over again.

Alexander smiled, that sunny, warm, open smile which had won Bridget's heart. 'Hallo, sir. I was just passing through Sturrenden after visiting friends in the Elam valley overnight, and thought I'd look Bridget up. I'd heard she was back from her travels and living at home at the moment. Is she in, by any chance?'

Except at work nobody else had ever called Thanet 'sir'. It went with Alexander's public school background, his plummy accent, his lucrative job in the city, the Porsche which had so impressed Bridget's brother Ben the first time he saw it.

Reluctant to admit that yes, Bridget was in, Thanet was saved from the temptation to lie by his daughter's voice.

'Alexander!'

Somehow Bridget had managed to infuse astonishment, disbelief and delight into the speaking of his name and Thanet saw with sinking heart that her face was aglow with welcome.

'Brig! It's good to see you!'

Brig. Thanet had forgotten how the abbreviation used to set his teeth on edge. He had no option now but to stand aside and watch helplessly as Alexander took both Bridget's hands and said, smiling, 'You're looking great!'

Thanet himself, he realized, had spoken not one single word since the moment he opened the door.

Bridget and her mother had been in the kitchen, cooking. Until the doorbell rang it had been the sort of Sunday which, given Thanet's job as a detective inspector in Sturrenden CID, hardly ever happened and was even more rare now that the children were grown up and had so many interests of their own. The four of them had been to church together, even Ben reluctantly joining them for once. It was a glorious July day and Thanet had been looking forward to a pleasant Sunday lunch en famille and a lazy afternoon in a deckchair in the garden.

Now, Joan came out to greet Alexander and then she and Thanet retreated to the kitchen, leaving the two young people alone.

'What a nerve!' said Thanet. 'Turning up out of the blue like that, after the way he treated her! I hope he doesn't think he's going to take up where he left off!'

Bridget had been head over heels in love with Alexander. He had dazzled her, enchanted her, then dropped her a year later without warning, saying that he didn't feel ready for a long-term commitment.

'That was eighteen months ago. Perhaps he's changed,' said Joan.

'Ever the optimist, aren't you? Nobody would believe you're a senior probation officer!'

Joan grinned. 'It's precisely because I'm an optimist that I *am* a probation officer! You do realize we'll have to ask him to stay to lunch.'

Thanet groaned. 'Oh, no.'

'Oh yes.'

The telephone rang. Ten minutes ago Thanet would

have answered it with reluctance. Now he hurried into the hall and snatched the receiver up with alacrity. And Hallelujah, yes, it was Pater, the Station Sergeant.

'Don't tell me!' said Joan, when he returned to the kitchen.

'A fatal accident, apparently. Chap's fallen off a ladder and broken his neck. But it sounds as though there could be something fishy about it. I'd better go and see for myself.'

'No need to look so pleased!' said Joan, following him into the hall.

Thanet grimaced as Alexander's hearty laugh emanated from the sitting-room. 'All right, I admit it,' he said, lowering his voice, 'If I had to choose between turning out on my weekend off and Sunday lunch with Alexander, there's no doubt which I'd go for.'

His car had been parked in the drive and the interior was stifling, the steering wheel almost too hot to hold. Suppressing the desire to back into Alexander's Porsche (a white one now, he noted) he switched the cold air blower on full and drove through the Sunday quiet of Sturrenden's normally busy streets wondering how he would feel if Bridget did take up with Alexander again. He would, he supposed, grin and bear it. There wasn't really any alternative; if he didn't want to bring about the unthinkable and alienate her. And it was, after all, her happiness that really mattered. But if Alexander let her down again . . . Thanet found he was gritting his teeth. Calm down, he told himself. It's beyond your control. Just wait and see.

With an effort he switched his thoughts to the little information he had been given about this apparent accident. The dead man, a Fred Scotcher, had been found by a neighbour, but there had been some mention of a family row earlier on this morning. Thanet hoped Lineham would be there before him. He and the sergeant had worked together for so long that conducting an investigation without him was like operating with one hand tied behind his back.

Scotcher had lived on a small council estate on the other side of town. Judging by the ambulance and the cluster of police vehicles his semi was the last in the row in a little cul-de-sac which ended abruptly as if further building had been intended and the council had changed its mind or run out of money. A chain-mesh fence ran across the end of the road and beyond there was a ragged coppice of trees whose summer foliage added a welcome touch of green to the drab surroundings. As usual the first whiff of drama had drawn people out of their houses, eager to enliven their Sunday, and heads turned and tongues wagged as Thanet drew up.

Lineham was waiting at the front gate and came to meet him.

'A real scorcher today, isn't it, sir.'

Still feeling disgruntled Thanet suppressed the desire to snap, *We didn't come here to talk about the weather, Mike.* 'Yes. Doc Mallard's here already, I see,' Thanet nodded at the police surgeon's ancient and much-loved Rover. 'That was quick.'

'Got here a few minutes ago,' said Lineham.

'Where's the body?'

'Round the back.'

Thanet braced himself. The moment he always dreaded was at hand and he experienced the familiar clenching of his stomach muscles, the churning sensation in his gut. He glanced at Lineham, wondering if the sergeant had ever suspected his superior's most private weakness. For the truth was that, even after all these years in the force, Thanet still shrank from that first sight of the corpse. In the early days he had felt ashamed of doing so, had tried every trick in the book to overcome this chink in the armour with which every policeman must learn to protect himself, but gradually he had come to realize that these moments of vulnerability had become, paradoxically, one of his strengths, a necessary spur to the energy with which he pursued the ensuing investigation. It was therefore with a resigned acceptance that he rounded the corner of the house and stopped to take in the scene before him.

Doc Mallard was kneeling beside the body, bald head sensibly protected from the heat of the midday sun by a rather dashing panama with a striped riband. A couple of Scenes-of-the-Crime Officers were standing by, waiting for him to finish. No need to ask if they had taken shots of the body before Mallard started his examination. Thanet knew his team and they were highly trained. He took in the aluminium ladder lying close by, the tin of white paint splattered across the unevenly-laid multicoloured paving stones of the patio and glanced up at the half-painted guttering under the eaves of the house. A simple accident, then? A fatal fall?

'Morning, Luke.' Mallard glanced up at him over his half-moons. 'Or should I say "afternoon"?'

'I always say "morning" until I've had my lunch,' said Thanet. *Now, look at the body.* He took a deep breath and did so.

This time it wasn't so bad. There were no marks of violence on Scotcher and had it not been for the awkward way in which his legs were splayed, the unnatural angle of head to body, he might have been asleep. He was in his late forties, Thanet guessed, a big man, well over six feet and heavily built, with a prominent belly and a mat of hair on chest and arms. He was stripped to the waist and wearing shorts.

'Not a very prepossessing specimen,' said Mallard, closing his bag with a snap and heaving himself to his feet.

'No,' agreed Thanet, taking in the thick lips, pouches beneath the eyes, coarse black stubble on unshaven cheeks and chin.

'And something of a drinker, I'd guess.' Mallard glanced at Thanet. 'I suppose you want to hear the usual? Yes. Well, you can see for yourself that it looks as though his neck is broken and I'd say he hasn't been dead long – sometime in the last two or three hours, probably. It's difficult to make an accurate estimate on such a hot day, as he's been lying in full sun.'

Thanet glanced at his watch. 12.45. 'Would death have been instantaneous?'

'Quite possibly but not necessarily.'

Thanet glanced at Lineham and could see that his sergeant was thinking the same thing. *A great help!*

Doc Mallard had noticed. 'Oh, I know you'd like me to give chapter and verse now, this minute, but spinal injuries are a complex matter and I really can't commit myself at the moment. Sorry, but there it is.'

'Will you be able to be more specific after a post-mortem?'

'Again, quite possibly but not necessarily!' Mallard gave a mischievous grin. 'That'll brighten up your Sunday!'

When Mallard had gone Lineham said, 'Perhaps one of the neighbours will be able to give us some idea when it happened. That aluminium ladder would have made a hell of a clatter when it came down.'

'Perhaps. Anyway, what's this about a family argument, Mike?'

'PC Denham tells me that according to the neighbour who found the body there was an almighty row at breakfast time. I haven't spoken to the man myself, so I don't know the details. I thought you'd want to interview him personally. Mrs Scotcher doesn't know what's happened yet. Her mother lives with them and she always takes her to church on Sunday mornings.'

'They should be back by now, surely. It's nearly one o'clock.'

Lineham shrugged. 'I agree.'

Thanet glanced at the SOCOs. 'Got all the shots you want of the body? In that case, they can take him away now. Then we'd better go and have a word with the neighbour, Mike. What's his name?'

'Bevan.'

Thanet groaned. 'Another Welshman.'

'Oh come on, sir. They're not all like Draco, you know!'

Superintendent Draco was the scourge of Sturrenden police headquarters and Thanet had frequently crossed swords with him in the past.

'I haven't met enough of them to have an informed opinion, thank goodness.'

Lineham laughed. 'Who's always saying we can't afford to be prejudiced?'

Bevan was in his fifties but judging by his hairstyle, striped shorts and brightly coloured hawaiian-style shirt was obviously trying to forget the fact. The latter was unbuttoned half-way down to his waist and a medallion on a gold chain nestled coyly in his chest hair. When Thanet saw Mrs Bevan he realized why; she was a good twenty years younger and wearing one of the shortest, tightest mini-skirts he had ever seen. Bevan's eyes were snapping with excitement and he led them into the sitting-room with alacrity, offering them tea, coffee, cold drinks, whatever they fancied.

Thanet declined, politely. 'If you could just tell us what happened . . .'

The Bevans had left at around 10 o'clock to do their weekly shop at the supermarket. Afterwards they had called in at a local garden centre before arriving back home at about 12.

'And as soon as we pulled up outside the house we could hear that bloody radio of his going full blast, couldn't we, Luce?' Bevan's Welsh accent was becoming more pronounced as his story gained pace.

Radio? Thanet remembered now: there had been a huge portable radio standing on the back doorstep of

Scotcher's house. He had noticed it but not really taken it into account. But if it had been making that much noise . . . He glanced at Lineham and could tell that the same thought had occurred to the sergeant: so much for the hope that one of the neighbours might have heard the ladder fall.

His wife was nodding. 'Belting out, it was. Well, we like a bit of music, don't we, Des. Livens the place up. But the din that man used to make! Drove us round the bend, didn't it?'

'You bet it did. And specially in the summer when you were out in the garden, working on your tan . . .' Bevan shot his wife a lascivious look and put his hand on her bare thigh. She responded by running her tongue over her lips and wriggling a little closer to him.

They were enjoying this, Thanet realized, getting a buzz out of the drama and excitement. Scotcher certainly wouldn't be mourned in this house.

'I think he used to turn it up full volume just to annoy us.'

'So what did you do?' said Lineham.

'What d'you think? Went straight round to tell him if he didn't turn it down I was going to call you lot. I mean to say, you do a hard week's work – and I work Saturdays, too – then on your only day off you do the shopping and come home looking forward to a nice cool beer and a sit out in the garden and what do you find? That you can't even open your back door without your eardrums being bloody perforated!'

'He drove the whole street mad,' said Mrs Bevan. 'But no one had the guts to tackle him about it, except Des.'

Bevan preened himself at her admiring look. 'Great big bloke he was, see. I don't mind telling you I was nearly pissing in my pants, but this was the last straw.'

'He was such a bully!' said Mrs Bevan. 'Used to knock that poor wife of his about something terrible.'

'Perhaps we could come back to that in a minute,' said Thanet. 'If you could just finish telling us what happened, Mr Bevan.'

Bevan shrugged. 'Not much more to tell. I went steaming round to the back of the house, where the din was coming from, and there he was. Dead as a doornail.' Bevan could not disguise his satisfaction.

'How did you know, sir?' said Lineham. 'That he was dead?'

'Well, obvious, wasn't it, man? I mean, with his neck all crooked like that . . . Of course, I just checked, to make sure.'

'What did you do, exactly?'

Bevan screwed up his eyes, thinking. 'Just what anyone else would have done, in the circumstances. I mean, I could see he wasn't breathing, not so as you could tell, but all the same I laid my hand against his cheek, to see if he was still warm. He was, so I tried to find the pulse in his neck, and couldn't. So then I went into the house – the back door was open – and dialled 999. Then I came home.'

'I presume it was you who turned off the radio,' said Thanet.

'Oh, yeah, well, it seemed sort of, well, indecent, like, to have music blaring out with him lying there like that. Anyway, I wanted a bit of hush to make that phone call.'

'You said he knocked his wife about, Mrs Bevan,' said Thanet.

'Used to go down the pub, Saturday nights,' said Bevan, 'and come home roaring drunk. Sunday mornings, regular as clockwork, there'd she be with bruises, black eyes and God knows what.'

'She used to try and hide it, avoid us if she could, but we knew, didn't we, Des? Everyone did. If you ask me, he got his just deserts.'

'Did she ever report it, do you know?' said Lineham.

Bevan shook his head. 'Too shit-scared, I should think.'

'I understand there was a family row earlier on this morning. If she never stood up to him, then who . . . ?'

'That was Tim,' said Bevan. 'Their son. Poor little sod, I should think it used to make him sick to the stomach, the way his dad used to treat his mum.'

'You think that was what the row was about?'

'Just a guess,' said Mrs Bevan. 'These walls are thin, but not so thin you can actually hear words, if you see what I mean. Just raised voices.'

'And it was definitely Tim and his father who were arguing?'

They both nodded.

'How old is the boy?' said Lineham.

'Sixteen.'

'And well grown?'

'Not really, no,' said Bevan. 'A bit undersized if anything, wouldn't you say, Luce?'

'Yeah, definitely. Looks a good couple of years younger, I'd say.'

'And had he stood up to Mr Scotcher before, to your knowledge?' said Thanet. It wouldn't be the first time a lad had turned on his father after years of watching his mother abused.

'No,' said Bevan, glancing at his wife for confirmation, 'not so far as we know, anyway. Scotcher used to knock him about, too.'

'No doubt about that,' said Mrs Bevan.

'We understand that Mrs Scotcher's mother lives with them,' said Thanet. 'From the way you describe her husband he doesn't sound at all the type to take his mother-in-law in.'

Bevan gave a cynical laugh. 'You can say that again! No, the only reason he gave her a home was because he wanted to buy his council house and she had a bit of cash. She used to live with her sister and they owned a little two-up, two-down in Victoria Street. Then the sister went gaga and had to go into a home and Beryl's mum got Parkinson's and found it more and more difficult to look after herself. So Scotcher said if she sold up and took her share of the proceeds to help him buy next door, she could come and live with them. Which she did.'

'So how did it work out?'

Bevan shrugged. 'All right, so far as I know. How can you tell? You can't see through bricks and mortar and when Scotcher was home we weren't exactly on visiting terms. But Luce goes around sometimes when she has a day off, and says Beryl and her mum got on well enough.'

His wife was nodding. 'Very fond of each other, I'd say. But I couldn't help feeling sorry for the old lady. I mean, it can't have been much fun for her, can it, living in the same house as that brute, watching him knocking her daughter and grandson about and not being able to do a dicky-bird about it.'

'I believe Mrs Scotcher usually takes her mother to church on Sunday mornings.'

'That's right. Glad to get out of the house for a bit of peace and quiet, if you ask me.'

'What time do they leave?'

'Ten-fifteen. Something like that. The car was still in the drive when we left about ten this morning, wasn't it, Luce?'

'And they get back at what time?'

'Just before twelve, usually,' said Bevan. 'But sometimes they go and visit the old lady's sister afterwards. The nursing home is the other side of Sturrenden. Scotcher usually had the car, see, so it's a good opportunity for Beryl to drive her mother over.'

So here was the probable explanation of their absence. Thanet had left a message that he was to be informed the second they returned.

'I expect that's where they are today,' said Mrs Bevan. 'Poor Beryl. What a shock for her!'

'Poor Beryl my foot!' said her husband. 'If I was her I'd be dancing on his grave!'

And she wouldn't be the only one, by the sound of it, thought Thanet.

'So what happened after this row?' said Lineham. 'Did things quieten down?'

'Not until Scotcher threw Tim out,' said Bevan. 'I was getting the car out and I saw what happened.'

Thanet and Lineham waited.

'He just chucked him out. Literally,' said Bevan. 'Front door opened and the next second Tim was sprawling on the front path. Scotcher saw me watching and if looks could kill I'd have dropped dead on the spot. Then he went back in, slamming the door behind him. Tim picked himself up and I went to see if he was all right.'

'And was he?'

'His face was grazed and he was limping. But there were no bones broken, so far as I could see.'

'What did he do?'

'Made off down the street.'

There was a knock at the door. Mrs Scotcher and her mother were back, apparently, and Thanet hurried to meet them. He was pleased to see that there was a policewoman beside them and that the ambulance had already gone.

They were standing by a rusting, dented Ford, looking bewildered, two diminutive figures whose clothes at once proclaimed how they had spent their morning. The old lady was wearing a neat, navy Crimplene two-piece with a white blouse beneath. On her head was a navy straw hat decorated with white daisies. The daisies, Thanet noticed, were nodding and swaying as if in a high wind, and he remembered what Bevan had told them: Parkinson's disease. She looked frail and exhausted, as if only an effort of will were keeping her upright.

Her daughter, who was supporting her with one arm around her waist, was wearing a drab, high-necked, long-sleeved summer dress. To conceal the bruises? Thanet wondered. Perhaps her hair-style had been chosen for the same reason; the long, lank brown hair straggled forward across her cheeks and shoulders on either side. Her fringe just cleared her eyebrows and beneath it two frightened eyes peered out at Thanet.

'Mrs Scotcher?'

'What is it? What's the matter? Is it Tim – my son?'

Tim was probably the one person, apart from her mother, who mattered most to her in the world, thought Thanet. Not surprising, then, that her first fear should be for him. She obviously thought he might have come back while she was out and was afraid of what her husband might have done.

'No, your son is fine, as far as we know,' he said gently. 'Shall we go inside?' This was not the place to break the news of her husband's death to Mrs Scotcher with all the neighbours watching avidly for her reaction. He gestured for the WPC to accompany them.

The three of them held back while the old lady tottered up the path, helped by her daughter. In the sitting-room Beryl Scotcher eased her mother into an upright armchair, then turned to face the detectives. 'Tell me what's happened.' She took a deep breath, clearly bracing herself against bad news.

'It's your husband.'

'Fred?' She turned her head sharply towards the back window, noticing for the first time the policemen moving about there. Her hair caught on her shoulder on one side, dragging it away from her cheek and revealing a bruise down one side of her face, terminating in a ragged gash high up near her forehead. She saw him looking and tugged her hair forward self-consciously. 'There's been an accident?'

'He fell from a ladder. Mrs Scotcher, wouldn't you like to sit down?'

She shook her head. 'Is he . . . ?'

'Yes. He's dead, I'm afraid. I'm sorry.' But would she

be, he wondered, when the news had time to sink in?

She drew in her breath sharply. 'Dead,' she whispered. 'D'you hear that, Mother?' she said, raising her voice. 'Fred's dead!' She gave a mirthless laugh. 'Fred's dead,' she repeated. 'That rhymes, doesn't it.' She felt for the nearest chair and sank down on to it. 'I can't believe it.'

The WPC moved closer to her and put a consolatory hand on her shoulder, but she seemed unaware of it.

Thanet glanced at the old lady. For the last few minutes he had been conscious of a background of sound to their conversation, an irregular susurration which was unfamiliar to him. Engrossed in Mrs Scotcher's reaction he hadn't tried to identify it but now he recognized its source. Her mother had taken out a rosary and the pronounced tremor in her hands was causing the tiny amber beads to tap against each other, producing a muted clicking sound. Now she spoke for the first time, in a curious monotone which Thanet later learned was characteristic of Parkinson's. 'What did you say, Beryl?' Then, as she got no response, she raised her voice. 'Beryl, what did you say?' she repeated. There was still no reply and she looked up at Thanet, her clouded blue eyes questioning, her head shaking. The beads whispered their accompaniment as her hands moved restlessly in her lap. 'What did she say?'

Thanet bent over her. 'That your son-in-law is dead.'

'Fred?'

Thanet nodded.

'You're sure?'

Another nod. 'I'm afraid so.'

The fog in the blue eyes suddenly cleared, miraculously, and a spark of unmistakable relief appeared. She looked at her daughter, who was sitting staring blankly into space. 'Thank God!' she said. 'Good riddance!'

'Mum!' Mrs Scotcher was shocked out of her

trance-like state.

'No point in pretending, is there? He was a bad lot,' the old woman said to Thanet. 'And no one could deny it.' She refocused her attention on her rosary, withdrawing from the conversation.

'Look, Mrs Scotcher,' said Thanet. 'I'm sorry to trouble you at a time like this, but if you do feel up to answering a few questions, perhaps we can get the matter cleared up and leave you in peace.'

She compressed her lips. 'Go ahead.'

She couldn't tell him much more than he had learnt already. They had left for church, 'mass' she called it, around 10.15 and after the service had visited Beryl's aunt in the nursing home. 'It's our only chance to get over there, see,' she said. 'Fred needed the car for work and you can't get there by bus.' She glanced briefly at the window through which the ancient Ford could clearly be seen, and Thanet could almost hear her thinking, *Now we'll be able to go whenever we like.* The benefits of her husband's unexpected demise were beginning to sink in.

Unless she had already anticipated those benefits and had speeded him on his way?

'What was your husband doing when you left?'

'He was round the back, painting the house.'

'You went out to say goodbye to him?'

She shook her head. 'He didn't like being bothered when he was busy.'

What utter misery it must be, thought Thanet, to be trapped in such a marriage as that. No love, no warmth, no shared companionship to compensate for the rough patches that invariably come along. And all the time, fear of when the next blow would fall.

'Anyway, the radio was on so loud he wouldn't have heard me if I had.'

'We understand that there was . . .' How to put it tactfully? '. . . some sort of family argument at breakfast time.'

For a brief moment the tapping of the rosary beads ceased.

Mrs Scotcher bit her lip and frowned, but did not say anything.

'Mrs Scotcher?' Thanet persisted. 'What was the argument about?'

She clenched her teeth and stared at him. She wasn't going to tell him, that was obvious. Not surprising, really, especially if the Bevans had guessed correctly and the row had been about Scotcher's treatment of her.

The old lady, Thanet was sure, was listening. He turned to her. 'Could you tell us, Mrs . . .?'

'Finch,' she responded, automatically. 'What did you say?'

'The argument, at breakfast. What was it about?'

The old woman looked at her daughter. Following her gaze Thanet caught the tail end of a frown. Enough, between these two, for Beryl Scotcher to convey her message. *Don't tell them.*

'What argument?' said Mrs Finch, the blue eyes guileless.

Thanet shrugged, mentally. If they were determined not to talk about it there was nothing he could do to make them. Nor was there any point in bringing up the fact that they knew Scotcher had thrown Tim out. He stood up. 'Well, I think that's all for the moment. We'll just take another look around the back, then we'll be off.'

With the body gone and SOCOs finished on the patio, Thanet and Lineham could move about freely and discuss how the apparent accident could have occurred. The enormous portable radio still stood on the back doorstep and the aluminium ladder had, by Thanet's request, been left exactly where it fell. Both had obviously been dusted for fingerprints. Now they picked the ladder up and leaned it against the wall below the point where the fresh paint on the guttering ended. The unevenness of the paving stones was such that it was difficult to find a stable position.

'Hmm,' said Thanet, considering.

'Very short, for the job he was doing,' said Lineham.

'I'm taller than you. Steady the ladder while I go up and see how far I can reach.'

Even allowing for a paintbrush, they agreed, Scotcher would really have had to stretch, to reach the guttering.

'No doubt about it, it could well have been a straightforward accident,' said Thanet.

'On the other hand, if the ladder was unevenly placed and he was stretching up and perhaps reaching out sideways and somebody had come along and given it a shove, or a tug . . . I shouldn't have thought it would have required that much force.'

'True.' Thanet's tone was abstracted. He was obviously thinking of something else. 'It's just occurred to me, Mike. I wonder if the paint might help forensic pinpoint time of death? Damn. Hope it's not too late. Slipped up there, didn't we. Should have thought of it earlier.' He called the SOCOs over and asked them to check how dry the new paintwork was and to give the lab this information together with the paint tin Scotcher had been using.

'Sir . . .' Carson, who had been doing house-to-house enquiries, came around the corner of the house. 'There's a witness who lives across the road . . . I think you'd like to hear what he has to say.'

'What's it about?' said Thanet, as they walked down the drive.

'The son,' said Carson, lowering his voice as he glanced back at the house.

'And the witness's name?'

'Tenant.'

Tenant lived directly opposite the Scotchers' house in one of a row of four semi-detached bungalows, old people's housing, Thanet guessed. A face was peering out at them from between the net curtains at the front window. It disappeared as they unlatched the gate and their knock was answered by a little apple-cheeked woman in her seventies, with sparse white hair.

'Mrs Tenant?' Thanet introduced himself and Lineham. 'May we have a word with your husband?'

She led them into the room on the left. It smelt of old age and sickness and was overpoweringly hot. Despite the heat of the day a gas fire was turned full on. Tenant was sitting in a high-backed armchair beside the window. He was wearing pyjamas and dressing gown and two tall cylinders stood beside him, an oxygen mask dangling from one of them. His feet were propped up on a footstool and Thanet noted the swollen ankles which bulged above his carpet slippers. A Bible lay open on his lap. 'You won't mind if I don't get up?' His voice was weak, breathy. He raised his hand slowly and tapped his chest. 'Emphysema.'

'Not at all.'

At his wife's invitation Thanet and Lineham sat down. Mrs Tenant went to stand beside her husband, one hand protectively on his shoulder.

'Now try not to get too worked up, Des.'

'Don't fuss, Flo.'

'I understand you have something to tell us, Mr Tenant,' said Thanet.

Tenant nodded. 'It's about the boy.' And he glanced out of the window, across the road.

From his armchair he had a clear view of the front of the Scotchers' house, Thanet saw. 'Tim?'

Tenant nodded.

'You saw him thrown out this morning?'

Another nod.

'We both did,' said his wife. 'That great bully of a man. We can't pretend we were sorry, when we heard he was dead. We wouldn't have said anything about what happened later, but we don't like telling lies.' She glanced at the Bible. 'So when the other policeman asked us outright if we'd seen anyone go in or out of the Scotchers' house this morning, Des felt he had to speak up, didn't you, love?'

'So what did you see, Mr Tenant?' said Thanet. The heat in the room was suffocating and he took out his handkerchief and mopped his forehead, wishing he had thought to remove his jacket before sitting down. It would look too obvious to do so now and would also break the flow of the interview, which was going nicely. He'd just have to suffer in silence. He glanced at Lineham and saw that he, too, was sweating.

'He came back. Tim,' said the old man.

'Oh?' Thanet's interest sharpened, discomfort forgotten. 'What time was this?'

'Quarter or ten to eleven.'

'You're sure of the time?'

'Des was waiting for Morning Worship to begin at eleven, on the telly,' said Mrs Tenant.

'You saw Tim too?'

She shook her head. 'I was in the kitchen.'

'Tell me what happened,' said Thanet.

The old man spoke in short sentences with long pauses in between, breath labouring. 'Saw him come along the street. Slowly up their drive. Warily.' He looked at Thanet to see if he understood.

'You think he was watching out for his father.'

A grateful nod. 'Went in.'

'By the front door? He had his own key?'

Another nod.

'How long was he in the house?'

'Ten minutes? Programme started just after.' There was a long pause while Tenant struggled to catch his breath. He looked at his wife.

'Mask?' she said.

He nodded and she unhooked it, handed it to him and when it was in position twisted the valve on the cylinder. There was a faint hissing sound and the old man took deep, slow, grateful breaths.

They all waited. Eventually he lowered the mask. 'Carrying a bag,' he said. 'Holdall.'

'When he came out, you mean?'

Tenant nodded again.

Thanet rose. 'Well, thank you very much for telling us this, Mr Tenant. We'll leave you in peace now. I hope you haven't found this too exhausting.' He gave the old man a warm smile. 'We appreciate the effort it has cost you.'

Mrs Tenant followed them out.

In the hall Thanet paused. 'Did you by any chance see Mrs Scotcher and her mother leave for church this morning?' He guessed that, housebound as she was, she and her husband both spent a lot of time looking out of the windows.

'Yes, I did.'

'Would you tell us about that?'

She looked puzzled. 'Not much to tell.'

'All the same . . . Any details you can remember.'

She frowned, thinking. 'Well, Beryl came out first. The car was already in the drive because her husband had backed it out to get at his ladder and stuff, earlier. She always has to reverse it down on to the road for her mother to get in – the drive is too narrow. There's no room for the passenger door to open. So she always backs on to the road like she did today, then goes back to fetch her mother. Poor soul. As you'll have seen, Edie's got Parkinson's really bad.' Mrs Tenant sighed. 'Old age can be a dreadful thing, if you're ill. Well, you saw my husband . . . We're only thankful I'm fit enough to look after him. But you don't want to hear all this. Where was I? Oh, yes. Beryl helped her mother down the drive and into the car and off they went. Is that what you wanted to know?'

'Yes. Just one further point, though. I gather from what you say that you saw Mr Scotcher earlier on.'

'Yes. Getting his stuff out of the garage, like I said. He's been painting the house at weekends for the last couple of weeks. Started at the front, worked his way around, always playing that radio of his full blast. We were relieved when he got to the back, I can tell you. Even with the windows shut you could hardly hear yourself think.'

'What time was it, when you saw him?'

She frowned, considering. 'Just after the Bevans went off in their car, I think it was. Yes, that's right.'

Soon after ten, then. Thanet thanked her. 'You've both been very helpful.'

'No trouble.'

'Phew!' said Lineham, as they walked back down the path, taking out a handkerchief and wiping it across forehead, cheeks, and around the back of his neck. 'If we'd stayed much longer in there I think I'd have passed out. How do they stand it?'

'I suppose if you're sitting around all day you don't generate much body heat and need extra warmth.'

'But on a day like today . . .'

'Anyway,' said Thanet. 'We'll go and sit in the car while we chew over what we've learnt this morning.'

'Let's use mine. It's in the shade.'

Inside they wound all the windows down.

'What d'you think, Mike?'

'Looks as though the boy's scarpered, doesn't it?'

'Yes. The question is, why?'

'I'd guess he'd had enough and decided to move out, came back to fetch his stuff. He obviously hoped to slip in and out without his father knowing.'

'I agree. The question is, is that all he did, when he got here?'

'He'd have heard the radio, known his father was out at the back, possibly knew he'd be up a ladder, painting . . . It would have been easy for him to nip out of the back door and dislodge it, it would only have taken a few seconds. If Scotcher had been concentrating on what he was doing he wouldn't have heard him down below, with all that noise.'

'True. We'll have to try and find the boy. But there are a couple of other possibilities, Mike.'

'Mrs Scotcher, for instance.'

'Yes. D'you think she'd have had enough strength to do it?'

Lineham considered. 'Difficult to tell. If she chose her moment, though, when his balance was precarious . . . well, it's possible, I'd say. If his weight was badly distributed it might not have taken much to topple him.'

'Mmm. The trouble is, no one saw him after the Tenants.'

'Yes. For all we know, he might have come off that ladder before his wife left for church.'

'Exactly, Mike. But even if he did, Doc Mallard said he couldn't commit himself as to whether death had been instantaneous. So unless forensic come up with a definitive answer on the paint . . .'

'If it did happen early on it's nasty to think of him lying there dying slowly with that pop music belting out.' Lineham pulled a face. 'Positively macabre.'

'Yes. But there's no way of knowing, is there, not until the lab and PM results come through. Let's hope they get a move on. Until then I can't see that there's any justification for treating this other than as a straightforward accident. If Scotcher hadn't been the sort of man he obviously was, I probably wouldn't be thinking twice about it.'

'I know. A real brute by the sound of it, wasn't he. In the circumstances it wouldn't be surprising if one of them had been tempted to get rid of him for good.'

'And that includes Bevan. Don't let's forget him. I imagine he was in a steaming temper when he went around to ask Scotcher to turn the radio down.'

'Yes. I can just imagine what would have happened if Scotcher had just refused pointblank, Bevan grabbing the ladder and shaking it in a fury. That's a point, sir! If Bevan's prints were on the ladder . . . It wouldn't prove a thing if either Tim's or Mrs

Scotcher's were on it, of course. They could both claim to have handled it at some other time.'

'Quite. And I suppose it would help if the medical evidence were unequivocal, but I've got a nasty feeling it isn't going to be. Ah well, there's nothing we can do about that. We'll just check and see if we can find out from Mrs Scotcher where Tim is. He might have left a note.'

'You think she'd tell us, even if she knew?'

'I doubt it. But we have to try.'

They got nowhere, however. There was nothing more to be done here for the moment so Thanet put Carson on to trying to track Tim down and, leaving a man to watch the house in case the boy returned, he and Lineham went back to headquarters to write up their reports. When Thanet eventually got home at around six he was relieved to see that Alexander's Porsche was no longer parked in front of the house.

'He's gone, then,' he said to Joan, who was sitting out in the garden with her feet up, reading the newspaper. He bent to kiss her. 'That's a relief, anyway.'

'Not such a relief when you hear that Bridget is with him. He's taken her down to the coast.'

'Oh, no!' Thanet sank down on to an adjacent deckchair. 'I was hoping she'd send him off with a flea in his ear. I should have known better, when I saw the way she looked at him when he arrived.'

'You need a nice cold beer,' said Joan, swinging her legs off the stool and standing up. 'Stay there and I'll get it for you.'

'I think I'll just change into something cooler first.'

It was a relief to relax in the garden and to light his pipe at last. Although he had cut down on his smoking considerably Thanet had long ago decided that he wasn't going to give it up altogether. The heat of the day had faded now and as Thanet puffed contentedly and sipped his beer he and Joan chatted about the case. He had always discussed his work with her except on one memorable occasion when it transpired that she was probation officer for one of the suspects, a problem which they had always dreaded and had not been easy to deal with when it arose.* She was an excellent listener and it was often through talking to her that he had worked his way towards the solution of a case. This time, however, there wasn't much she could add.

'Poor woman,' she said with a sigh, when he had finished. 'What a miserable life! The trouble with these battered wives is that they're usually just too terrified to do anything about it. Either because they're afraid that whatever they do and wherever they go their husbands will seek them out and make them pay for it, or because, like her, their hands are tied by their family situation.'

'Her mother, you mean.'

'Yes. It sounds as though she's fond of her and wouldn't have dreamt of abandoning her, especially to a man like him.'

'No doubt about that, I'd say. I imagine Scotcher would have had the old lady in a home before you could turn around.'

'Exactly. Oh dear. I do hope his wife had nothing to do with it.'

'So do I. Or his son, for that matter. The boy's had a miserable enough life up to now, by the sound of it.' Thanet sighed. 'I sometimes wish I didn't have a conscience. Then in a case like this I could just put in an accident report and that would be that.'

'But you'd always wonder, wouldn't you? Anyway, you know perfectly well that in your heart of hearts you feel that murder can never be justified, however horrendous the circumstances. Understandable, yes, excusable, no. In any case, it could well have been this

* See *Element of Doubt* (1987).

neighbour, Bevan, in which case I imagine you'd feel quite differently.'

'Yes, I know.'

No more was said on the subject. Besides, Thanet had something else on his mind. How could he react, behave, when Bridget and Alexander got back? All evening he was on edge, one ear cocked for their return, but by the time he and Joan went to bed there was still no sign of them.

'He's probably taken her out to dinner somewhere,' said Joan as she switched the light out. 'There's no point in worrying about it, Luke. If she decides she wants to start going out with him again there's absolutely nothing we can do.'

'I know.' But he couldn't help himself and it wasn't until after midnight, when he at last heard Bridget arrive and come quietly upstairs that he was able to go to sleep.

In the morning, when he took Joan her cup of tea in bed, she glanced at his face and said, 'Bad night?'

He grimaced. 'Not too good.'

'Bridget, or the case?'

'Bit of both, I suppose.'

'Well as far as the case is concerned, don't forget that as you said yourself, it may have been precisely what it seemed, a straightforward accident. Perhaps the post-mortem will help to resolve the matter. When's it being done?'

'Today, with any luck.'

'Good.'

'I don't know that it will help much, though. Doc Mallard was a bit evasive. I suspect spinal injuries can be difficult.'

And he was right. The PM had been scheduled for that morning and around midday Mallard called in at the office to give a verbal report.

'Not that you're going to be too pleased with what I have to say,' he said, propping himself on the edge of

Thanet's desk. 'No problem about cause of death. The spinal cord was severed, as we thought. But time of death is another matter.'

'Why? What's the problem?'

'Well, as I said, body temperature didn't help in this case because it was such a hot day and the body was lying in full sun. And spinal injuries are tricky. There's no doubt that death would have occurred when the cord was severed but that might not necessarily have happened when he actually fell.'

'It might have, though?'

'Oh yes, certainly.'

'But if he didn't die instantly, how long might it have taken?'

'For him to die?' Mallard shrugged. 'He wouldn't have, not of his own accord, so to speak. He'd still be alive now – paralyzed, probably, but still alive – unless something happened to complete the transection of the cord.'

'What, for instance?'

'Even the slightest unskilled movement of the head could have been enough. It's always happening. There's an accident, some well-meaning person comes along and tries to make the poor chap comfortable and – ' Mallard snapped his fingers, 'he's dead! This is why, in the case of neck injuries, it's best to leave well alone, and why ambulance personnel take such extreme care in moving the injured person. D'you know if anyone did move him or even touch his head before I arrived on the scene?'

Thanet and Lineham looked at each other.

'Bevan!' said Lineham, and described what Scotcher's neighbour had done.

'Well, there you are, then. That's exactly the sort of thing I mean. The final severance might well have occurred then.'

'But there's just no way of knowing?' said Thanet. 'The condition of the stomach contents, for instance?'

Mallard shook his head. 'The nerves which control the respiratory and digestive mechanisms run through that cord. The initial injury could well have been sufficient to inhibit the latter without destroying the former.'

'Bevan did say Scotcher wasn't breathing when he found him,' said Lineham.

Mallard slid off the desk, preparatory to leaving. 'Well, if you're prepared to take his word for it . . . But you know as well as I do how wrong the layman can be about that. So there you are, Luke. There's no point in asking further questions because I can't tell you any more than I have already. In any case you know by now what I always say as far as medical matters are concerned.'

' "Nothing is always so and nothing is never so," ' chanted Thanet and Lineham together.

'Very succinctly put!' said Mallard, 'Though I did coin the expression myself. Sorry I can't be of more help.' And he breezed off, leaving Thanet and Lineham in a state of gloom.

'Just as I feared,' said Thanet. 'It leaves the whole thing wide open. Scotcher could have died instantly, as the result of an accident, either before his wife left for church, or when Tim came home, or when Bevan touched his neck looking for a pulse. Or any one of them could deliberately have given that ladder a shove. I've got a nasty feeling we're not going to get anywhere on this one, Mike.' Thanet felt disgruntled. What was the matter with him? Only yesterday he had been saying to Joan that he wished he could put in an accident report with a clear conscience. Now, unless forensic could help on the question of the dryness of the paint, or new evidence turned up such as Bevan's prints on the ladder, Mallard had given him the perfect excuse for doing so. So why wasn't he rejoicing? The truth was, he hated leaving matters unresolved. This was one of the things, he knew, which made a good detective: you never gave up if you could help it. You just went on and on, seeking, sifting, eliminating until with any luck you got there. Only too often, of course, you didn't, but Thanet's track record in cases of this sort was excellent and now, he realized, his pride was about to be dented. Which might not be a bad thing. Vanity, in a policeman, could be dangerous.

'Doesn't look like it,' said Lineham.

'Sorry . . . Look like what?'

'As though we're going to get anywhere on this one,' said Lineham patiently. He was used to Thanet's moments of abstraction, they were often fruitful, and now he glanced hopefully at him before saying, 'It's a pity Carson hasn't been able to find the boy, though. Tim would at least have been able to tell us if his father was still alive just before eleven.'

'He might not know. I'd guess he would have done his level best to keep right out of his way. But I agree, it is a pity, I really would have liked to talk to him. But now, well, in the circumstances I can't see Draco authorizing a wide-scale attempt to find him, and I don't feel, myself, that it would be justified.'

'Perhaps he'll turn up of his own accord, if he hears that news item we gave to Radio Kent.'

'Perhaps.'

Meanwhile, there was other work to do and they got on with it. But Thanet was pleased when they got back from their lunch break to find a message on his desk.

'Looks as though you were right,' he said to Lineham. 'Tim's turned up. Got home half an hour ago. Let's go.'

But they were delayed by a call from the lab. Lineham pulled a face as he put the phone down. 'Great help that was.'

'What did they say?'

'Apparently Scotcher was using an acrylic – that is, water-based – paint. On such a hot day it would have dried almost instantly.'

So that was that. Another avenue closed off. Thanet shrugged philosophically. He was used to disappointments such as this, they all were. 'Come on, let's see what Tim has to say.'

At the entrance to the cul-de-sac Thanet pulled up for a word with the officer who had sent the message. 'He still in there?'

'Yes, sir.'

'Good.'

In contrast with yesterday the street was deserted. Mrs Scotcher answered their knock. The bruising on the side of her face was now much more obvious as the black and greenish-yellow discolouration spread across her cheek.

'I believe your son is home now. If we could have a word . . .?'

She stood back reluctantly and went to the foot of the stairs. 'Tim?' she called. 'Come down here a minute, will you?' She pushed open the sitting-room door. 'In here,' she said to the two policemen.

Her mother was in the high-backed armchair again and when she saw who it was she began to struggle to stand up.

Mrs Scotcher crossed to help her. 'What d'you want, Mum?'

'My rosary.'

'I'll get it. Where is it?'

'In the kitchen.' Mrs Finch was on her feet now and she shook off her daughter's hand. 'I can get it myself. You know what the doctor says.'

They were watching her slow progress across the room when Tim came in. It looked as though he had inherited his mother's genes as far as size was concerned, Thanet thought, though there was plenty of time yet for him to put on a sudden spurt in height. Thanet agreed with Mrs Bevan: the boy looked a good two years younger than his age. At five feet three and with so slight a build it must have taken a lot of courage to stand up to that great bear of a man on his mother's behalf. The graze on his cheek was still red and angry, discoloured with an excess of iodine applied by an inexpert hand. Thanet had a sudden vivid mental picture of Mrs Scotcher bending over her son, cotton wool in one hand, iodine bottle in the other, dabbing tenderly at his cheek, wincing in sympathy as she did so. The boy saw Thanet glance at the abrasion and put up his hand defensively, to conceal it.

'It's the two policemen, Tim,' said Mrs Scotcher. 'The ones I told you about.'

'We just wanted a word about yesterday,' said Thanet. 'D'you mind if I call you Tim?'

The boy shook his head, his eyes wary.

'May we sit down, Mrs Scotcher?'

'Help yourself.'

Thanet and Lineham took two of the chairs from around the dining table and Mrs Scotcher and Tim sat down close together on the sofa, both of them on the very edge of the seat. It wasn't surprising that they were tense, uneasy, of course, Thanet thought; even the innocent find an interview with the police an ordeal. While they were all seating themselves the old lady came back in and shuffled to her chair. As soon as she was settled the muted clicking of her rosary began, jerked this way and that by the uncontrollable movements of her hands. For her, Thanet realized, it was probably as much a comfort object as a means to devotion.

'Now,' he said to the boy, 'there's no need to be alarmed, Tim. We're just trying to clear this matter up, find out exactly what happened. I'm sorry about your father.'

The boy's lips tightened, but he said nothing.

So far, Thanet realized, he hadn't said a single word. A direct question was called for. 'How did you hear what had happened?'

'On the radio.' His voice was rough, had not yet completely broken. Thanet was not surprised in view of his apparent immaturity.

'You do understand, don't you, that when there is a sudden death like this we have to look at all the circumstances surrounding it?'

The boy nodded. His hands were tightly clasped between his knees and Thanet saw the knuckles whiten.

It had never been Thanet's way to bully witnesses unless they thoroughly deserved it and he knew that he wasn't bullying this lad now. All the same, he was beginning to feel as though he was and he didn't like it. Perhaps he should hand over to Lineham? And put the sergeant in this uncomfortable position instead? Don't be a coward, he told himself. You've got to do it, so get on with it.

'Now, we gather that yesterday morning there was an argument, around breakfast time?'

The boy glanced at his mother, who shook her head. *I haven't told them anything.*

'Between you and your father, I believe.'

Tim compressed his lips. He was looking down now, avoiding Thanet's gaze, and suddenly he bent forward and retied the lace on one of his trainers.

'Tim?' said Thanet. There was absolutely nothing he could do to make them tell if they didn't want to. But he couldn't give up yet. 'It was about your mother, wasn't it? The way he treated her. The way he . . .' Thanet stopped. He'd been going to say, 'The way he knocked her about,' but even as the words formed in his mind, were about to issue from his mouth, he realized he couldn't bring himself to say them. Hadn't this family suffered enough, without having their private humiliation dragged out in public? And yet . . . if one of these two had in fact rid themselves of Scotcher's unwanted presence in their lives, who was he, Thanet, to decide they should get off scot-free? He had no right, no authority to do so. In any case, no one man should have to carry the burden of such decisions alone, it was entirely right and proper that they should be left to a court of law, to the jury of twelve who share equally the responsibility for making them. He tried again. 'I know all this must be painful for you. No one wants to have his private affairs discussed in public. But it has to be done. You do realize that there will be an inquest, don't you?'

'An inquest!' said Mrs Scotcher in dismay. It was clear that she had either not known or had chosen to forget that there would be one.

Briefly, the beads stopped clicking. So Mrs Finch was listening too. Thanet hadn't been sure until now.

'There always is, in the case of a sudden death like this. The questions I am asking are very much the sort of questions that will be put to you then. And I'm afraid it won't be so easy on that occasion simply to refuse to answer. The coroner won't allow it. So, would you like to tell me now, what the argument was about?'

They consulted each other with a glance. Then Mrs Scotcher shook her head. 'I'm sorry,' she whispered. 'We can't talk about it. Not at the moment. Later, perhaps, if we have to . . .'

'Very well, it's your decision. So let's move on a little. The result of that argument, I believe, was that your husband threw Tim out. Literally threw him out. You can't keep that sort of thing quiet, of course, not in a street like this, especially on a Sunday when everybody is at home. And then, around 10.45, Tim was seen to return, to let himself into the house and to leave ten minutes later carrying a bag. You'd come to collect your gear, I imagine?'

The boy nodded. Three words was all he'd yet managed to get out of him, thought Thanet. 'So, would you mind telling us exactly what you did while you were in the house?'

It was a painful process, extracting this information. Tim's answers were, whenever possible, monosyllables or at best brief phrases. Thanet had hoped that the boy would loosen up as the interview progressed, but this didn't happen. He rarely met Thanet's eyes and he fidgeted constantly, picking at a frayed patch on his jeans, twitching his toes, crossing and uncrossing his legs.

Apparently, wishing to avoid his father at all costs and hoping to slip in and out of the house without being seen, Tim had waited until mid-morning to return. He knew that his father intended to continue painting the house that day and was hoping that by then Scotcher would be engrossed in his work. He also knew that his father tended to play the radio loudly during his do-it-yourself activities, and had counted on the fact to help him to remain unobserved.

And this, according to Tim's story, was what had happened. Once indoors he had gone straight up to his room, which was the small bedroom above the front door. He could hear the radio blasting away but hadn't risked even a peep out of any of the back windows in case his father caught a glimpse of him. He had packed as quickly as he could and left.

'So you didn't actually see your father at all?'

Tim shook his head. 'No.' He stared hopefully at Thanet. *Is that all?*

But Thanet wasn't finished yet. 'The problem is, you see – or one of the problems, I should say – is that no one seems to have seen him after he went around to the back of the house to start painting. You did tell me you didn't go out to say goodbye before leaving for church, Mrs Scotcher?'

'That's right.'

'And neither did your mother?'

The old lady had indeed been listening. The shaking hands stilled and the whispering undercurrent of sound stopped momentarily as the faded blue eyes met his. 'No, I didn't.'

'Inspector!' said Mrs Scotcher suddenly. 'Would he . . . Would he have died instantly? I mean, would he have . . . lingered on at all?'

'I'm afraid we just don't know. It's impossible to tell.'

'Oh God,' she whispered. She glanced at Tim and Thanet knew what she was going to say. *Don't say it,* he thought. *It'll only make things worse for him.* But she went on, 'Are you saying he might have been lying there, still alive, when Tim was in the house?'

With one eye on Tim, Thanet lifted his hands in a gesture of helplessness. 'I'm sorry. We really don't know.' Any minute now, he thought. Any minute now he's going to crack. The boy had gone rigid. He was gaping at his mother, his eyes wide and staring. Suddenly he shot up out of his seat, as if catapulted.

'What does it matter?' he shouted. 'Why pretend? He's dead now, that's what matters! And I'm glad, d'you hear, I'm *glad!*' He turned on Thanet. 'If you knew what he was like, you just wouldn't care what happened to him, you wouldn't be sitting there banging on with all these questions!' Suddenly tears gushed from his eyes and poured down his cheeks and he dashed them away with an impatient hand. He was beside himself with grief, anger, guilt, all the pent-up emotion perhaps of years. 'He didn't care about us, that's for sure. Look at the way he treated us – knocking Mum about – oh yes, what's the point in hiding it? And me, too. And Gran! Threatening to put her in a home, after she'd put up the money to buy this place for us! And the way he used to think up ways to upset her, as if she didn't have enough to put up with already! Only yesterday morning . . . He knew how much she loves her rosary, how she hates going to mass without it. So what does he do, because he's angry with me for daring to stand up to him for once? Turns on her and says the clicking is driving him mad, he can't stand it a moment longer, and grabs it away from her, shoves it in his pocket, that's what! That's the sort of man he was!' Abruptly, he ran out of steam, collapsed on to the sofa beside his mother and buried his face in his hands.

The brief, appalled silence which ensued was broken only by the sound of Tim's sobbing and the whisper of the amber beads in Mrs Finch's hands. All eyes but his had turned to the rosary in her lap and it was obvious that his mother, Thanet and Lineham were all asking themselves the same question. *In that case, how did she get it back?*

The old lady did not look up, but her shaking fingers had tightened on the object which had no doubt given her consolation through some of the darkest hours of her life, gripping it so hard that the clicking sound almost ceased.

Alerted by the sudden tension in the room Tim raised a tear-stained face. 'What?' he said. He glanced from his mother, to Thanet, to Lineham. 'What?' he shouted.

'Mrs Finch,' said Thanet gently. 'Is this true?' She wouldn't have the strength, he told himself. She surely wouldn't have had the strength to dislodge that ladder?

At last she sighed, laying the beads down and stroking with one shaking finger the crucifix which depended from them as if making a silent prayer for forgiveness. Then she raised her head and met Thanet's gaze squarely. 'Yes.'

He said nothing, waited. They all did.

She sighed again. 'I went into the kitchen to fetch my glasses. I needed them, to go to mass. Beryl had gone to get the car out. That radio of his was blaring away. I picked my glasses up and then there was a scraping sound and suddenly, all in a flash, the kitchen went dark and then light again and there was a sort of dull thump and a clatter.'

A pretty graphic – and accurate – description, thought Thanet, visualizing it all.

'I guessed what had happened. I went to the door and looked out. And there he was, ladder on the ground, paint all over the place. He was quite still and my rosary was dangling out of his pocket. So I went out and picked it up. Beryl was just coming back in as I went into the hall.'

. Her daughter was staring at her as if she'd never seen her before. 'Mum . . .' she whispered. 'You didn't say a word.'

'You didn't know your husband had taken your mother's rosary away, Mrs Scotcher?' said Thanet.

'No. When Tim started sticking up for me Fred went for him and I tried to get between them. So he shoved me out the room and slammed the door.'

'That was when he turned on Gran,' said Tim. 'Asked her what she was staring at, then snatched her rosary away from her.'

'But Mum,' said Mrs Scotcher, asking the question in all their minds. 'Why didn't you tell me? We could have called an ambulance.'

The old lady sighed once more. 'I know. And I expect I shall have that on my conscience for the rest of my life.' The tip of her finger touched the crucifix again. 'But at the time . . . Look at the state your poor face is in! You can't imagine how hard it's been for me to sit here, a useless lump, and watched you knocked about like that, and Tim, too. So when I saw Fred lying there, God forgive me but all I could feel was relief, that you'd be free of him at last.'

There was something else Thanet had to know. 'Was he still alive?'

'I don't know. I didn't look at him properly and I certainly didn't touch him.' She shivered, as if the thought was repugnant to her – which, thought Thanet, it probably was.

'I hope you can understand that, Inspector, but I didn't *want* to know. I knew that if I did and he was still alive I would have to do something about it. And

I'll just ask you this. In the circumstances, what would you have done?'

'I didn't give her an answer, of course,' Thanet said to Joan later, 'but I must admit that in my heart of hearts I couldn't bring myself to blame her.' They were in the kitchen and Joan was putting the finishing touches to supper.

'And as she hasn't actually committed an offence, she won't have to face prosecution.'

'No. We still don't know, and we never will know now, exactly when he died.'

'But at least you're satisfied, that you know what happened.'

Thanet grinned. 'I hate loose ends.'

Joan handed him some cutlery. 'Lay the table, will you? This is just about ready.'

'Sure.' He went off obediently and when he came back said, 'Only three of us tonight?'

'Oh, I forgot to tell you. Bridget is going out with Alexander again. He's picking her up shortly.'

Thanet grimaced and Joan set down the dish she was holding and came to grip his upper arms. 'Luke. You know what we said.'

'Yes, yes. But that doesn't mean I have to *like* it.'

'Just act as though you do, that's all.'

'All!'

There was a ring at the bell.

'That'll be him,' said Joan. 'Now . . .'

'All right, all right,' said Thanet, holding up his hand. 'I'll do my best.' He went to the front door and flung it wide. 'Alexander!' he said heartily. 'Come in. Bridget won't be long, I'm sure.'

His daughter's radiant face as she came down the stairs was sufficient reward.

Inspector Luke Thanet

I'm going to tell you a secret.

When I wrote the first Thanet book, *The Night She Died*, I realized that the most important decisions I would have to make would be about my detective. If, as I hoped, I was going to write a series, I knew that above all I would have to *like* him. The prospect of living year in, year out with someone who would get on my nerves did not appeal to me! I also decided that I would have to make him young enough to last me out. Each book would be a complete mystery story in itself but an added interest would be the long-running serial story of the Thanet family. In the early books they all aged by two years a year but suddenly slowed down when I realized that at this rate Thanet would have to retire before I did!

Thanet, then, would be above all an ordinary man. I knew I was taking a risk. It's so much easier to write gripping novels about the eccentric, the bloodthirsty, the evil and the bizarre.

And so it was a surprise to find how very popular Thanet has proved to be. In fact, I sometimes wonder why I bother to put in the detective story at all! Because almost invariably, someone who is reading one of my books will say, 'It's the one in which Bridget (Thanet's daughter) was worried about her O levels'. Or, 'It's the one in which Ben (Thanet's son) was glue-sniffing'.

And the secret?

Don't tell anyone, but Thanet is really me (in male form, that is). Sheer laziness on my part, and that's the truth of it. I never have to wonder what he would think/say/do, because his attitudes are my attitudes, his philosophy of life is mine.

So there you are, now you know.

Dorothy Simpson

Dorothy Simpson was born and brought up in South Wales. She read modern languages at Bristol University before moving to Kent, the background for the Inspector Thanet novels, to teach French at Dartford and Erith grammar schools. After her marriage she worked for thirteen years as a marriage guidance counsellor before turning to writing full-time.

Her books have been translated into many languages and her sixth, *Last Seen Alive*, won the Crime Writers' Association Silver Dagger.

She has three children, all now married, and still lives in Kent with her husband.

Also by Dorothy Simpson

A Taste of Freedom

Margaret Yorke

A Taste of Freedom

Frances Fanshawe decided to commit murder while waiting at the crematorium for Denis Wilson's funeral cortège to arrive. She had parked her Metro under some trees among the cars of other mourners who were emerging from them, sombrely clad, speaking in muted tones, smiling but not laughing.

Denis wouldn't have minded a laugh or two, thought Frances, exchanging her scuffed brown pumps for black patent shoes with small heels. She took a deep breath and opened the door, stepping from her car, pulling down her black pleated skirt last worn at her own husband's funeral six months ago. It had been winter then, a cold raw day with the trees bare and the ground hard with frost. Now it was warm and sultry; not a leaf stirred in the branches overhead. There had been no rain for ten days, all through the weary hours of Denis's dying. She had heard every detail from Carol, who had daily visited the stricken household, then made all her acquaintances in Little Ferringham aware of her neighbourly conduct. She had done the same when Jim, Frances's husband, had died, forcing her way past Frances up the stairs and into the sickroom where Jim lay, in a coma it was true, but how could anyone be certain that he could not understand Carol's torrent of speech, her comments on his appearance, her words of sympathy? Relief had come only with death – relief for him, but not for

Frances, who ever since had been the recipient of relentless support from her friend.

For they were friends, weren't they? Or so everyone said. Carol had not deserted Frances, despite other claims on her compassion. Here she was now, driving up in her Honda Accord, slowing as she recognized Frances, lowering the window to utter a reproof.

'Why didn't you wait? I told you I'd collect you,' Carol said. 'I thought you'd collapsed or not felt able to face this place again. I walked all round the house knocking on doors and peeping in through windows. I could have been late.'

'Well, you're not,' said Frances. 'I said I had things to do on the way. Couldn't you have looked in the garage to see if the car was out?'

But Carol's window had risen again and she was driving on to find a parking place. Frances thought she heard a mutter about keys.

Carol had once had a key to Frances's house. She'd kept an eye on things when Frances and Jim went away: picked up the post, checked the pipes – poked about, Jim had said, sure that his papers had been disturbed. In his retirement he was writing a book about garden ornaments, ranging from statues to gnomes. It had never been finished. They'd been to Lamport House to look at the site of the first garden gnomes to come to England, brought from Nuremberg. A classicist friend of Jim's had said they had priapic connotations, hence so many found fishing or with other extensions to their pixie persons. Frances said that was nonsense; the Lamport ones were miners. Jim had planned further research in Germany, but illness defeated him.

In those last days, Carol had come in and out of Ivy Lodge constantly. She had shopped and fielded telephone enquiries; after a while, exhausted and distressed as Frances was, she had found it easier to fall in with Carol's plans for their welfare than to protest, but Carol would not be turned away when Jim had briefly regained consciousness, entering the bedroom to ask in an exaggerated whisper how he was, causing Frances to turn her head, and by the time she had muttered some reply and looked back at Jim, he had lapsed again into his coma, never to be roused. Unreasonable though she knew it to be, Frances felt that Carol had deprived her of a precious last moment's communion, even a final word.

Afterwards, Carol had organized Frances's existence, for which, briefly, she had been grateful after her son and daughter had returned to their own lives, one a physics lecturer at a northern university, the other a doctor, who had thought her father's last days should have been spent in a hospice, or at least a hospital, although admitting that excellent support had been provided by the local team of doctors and nurses.

'Of course, you had Carol, too,' her daughter had said, approvingly. Her intentions were benevolent but she was anxious to return to her own patients, who would provide a barrier against the shattering sense of loss she was experiencing since her father's death, an emotion she had not expected as she had already, intellectually, accepted the inevitable.

Now Maggie Wilson, Denis's widow, might receive the same dedicated care from Carol, which, Frances hoped, should relieve the pressure upon her. Would Maggie tolerate it?

'I don't think this is nearly as well run as the crematorium where we held my mother's service,' Carol said. She had caught up with Frances and taken her elbow, propelling her towards the group of people clustered outside the chapel, waiting for admittance. 'The parking area is better arranged, and it's cheaper, too,' she continued. 'Not that that was any consideration, naturally.'

Frances resolved to kill her as they left after the service, with Carol insisting that they go to the cinema that evening.

'This will have brought it all back to you, and it's bad for you to brood,' she declared. 'I'll collect you at six o'clock.'

'To see what film?' Frances managed to ask.

'It doesn't matter. We'll pick one when we get there,' Carol said. 'That's the joy of these multi-screen complexes.'

They had been invited back to the Wilsons' house, opposite Ivy Lodge where Frances lived. Cold ham and chicken, quiches, salads, fruit and cheese were laid out in the dining-room. Maggie's two daughters and their husbands had everything in hand and Maggie herself was calm. She had removed the wide-brimmed black straw hat she had worn earlier, and, in a black and white printed cotton dress, looked cool and composed as she spoke to her friends. There was a burst of laughter: that was right, thought Frances. These occasions were reunions, times when old feuds might be refuelled but some wounds might be healed. Frances did not know of any tensions among the Wilsons; no marriages had so far broken up, and the grandchildren were still infants, left behind today. Frances supposed the other grand-parents were looking after them. Would her children ever marry, ever breed? Jim had wished they would.

'It would be nice for you,' he'd said. 'Give you a stake in the future.'

He'd meant that they would give a purpose to her life, without him. Well, she had one, born today. She would eliminate Carol before she was swallowed up by her completely.

It wasn't seemly to be thinking like that now, she thought, sipping the rather good wine the elder son-in-law had provided. He was something in the City. Frances watched him, a big broad-shouldered man in a well-tailored suit, a kindly person, she felt sure. She saw him give his wife's arm a reassuring squeeze. In spite of what one read in the press, there were still strong marriages, centres of strength and harmony in the troubled world. Hers had been one of them, perhaps too strong for the children, from whom she sensed herself so distant nowadays, knowing they felt guilt at not spending more time with her during Jim's illness. They'd grown used to it, accepted his failing health.

She had enough money to go on living at Ivy Lodge and her own health was good. And, as her daughter emphasized to her brother, Carol kept an eye on her.

Why didn't Carol get a job? Either a proper one, in an office or a dress shop, where she'd be paid, or something voluntary, to keep her occupied and prevent her seeking intrusive acts of kindness to perform? In spite of her husband's good position – he worked in the Middle East and was seldom home – she was always sponging, though her own house had been done up regardless of expense. In March, she had suggested that Frances needed a break and arranged a long weekend in Bournemouth for them both. In May, they'd gone away again, to Bath. Frances had paid for both of them, each time. Carol had simply told the hotels she would settle later with her friend, but she had never done so. Was Edward simply mean, keeping her so short?

If I don't get rid of her, she'll eat me up, thought Frances, nibbling at a slice of the Wilsons' Stilton. Carol would not, it now appeared, be diverted by ministering to Maggie, for Maggie was going to sell her house and move to Yorkshire, close to her younger daughter who was married to a farmer. They took in bed and breakfast guests, and Maggie would be useful either helping with them or looking after her grandchildren.

'An unpaid baby-sitter,' was Carol's caustic comment.

'Why shouldn't she be?' demanded Frances.

'Why shouldn't who be what?'

'Why shouldn't Maggie baby-sit her grandchildren, for love? I'm sure she loves them.' Frances would love hers, if they were ever born.

'She'll be taken advantage of,' said Carol.

She had followed Frances home, insisting that they both needed cups of tea – quite unnecessary since Maggie and her family had provided coffee for their guests.

'Do you regret never having children?' Frances asked, stretching past Carol to reach the pretty Spode teapot down from its high shelf. Carol somehow always got in the way whenever she was in Frances's kitchen. Now she was by the sink, when Frances wanted to warm the pot with water from the tap.

'It wasn't to be,' said Carol firmly.

Few people in Lower Ferringham had met her husband, Edward. They had moved into Willow Cottage seven years ago, when Edward took up his post abroad. Carol could not, she said, survive in so hot a climate. Now and then he returned on short leaves, and sometimes she met him in Paris or Vienna or in Italy. He must draw a good salary; Willow Cottage had been submitted to such drastic treatment that Maggie thought it should feature in *Country Living* or some other glossy magazine; she had suggested it, but Carol said that would be a form of prostitution.

Jim and Denis had been quite malicious about Carol. They had been subjected to her pretty pouts and kittenish ways, which twenty years before might have been appealing, as they both admitted. Finding the two immune, she'd kept her distance, entering village life by way of the dramatic society – she'd been Elvira in *Blithe Spirit* and was very good, everyone agreed – and dreaming up ideas for entertaining the 'dear old folk' as she called the rather lively Senior Citizens' club, which already went in for ballroom dancing and excursions to historic houses with no encouragement from her.

'She'll soon be an old folk herself,' Denis had said, unkindly and inaccurately.

No one knew Carol's age. She was small, with light blonde hair, a slim figure, and a porcelain complexion. No blemish had ever dared to surface on her perfect cheek, said Jim, and Denis wondered how Edward had ever tackled anything as earthy as a sex life with such a doll.

'Perhaps he never did,' said Jim. 'He gets few chances now. Maybe he's got a comely mistress in the desert.'

'Carol's tough,' said Maggie. 'She gets what she wants from life. He pays the bills.'

'And you reckon she wants a single life in spotless Willow Cottage,' Jim remarked. 'Abandoning her mate. Or, like a spider, eating him.'

But Edward wasn't dead. He did appear, dimly visible, from time to time.

While both couples were intact, they had not foreseen how Carol would become a limpet, clinging to the fringes of their lives, waiting for her hour to come, but she always discovered who was going on holiday and insisted on holding their keys, invigilating their houses in their absence. Carol drew curtains across windows in the evening, and pulled them back each morning; she retrieved mail from the mat and arranged it neatly, bills and letters separated. She walked dogs and tended houseplants when people kept hospital appointments, and drove selected persons to out-patient clinics, waiting hours for them.

'She's very thoughtful,' Frances said.

'And doesn't she let you know it,' Denis commented, for Carol never hid her light beneath a bushel but openly proclaimed her benefactions.

In the end, on the day of the funeral, she never went home but remained at Ivy Lodge until it was time to leave for the cinema, to which Frances had no desire at all to go.

She sat there scheming in the darkness while a gentle comedy flickered before her unseeing eyes.

How could Carol be removed?

Or should she move away herself? It would be a less drastic answer to the problem. Carol, left behind, would soon find someone else to batten on. Frances thought of all the things she'd done simply because Carol had insisted. She'd gone to bridge lessons when she would have preferred to learn to paint, and now she was committed to arranging bridge sessions every Tuesday evening. Carol, a keen and efficient player, never held one at Willow Cottage, but she did help Frances serve the sandwiches. In fact, one was seldom invited to Willow Cottage because Carol was always in other people's houses or involved in a community activity.

Frances wondered if she hated Carol. What was hate? A revulsion in the stomach, a clenching of the guts? Surely no one as virtuous as Carol could earn hatred? She deserved appreciation; wasn't it mean-spirited of Frances to resent her helpfulness?

Once, making a dental appointment after a filling crumbled when she bit an apple, Frances had found herself hesitating before agreeing on the time, feeling she should consult Carol in case she was not free to take her to the surgery. How ridiculous! She'd taken herself there for years, long before Jim died. She wasn't a woman who had never learnt to drive, but Carol implied that she was scarcely competent behind the wheel. If she was not careful, she would lose all confidence in her powers. As a consequence of this, in a burst of rebellion, Frances had had the house locks changed and had outwitted Carol over the journey to Denis's funeral.

What a pity she couldn't tell Maggie what she planned to do. They'd have had a great laugh about it while Maggie told her it was a good joke. But how else could she divorce herself from Carol? Frances was only fifty-eight – not old. She'd like to go on travelling. With no Jim, it would be more difficult but there were escorted tours she could take. She'd sent for some brochures: Australia was a possibility, next winter. Carol, though, would expect to go with her and would intend Frances to pay.

In the cinema, she contemplated poison. Paraquat, she thought, or laburnum seeds: something that was readily to hand. She wouldn't hurry. Planning was the essence.

Carol received a shock when, three weeks later, she learned from Maggie, busy packing up her house, which was already on the market and with several people interested, that Frances had left to spend two weeks in the Lake District.

'Didn't you know?' asked Maggie innocently, though Frances had told her she was planning to conceal her escape.

'Without me?' Carol exclaimed. 'Alone? She'll never manage. I've done everything for her since Jim was taken.'

'Too much, perhaps,' Maggie daringly replied. 'You've been almost too kind. Given up too much of your time.'

'What? For a friend? Impossible,' said Carol. 'I'd have done the same for you, Maggie – I've tried to, goodness knows, but you haven't seemed to want me.'

'Don't take it to heart,' said Maggie. 'I'd made my plans with Denis, before he died.'

'Well, you've got spunk,' said Carol. 'Frances is a poor dear, isn't she? She needs someone to make decisions for her. Where has she gone? To a hotel?'

'She's taken a cottage,' Maggie said. 'She's sharing it with an old school friend – Barbara someone or other.'

'Oh – oh, is that right?' Carol could barely utter. 'She never mentioned it,' she added. 'Perhaps she couldn't bring herself to do it – to hurt me so. I've turned down

invitations for her – I'd been asked to go on a cruise
with someone, all expenses paid, but of course I
refused because Frances needed me. But she's been
taking me for granted, that's the pity of it.'

'Find someone else to help, Carol,' Maggie advised.
'Frances must manage without you.'

'Maggie, not everyone is strong, like you. Frances is
a weak sister. Where would she have been during all
these weeks without me?' Carol said.

In Greece, perhaps, or Rome, thought Maggie, but
the Lake District was a start. Frances had arranged it
all by post and telephone, without a word, only telling
her just before she left. She'd explained that Barbara,
who had never married, was a headmistress whose
holidays were in progress now. They would explore
Wordsworth country and see where Beatrix Potter had
lived, Frances had said, and they would go walking
over the fells.

'She's not alone,' Maggie pointed out, as Carol
dabbed a lace-edged hanky to a lustrous, still large eye.
'She's just with a different friend, that's all.'

'She's got to get there on her own, though. Drive all
that way,' said Carol. 'I'd have taken her, and fetched
her back again if she was determined on leaving me
out of her arrangements.'

'You would have embarrassed her,' said Maggie.
'She wouldn't want to be beholden.' Maliciously, she
was enjoying Carol's discomfiture.

'She's beholden already.' Carol's tone was waspish
now. 'And what about Ivy Lodge? I – she's had the
locks changed – something went wrong with the old
one, it got stuck. She's forgotten to give me a new key.
She'll be counting on me to keep an eye on things
while she's away.'

'I shouldn't think she will,' said Maggie. 'She hasn't
asked you to, has she? Let it go, Carol. Why don't you
take Phil Dawson in to visit Margery in hospital? You
know he's lost his licence and can't go without a lift.'

'He broke the law,' said Carol, frowning.

Phil had amassed surplus penalty points for a defective tyre, a parking offence, and for travelling at forty miles an hour in a thirty mile an hour zone. His pregnant wife, suffering from oedema, would probably be in hospital until the birth.

'He could do with some help,' said Maggie, who had taken him in twice. The bus journey was difficult and took a long time. Phil was the school caretaker, and on his second marriage.

'He can go by public transport,' Carol said curtly. Then she began telling Maggie how she had washed and ironed the choir's surplices ready for a wedding that afternoon because their parents couldn't be trusted to do it properly.

Most of them could be, Maggie knew. Why was Carol so selective with her philanthropy? She had probably upset some mothers, now.

Wondering how Frances was faring on the way to Cumbria, Maggie enquired about Edward.

'Can we expect him soon?' she asked. When briefly allowed to meet him, she had quite liked quiet, saturnine Edward.

'Yes, as a matter of fact. Next week,' said Carol. 'Monday, probably.'

'Well, you couldn't have gone away with Frances, then, could you?' Maggie smiled.

But Carol wanted a reason not to be at home during Edward's visit. She did not answer, getting back into her car and driving away.

Frances had pulled it off, thought Maggie. That was good. She'd be all right. All she needed was some fine, sunny weather.

Luke sat on a bench watching the children. Some played on a seesaw, others used the slide, shrieking with delight, stretching limbs that had been cramped in car seats for hours. It was a good idea to have these playgrounds at roadside service stations.

He'd liked the activities they were enjoying, too. Always one for the open spaces, he'd truanted from school to haunt parks and commons, and even in wet weather he'd preferred bouncing a ball in the small patch of garden behind the house to being indoors, in the dry. But then life at home had been unpredictable; he'd never known what sort of mood his dad would be in when he got back from one of his cross-Europe journeys. He was a long-distance lorry driver, only really happy behind the wheel of his vast vehicle, king of the road as he'd called himself when Luke was small, swinging him up on his shoulder, sitting him on his knee in the cab so that he could pretend to be a driver, too.

Luke had come here in a lorry today, thumbing a lift from a roadside more than a hundred miles away. The man who had picked him up had stopped for a break; he said Luke could go on with him, as long as he returned in time. There'd be no waiting about.

With the sun on his face, Luke had forgotten time, sitting there absently gazing at the youngsters. One or two mothers eyed him doubtfully; men and youths watching kids were always suspect. He'd greeted one or two of the women, commenting on the weather, asking where they were bound for. His pleasant manner allayed their suspicions; he was a traveller, too.

At last he stood up and walked towards the lorry park, only to see the back of his benefactor's 40-tonner departing to the exit.

Luke cursed. Still, not to worry, he'd pick up another ride soon enough. He didn't mind where he went, as long as it was taking him further from the prison.

Being cooped up inside had been unbearable. There were men around him all the time, another in his cell. People didn't understand how he needed a life in the open. Institutions – schools, prisons, hospitals – and cramped flats and houses frightened him, made him ready to do anything to get outside. As a lad, he'd tried to run away to sea, as he'd read a boy did in a story, but it didn't seem possible these days; cabin boys weren't wanted now. He was retrieved and taken back to the children's home from which he had absconded.

His father had driven off one day and had not returned. Luke didn't know what had happened to him; perhaps he was dead. After that his mother had had a series of men friends, Luke's 'uncles', against whom he had rebelled until she had had him taken into care as beyond her control. It was true that he'd done some wild things; he'd stolen stuff and he'd hit the baby she'd had by one of the uncles. He'd nothing against the baby itself, but it made such a noise, yelling, and he couldn't get it to quieten down when he was left looking after it while his mother and the man went to a club. They both came back drunk and didn't see the bruise on the baby's back until the next day.

When he was sixteen, he was freed into the world, with a room found for him by the authorities and a job sweeping up in a factory. Neither had lasted long. Luke had gone stealing with some of his friends from the home; then he'd started sleeping rough. It wasn't long before he was caught breaking and entering, and when he confessed to earlier offences, he was sent to a young offenders' centre.

Kids these days got sent on safari to Africa and on adventure holidays, lucky sods, thought Luke, who wouldn't have minded that sort of punishment. He sauntered back to the cafeteria, where he might pick up some cash. People were careless with their purses, and left jackets hanging on chairs. He needed funds. He spent a little time prowling about and drank a Coca-Cola. He might get talking to someone and catch a lift in a car. Stealing one from here could be risky; he might be seen. He wasn't as quick at hot-wiring cars as some of his friends, and these days most of them had alarms and even immobilizers.

However, when he went outside again, having had no luck over money, he took notice when he saw the woman drive up in her Metro, close to where he was standing.

Frances didn't park in the first vacant slot she saw but cruised slowly along the ranks of cars until she noticed an older woman emerge from a Renault and begin rummaging in its boot. She was plump, and wore navy trousers and a blue shirt. Her sturdy rear view, and the curly grey hair visible when she stood up, holding a thermos and a mug, inspired confidence in Frances, who drew neatly alongside her. The woman, pouring coffee into the mug, glanced up, met her gaze, and smiled.

Frances smiled, too, and heaved a sigh.

'It's a relief to stop, isn't it,' said the woman. 'Leaving all that fast traffic.' Now she was unwrapping a pack of sandwiches.

'Phew. Yes, you're right,' said Frances. 'I'm not used to driving on the motorway.' She glanced at her watch. 'Goodness, I've got here quickly,' she exclaimed. 'I'm going to be early.'

The other woman was standing by her car, eating her sandwich, her hair ruffled by the slight breeze.

'It's good to get some air and stretch one's legs,' she said.

Frances got out of her car. She, too, had brought a picnic.

'I wonder how long it will take me to get to Kendal,' she said.

'Oh – not much more than an hour, I'd say,' said the other woman.

'I'm not quite sure where I am,' Frances confessed. 'I just thought it was time I stopped.'

'This is a good service area,' said the other woman. 'I always aim to reach it, when I go to Scotland.

Sometimes I eat my sandwiches inside, and buy a coffee, especially in the winter. Though I seldom drive up after November.'

'Do you often drive to Scotland?' Frances was impressed.

'Three or four times a year,' said the woman. 'My son lives near Dumfries. It's not far, once you cross the border.' She was munching away at her sandwich. Egg and cress, noted Frances, who was near enough to spy a wisp of cress take off and float away. Her own sandwiches were made of humble packet ham. 'Have you friends in Kendal?' the other woman asked.

'No. I'm renting a holiday cottage, with a friend I'm meeting there,' said Frances. The lie tripped glibly off her tongue, as it had to Maggie. 'I can't collect the key until five o'clock,' she added.

'Where have you come from?'

'Near Oxford,' Frances said. 'Not far from the motorway. And you?'

'Andover,' said the woman.

Hers had been by far the longer journey, yet she seemed to think nothing of it. Frances nodded.

'I must go to the cloakroom,' she said.

She hurried off, forgetting to lock her car, leaving the key in the dash. The other woman noticed this omission and decided that chatting had distracted her. She did not call her back; after all, she was there to guard the Metro.

Frances was gone for ten minutes. She had felt a huge sense of elation when she drew up safely in the parking area. She had done it – driven all this way without mishap. That would show Carol! She washed her face and splashed her wrists with cold water, then took a wander round the shop where she bought some fudge and two paperback romances – both purchases Carol would condemn. Heavens – the way she was thinking, anyone would imagine Carol was a tyrannical spouse, exercising control over her.

She did exercise control. That was the trouble. That was why she must be stopped. She could overwhelm other people, too, not just Frances.

Returning to the car, Frances did not notice a thin young man who walked a little way behind her, and to one side. The Renault driver, who did observe him, thought he was a harmless student returning to another car. He passed them both, eating an ice cream cornet, and stopped at a Mitsubishi Space Wagon close to them, standing in its shadow where he could overhear their conversation, ready to move away if the Mitsubishi owner reappeared. Neither of the women had noticed him before, loitering near enough to eavesdrop.

Frances's new friend was studying a map, spread out on the bonnet of her car. She understood the urge to talk which the Metro driver had displayed, the relief at making human contact after two or more hours isolated in a speeding metal box, dicing with the heavy lorries sitting on your tail, and the lurching vans which went just over the speed limit so that you had to, too, to get away from them.

'Here's Kendal,' she told Frances. 'And this is where we are now.'

'Oh, thank you.' Frances pored over the map.

'You left your car unlocked,' said the Renault driver. 'I expect you just forgot. It was all right, as I was here.'

'So I did!' Frances was shocked by her lapse and her colour drained away. 'Oh, what a fool I am.'

'No harm done,' said the woman. 'You'd have remembered if we hadn't been talking.'

'I hope so,' Frances gasped. An urge to pour out the story of Jim's death and Carol's invasion of her life almost overcame her, but she managed to resist it. This doughty woman was probably a widow too; she would despise such weakness, and quite rightly.

'I must get on,' said the Renault driver, having done what she could for this agreeable, if slightly witless person. 'You needn't hurry, as you're so ahead of your schedule.'

As if Frances had had anything remotely like a schedule in her mind! She laughed, recovered now.

'I'll potter along gently and find the place. Maybe there's a tea shop where I can pass the time till Barbara arrives,' she said.

'Good idea,' said the Renault driver. 'Well, goodbye. Enjoy your holiday.'

She had put away her map, and her picnic things. She climbed into her car, started the engine and drove off, with a friendly wave.

Frances also waved, then felt forlorn. Well, she'd get off, too.

Luke had heard most of their conversation, both before Frances went into the building, where he had followed her, except into the toilet, and later. Now he knew she was renting a cottage where she was due to meet a friend. If he was crafty, he might soon relieve her of her vehicle and her money; then he could be away to Wales, or maybe to the Highlands. You could lie low in either place, live off the land, exist in the open for months. Eventually the police would stop looking for him. After all, it wasn't as though he was a threat to society. He was in for GBH with intent, but he hadn't murdered anyone, and he hadn't meant to hurt that old man, the night-watchman; he just got in the way.

There must be a car here which he could take. The Metro woman had left hers unlocked; he'd heard the other woman say so. Someone else would have been just as stupid, or, if he searched about, he'd find some clapped out crate which he could soon nab. He'd catch the woman up, once he'd got wheels; he knew she'd be turning off for Kendal. The opportunity was worth a little risk.

He found an old cream Ford Cortina on the fringe of the car park. Its lock was broken, and he got it started in a few seconds, driving off quite quietly, so as not to attract attention.

He fell in behind Frances five miles up the motorway, and settled down to follow her.

Frances never noticed the Cortina. Luke stayed two cars behind, only moving up when sometimes the Metro took off, passing an obstructive vehicle. Frances was watching out for cars speeding to overtake her. Driving fast was exciting but she need not hurry now; she would reach Daffodil Cottage far too early to claim the key from Mrs Lampeter at Cross Farm, but once she had located both it and the cottage, she could relax.

She thought about the friendly woman in the Renault, who made driving up to Scotland sound so easy. She was older than Frances – quite a lot older, Frances had decided, but she had a bigger, probably more comfortable car. Frances patted the Metro's steering wheel affectionately; she liked her little car which fitted neatly into small parking spots.

The sense of release she had experienced when she left Lower Ferringham that morning had grown stronger as she progressed northwards. She had seen the cottage advertised in a Sunday paper, and that had given her the whole idea. It had sounded perfect – secluded, on the fringe of a hamlet, with two bedrooms, a bathroom and a garden, and the lake not far away. Within easy reach were sites of interest, and there was endless scope for walking. She did not know the area well, but she and Jim had once spent a weekend near Ambleside in late October, with early snow sitting on the hills beneath pale blue skies. They had found it beautiful.

Jim would approve her independence, her break for freedom, but her ultimate plan would horrify him. Would she have the nerve to carry it through? Was there no other way? What about Edward? Would he grieve, or be relieved? Above all, would it work? The answer lay with Carol.

She saw the sign for Kendal and turned off. Soon she had to turn again, and after a while she stopped to check the map. She did not notice the Cortina pass her and pull into a gateway further on as Luke waited for her to continue her journey. Reassured, Frances slid the car into gear and drove on. She thought about Wordsworth and his devoted sister; she recalled the adventures of Peter Rabbit. These were matters she must explore in the coming days so that she would have a story to tell when she went home, and she must buy presents, especially one for Carol: a monster gift for her. Or monstrous.

She still had more than twenty miles to go, and she travelled at a steady pace, between forty and fifty miles an hour when conditions allowed, more slowly when they didn't. Once or twice she noticed a cream coloured, shabby car a little way behind her but it did not hug her exhaust so she paid it scant attention. The other cars she met were mostly tourist traffic, in no hurry.

Clouds had formed now. The weather here could be dreadful, Frances knew; rain might fall for days. Well, she had two books and could buy more, and she had her portable radio, besides which there was television in the cottage; people expected the comforts of home these days.

She turned down a side road and after two miles or so reached a hamlet where there were several cottages dotted about in a valley. There was her destination, a small grey cottage some distance from its neighbour, with a slate roof and a New Dawn rose, still blooming but needing its dead heads cut off, sprawling up the front. As she got out of the car the clouds parted and a shaft of sunlight pierced the grey sky, shining on the blue-painted front door like an omen. Frances glanced up the road. Further on, along another lane, lay Cross Farm.

Returning to the car, she set off to find it, following
the twisting road uphill until she saw its sign beside a
gateway. Across country it wasn't far, she realized, but
by the road it was more than a mile. She drove on and
came to another hamlet where there was a pottery and
a guest house, then turned on to the main road leading
to the town. A 'Welcome Pack' of groceries would be
provided in the cottage, and she had brought supplies
from home; even so, fresh fruit and some wine, with
which to celebrate, would add to her pleasure, and
she'd have that cup of tea she'd mentioned to the
Renault driver.

Luke did not follow her. She'd be back. Besides,
there was the other one, her friend. He set off in the
opposite direction, keen to do some shopping of his
own. The Cortina was rather low on fuel, and he
hadn't got much cash to spare, not yet. He put in
fifteen litres; he'd have another car to drive quite soon,
but he must be prepared in case he had to shift this one
unexpectedly.

His plan was still vague, just an intention of stealing
from the woman and taking her car, or the other
woman's if it was a better one; he'd get her money too.
But he could hole up in the cottage, if he tied them
both up, till the hue and cry following his escape died
down.

That cottage would be comfortable, and the Metro
woman would be a pushover. She'd be so scared.
She'd think he was a wild man, out to rape her. He
wouldn't do a thing like that. Rape was sick. Luke
didn't hate women, but he didn't mind frightening
them occasionally.

When he returned to the cottage he met several cars.
Luke did not realize that the weekend was changeover
time for rented cottages, and in many guest houses
and hotels. He backed the Cortina through a gateway
into a field where it was hidden from the road by a

thick hedge which grew behind a stone wall. There were sheep in the field, but he didn't mind them as they scuffled round him in a heaving sea of wool. Once, he'd been on a country holiday sponsored by a charity, staying on a farm. It had been, to him, a sort of paradise, sleeping in a big room with several other boys, roaming over fields, learning to paddle a canoe and abseiling in a quarry. He'd hoped to go again but it had not been repeated, yet he'd behaved well all the time, never starting a fight and only punching one boy who had accused him of stealing some money he'd had hidden underneath his mattress. Luke had taken it; he'd used it to buy his mother a present as he had no money of his own.

Walking back from the field, he saw a Land Rover parked outside Daffodil Cottage. The front door was open. Luke walked past, glancing back once, and saw a woman in jeans and a yellow shirt come out of the cottage, close the front door and look at her watch. She climbed into the Land Rover and drove on, passing Luke, stopping at another cottage round a bend. Here, she got out of the Land Rover and took a large cardboard carton from it, carrying it up to the cottage and setting it on the ground while she opened the front door: then she heaved it up again and carried it inside.

Some sort of delivery service, Luke decided, unaware that Eleanor Lampeter was delivering the groceries she provided for her incoming tenants. Soon she emerged and drove off again, disappearing up the hill.

Luke took a chance. He cut across a field, circling round the second cottage and doubling back towards Daffodil Cottage, so that he approached from the garden side. Behind him was a belt of trees; this was a sheltered spot, with the river not far distant. He loped along, trying to look like a normal walker, wearing his sweatshirt, though it was very hot, keeping his blue and white striped prison shirt concealed. He must get another. It was lucky he'd had a sweatshirt on when he made his break. Coming up to Daffodil Cottage, he saw a stone wall separating its garden from a field in which two small ponies grazed. They ignored him as he walked by, a piece of grass between his teeth. Even if he were recaptured tonight, this taste of freedom made it worthwhile; he could live on the memory of it, shutting his eyes, thinking back to it above the smells of prison.

But he wasn't going to be recaptured. Once he had some money and a decent car, he'd get right away. You could do anything with a bit of money.

Soon he was over the wall and walking up the cottage garden, which was small, with a freshly mown lawn and some asters flowering beneath two Iceberg rose bushes. Luke knew what they were; he'd managed to get on a garden detail during a spell in a young offenders' institution.

A fanlight window in the kitchen was insecurely latched. Luke reached through and opened the bigger window below it. The next moment he was in the kitchen, panting with a familiar mixture of fear and excitement. He saw a box of groceries on the table, the neck of a bottle of wine protruding, a sliced loaf visible. He did not touch anything, but after closing the window and shutting the fanlight properly, he went upstairs. From here he'd have an advantage over whoever arrived next. He expected it to be the Metro woman but it could be her friend, or they might arrive together. There was room outside for both their cars on hard standing beside the cottage.

The two bedrooms were fair sized, each with a double bed, high old fashioned ones with valances. He could hide under one when the women arrived. It would be safer than the wardrobe; they'd have stuff to hang in there, skirts and that, he thought. After they'd unpacked, they'd go down to make a cup of tea. Wasn't that what women always did?

He felt a sudden desperate urge to urinate. Well, there was probably plenty of time. He went into the bathroom, which was spacious, having been made from what was a third bedroom, relieved himself into the white porcelain bowl, newly cleansed and sprayed with green fluid, then flushed it, watching the detergent foam as the water surged round.

He'd left his mark. He grinned to himself, adjusting his zip, making himself comfortable. The cistern, refilling, made a lot of noise and he felt anxious till it had stopped; what if the women arrived and heard it? But they didn't. He'd like a wash – a bath, even; he eyed the thick fluffy towels, one green, one yellow, with smaller ones to match. It would have to wait. You could spoil things if you rushed them; he'd learned that. He'd be patient.

He heard the Metro coming back. Frances had collected the key, as instructed, exchanging a few pleasant words with Mrs Lampeter. By the time she opened the front door, Luke was under the bed in the rear bedroom, from whose window he could, if necessary, drop on to the flat roof over the kitchen extension and escape across the fields.

But he didn't need to make a sudden getaway.

Frances took her time, settling in. She carried her bags into the small hall, setting them down, looking round with pleasure. What an adventure! She'd arrived without getting lost, nor had she had an accident; she'd found somewhere to park in a strange town, bought some extra supplies including a bottle of champagne, and had tea in a café. None of these would have struck her as remarkable achievements before Jim's death, but since then her confidence had dwindled, and Carol had deprived her of what remained. She'd been so feeble, Frances now reflected; she shouldn't have let Carol swamp her, should have thanked her for the help that had been welcome, then told her to keep away, being rude, if that was what it took. But Carol was persistent; she ignored discouragement, always needing to be in control.

Well, this time she'd been outwitted, and Frances had achieved a liberation.

Of course she didn't really mean to kill her. That was just a fantasy, she thought, humming under her breath as she unpacked the groceries left by Mrs Lampeter. In addition to the box of stores, there was a chicken in the fridge, and milk and cheese. Everything had been thought of: was renting cottages in this way a profitable enterprise? Frances supposed that in the days when farms needed several manual workers, these were tied cottages that went with the job; now, modernized, they earned another sort of income.

She opened the kitchen window, letting in the fresh, late summer air. A small smear of earth caught her eye on the sill but she thought nothing of it, though it was not in keeping with the perfect order of the place. Mrs Lampeter had told her to telephone if there were any problems.

'Otherwise, I'll leave you alone,' she said, smiling brightly, a pleasant woman, forty-two years old with teenage children now on holiday. 'When I first started renting out, I used to call round to see if everything was all right, but I soon discovered that not everyone wants that,' she said. 'Now I leave it to the guests, and there's an answerphone so that I'll always get the message, if I'm out.'

'That's fine,' said Frances. 'Thank you.'

Eleanor Lampeter dismissed her from her mind when she had gone. She seemed a competent person, and would not be alone when her friend arrived.

There was a clutch of tourist leaflets on the hall table. Frances glanced through them, sorting out the more interesting ones. She'd brought her Historic Houses book; there were castles and mansions she could visit. Hadn't Walter Scott lived somewhere in this area, or was she imagining that? She would check.

The sitting-room, which faced the road, was rather dark, with a single small window fringed on one side by an overgrown cotoneaster and on the other by a straggly Golden Showers rose. Frances was rather relieved to find that the efficient Mrs Lampeter was not quite on top of all her garden chores. If there were any secateurs in the cottage, Frances might cut the dead heads from the roses for her.

She had enjoyed inventing Barbara, giving her non-existent friend a past as a member of the school tennis six, a penchant for marshmallows toasted over the bars of an electric fire, red hair, an aptitude for mathematics which led her into teaching, and a youthful romance with a cathedral organist who was not the marrying kind. She almost believed in Barbara's existence herself. Her history could be embellished. Perhaps she'd had an illegitimate baby which had been adopted; in their day, that was what happened in such circumstances, ensuring a supply of infants for childless couples without recourse to technology. Frances briefly wondered what it would be like to know that you sprang from a test-tube and were not your father's child; that sort of thing had been managed previously by sleight, not science.

Thinking this, she sighed, and decided that Barbara had a current suitor, a widower of sixty who wooed her ardently and whom she was tempted to accept. She'd come away to contemplate the merits of the match: company, an escort on holiday, two living more cheaply together than apart, not that Barbara was impoverished. She played the violin, and he the cello, Frances decided; it seemed an ideal partnership, or would Barbara miss her independence? Frances would hold conversations with her imaginary friend about her dilemma, in the coming days.

She'd send Maggie a card tomorrow, reporting her safe arrival. Well, perhaps not tomorrow, as it was

Sunday, but on Monday, certainly.

At last she went upstairs, carrying her bags. She looked at the front bedroom – large, but, like the sitting-room, rather dark, its window small. Then she glanced at the bathroom – bright, looking modern, with a shower attachment above the bath. After that, she tried the other room. It faced towards the wooded hills. She saw the ponies in the field beyond the garden, and the deep green of the summer trees. She pushed up the sash and breathed in deeply. Then, suddenly, terrifyingly, her breath was cut off as a hand was held over her mouth and she was grabbed from behind.

'Not a sound out of you, or you're dead,' Luke hissed, his heart racing with excitement.

She tore at his arms, pulling at the stranglehold around her throat. Screaming was no use for there was no one to hear her. He twisted one of her arms up behind her back and she doubled over to defeat the excruciating pain, but as he dragged her away from the window she kicked and struggled hard. He forced her on to the bed, face downwards, kneeing her in the back to hold her down. Frances made spluttering, groaning sounds of protest, and he hit her face, telling her to be quiet. Tears of pain trickled down her cheeks and he seized the moment to fasten her hands behind her back with strong cord he had bought that afternoon. Kneeling on her, he stuffed a rag – it tasted cottony – in her mouth, then turned her over. Frances kicked at him but he caught her flailing legs, lashing them together. Then he stuck brown parcel tape across her mouth.

'Now we'll wait for your friend,' he said, with satisfaction at a job well done. 'I hope she won't be long.'

Frances could not work it out. She lay on the bed, struggling vainly against her bonds until, from sheer fatigue, she had to stop. She felt as if she would choke on the cotton he had stuffed into her mouth, and she could feel the pounding of her heart. What if she had a heart attack? She made an effort to calm down, trying to steady her breathing. No one ever won a duel by panicking; she must retrieve her wits.

He paced about, leaving the room and going to the front window to watch for the woman she was expecting. After a while she heard him go downstairs. He rummaged in the kitchen. Her hearing seemed suddenly acute as she realized he was opening drawers and cupboards. Perhaps he was hungry. What did he want? He seemed to know she was expecting a companion. Her immediate fear that he meant to rape her had worn off: at least that wasn't his priority. The fact that she was no glamorous girl meant nothing, she knew, where sexual violence was concerned.

When he returned, he was eating an enormous sandwich. Layers of cheese bulged out between two slices of the loaf which Mrs Lampeter had left in what seemed another life. Frances got her first good look at him. He was thin, dark, with long delicate hands. She'd never thought about the hands of criminals: surely murderers would have short, stubby fingers? Was he a thief? Why was he waiting for the mythical Barbara to arrive?

Of course, two beds had been made up and there were towels for two laid out in the bathroom. That was how he knew that someone else was due. He must have been already in the house, hiding somewhere, while she unloaded the car.

She moved her head and made noises in her throat. If he were simply a thief, waiting until Barbara arrived and then intending to rob them both and go, he'd know that they would be able to describe him, and he wasn't wearing gloves. His fingerprints would be everywhere, proof of his guilt if – when – he was caught.

He might have taken her money already. Trussed up like this, she wouldn't know. She'd left her handbag in

the sitting-room. He was welcome to it, if only he
would go.

He'd finished his sandwich. He wiped his hand
across his mouth and then down the side of his jeans,
after which he came across to look at her. She stared at
him above the gag, willing herself not to show fear,
counting in her head, 'One, two, three, four,' still
gazing at him, trying not to blink. If he hit her again,
her eyes might water as a reflex and he would think
that she was crying.

But he didn't.

'What's the time?' he asked suddenly. He had a flat,
south London accent.

Had he no watch? She made herself lie still, not
reacting, and he moved across to her and jerked her on
to her stomach again, so that her wrists were exposed,
then he tried to tear off her gold bracelet watch. It
didn't break but he hurt her and her head jerked back.
He bent lower to look at it, then roughly eased it past
the cords and over her hand, leaving her still lying face
downwards. Struggling, she managed to roll over so
that she could see him as he stood by the window.

'Nice watch,' he said. 'Valuable,' and he put it in his
pocket. 'It's getting on for seven. Your friend's late.
When did you expect her?'

Again she made grunting sounds and at last, to her
infinite relief, he tore off the sticky tape and as she
tried to push the gag out of her mouth with her
tongue, he grabbed the cotton stuff and yanked it free.

'Your friend. Where's she coming from?' he
demanded.

Frances had told Maggie that Barbara lived in
Manchester; that was not far from here, and wouldn't
do for an answer now. Should she say Land's End or
John O'Groats? Playing safe, she chose Inverness.

'It's in the north of Scotland,' she said. 'I thought
she'd be here by now, though. She must have had
some trouble on the way. Maybe she's broken down.'

'She'd phone,' he said. He'd seen the telephone downstairs.

'She doesn't know the number,' Frances told him. 'I made all the arrangements for the cottage.'

That silenced him.

'I'm thirsty,' Frances said. 'Could I have a drink of water, please?'

'I suppose so.'

He made as if to gag her again and she said, meekly, 'I won't call out. I promise. Anyway, who's to hear? There's no one else within a hundred yards.'

It was true.

'I'll get you some,' he said, quite willingly, and left the room.

What if there really were a Barbara, who would arrive while he was in the kitchen? Then she would call out, a warning shout, but he might have had enough time to hit her over the head before she could run away. He, after all, would be expecting her, while she would anticipate only seeing Frances. But although she was a fiction, Frances decided that she must maintain the pretence, decide that Barbara had been delayed in such a way that she had been unable to send any sort of message.

It was still light outside. Darkness would not fall for hours.

'What do you want?' she asked. 'Why are you waiting for Barbara?'

'I'm not sure,' he told her truthfully, and then added, brusquely, 'Shut up, or I'll stuff your mouth again.'

Luke had never been good at forward planning, but he was trying, now, to think ahead. Could he manage to keep two women captive for a week while he enjoyed the comfort of the cottage? They could take turns to cook for him. He was sure they would be good cooks; this one, Frances Fanshawe, whose name he had discovered from her driving licence, looked the homely sort, and her friend was probably just like her. Between them, they'd be able to make crisp pastry and squishy sponge cakes, and the sort of food he'd had on that country holiday so long ago.

He allowed Frances to visit the bathroom. Needing the toilet himself, he realized that she might, too, and he untied her hands and feet and let her go, standing outside the door, which he left ajar. When he heard the cistern flush, and she did not at once appear, he burst the door open, only to see her washing at the basin. She had both taps running and was splashing her face. Her bent back, the denim skirt creased, the checked shirt hanging out, filled him with an odd emotion: not lust – he would have recognized that. It was a sort of pity, though he could not name it.

Frances had seen instantly that she could not escape by way of the window. The flat roof over the kitchen might be reached by climbing out of it, but from there it was some way to the ground and she would only manage it if she had quite a lot of time. He'd be after her at once, and then she'd fall and break a leg. Her best plan was to play for time, make some sort of bond with him, if she could.

As he tied her up again, this time, at her request, binding her hands in front of her, she asked him if he would like to see his mother treated in this manner.

'Don't know where she is,' he said. 'Wouldn't bother me.' He turned away from her and went over to the window. 'You got any kids?' he asked her.

She told him about Giles and Felicity.

'Felicity? What sort of name is that?' he asked.

'It means happiness,' she answered.

'And is she happy?'

'I hope so. She's a doctor,' Frances said.

Doctors were rich. Would she pay a ransom for her mother? The thought flashed through Luke's mind. It might work. On the other hand, it would take time to set up, and once the other woman had arrived, snatching the better of the cars and all their money, plus some of the stuff from the house – the television, radio and microwave, for instance – might be the safest plan. Then he could put distance between himself and this fresh offence – for he knew it was one, and could attract a heavy sentence. He could finance himself for several weeks with what he'd get for loot taken from here, and he'd have the women's cheque books and their credit cards. He could force them to reveal their pin numbers and then empty their accounts.

'What's your son's name mean? Giles, you said,' he asked.

'It's a saint's name,' she replied. 'Like Francis in the male form. My name's Frances.'

'Why'd you call him that?'

'We just liked the name. Jim and I. My husband's name was James, always known as Jim,' she said. She kept her voice steady, though she felt tears filling her eyes as she mentioned him. 'Another saint,' she added.

'Luke was a saint, too, wasn't he?' Luke asked her.

'Yes.' Was that his name?

'Your friend. What about her? When's she going to get here?'

'I can't tell you. I don't know what's happened to make her so late,' said Frances. Then, greatly daring, she said, 'I could ring up.'

If he let her, whom should she ring and what would she be able to say that would help her out of this mess, without him realizing he had been tricked?

Luke, however, did not like the idea of her using the telephone.

'I'll do it,' he said. 'What's the number?'

Frances gave him her own, taking a chance that he would fail to recognize the code as not being one for Inverness. There would be no reply from Ivy Lodge.

'How will you explain to her why I'm not ringing myself?' she asked.

'I'll say you've hurt yourself – burnt your hand – nothing serious. I'm phoning for you,' he said promptly.

She nodded. It was plausible enough to satisfy Barbara, had she existed.

But Luke, going to the telephone, decided to tell Barbara that Frances didn't like the cottage and had gone home; he'd advise her not to come. He was a neighbour who'd found a rat in the living-room. That would put her off.

However, there was no reply, so his invention was not needed.

'She must be on her way,' he said, returning to his captive. 'She didn't answer.'

'Then she's had an accident, as I thought,' said Frances. 'You could ring the police and ask.'

She knew he wouldn't rise to that one. He gave her a look and left the room. Frances thought she heard the back door open. With her hands tied in front of her, movement was easier and she managed to swing her legs off the bed and stand up. It was difficult to balance; she lurched, unable to reach any support. Then, hopping awkwardly, as if she were in a sack race, she made her way to the window, nearly falling over but somehow succeeding in keeping on her feet. Looking out, she could see him in the garden in the dusk. Light streamed from the house, casting a bright stripe across the trimmed lawn. Frances watched him as he stood there, motionless, for several minutes. Then, fearing he would turn and see the white globe of her face against the darkness of the window, she moved away, hopping back to the bed where she lay plucking at the bonds around her wrists, trying to work them loose. Though how would it benefit her if she freed herself, unless he stayed out long enough to let her lock the door against him and telephone for help?

*

John Lampeter, getting up to do the early milking, saw
the Cortina when he looked out of the bedroom
window on Sunday morning. He always took a quick
glance at the weather as he pulled his clothes on, and
this morning it was dry but just a little hazy, promising
to be another fine day. In the rumpled bed behind him,
Eleanor still slept. On Saturday nights in the season,
after turning round the two cottages in the village and
those in the converted outbuildings at the farm, she
was always shattered. This weekend, Maisie Green,
who helped her, had broken her wrist, and though
able to do some things with one hand – dust, push the
Hoover, check drawers and cupboards – she was not
the reliable assistant on whom Eleanor had been able
to depend. The rentings were lucrative, and Eleanor
enjoyed running this side of the business. She was a
fashion journalist before they married, and he had
worried about transplanting her from Islington to the
remote Cumbrian countryside, but after a few uneasy
years she had adapted and seemed content, which was
as much as anyone could hope for in this life, he had
felt. Doing up the cottages and launching them had
given her an outlet for her energy and creativity. Now,
she said she would hate to live in town again.

He heard Rory, their fifteen-year-old son, lumber,
half asleep, along the passage to the bathroom, and
smiled. Good boy, he thought; Rory had helped with
the milking every morning in the holidays. They met
in the kitchen, where John swallowed a quick mug of
strong black instant coffee before going outside, and
Rory drank a mug of milk. They would have breakfast
later. Rory went into the yard with him, eating a
banana.

'There's a car in the four-acre field,' said John. 'Some
bugger sleeping rough, I suppose.'

'Yes. I saw it, too,' said Rory.

'We'll roust them out later,' John said. 'First things first.'

After they had had their breakfast – Eleanor was up by now and had cooked eggs and bacon, with fried bread and tomatoes – the two of them strode off to investigate. People sometimes set up tents in fields without permission, and John let some of them leave without comment if they departed promptly. They could be youngsters hitch-hiking round the country on a budget, just as Rory and his friends might do in a few years' time, in France or Germany. John wouldn't harass them if they tidied up and did no damage, but he'd prefer a request at the door. Then, he would almost always give permission, charging only a nominal sum per night. If they looked like students, Eleanor would often invite them in for supper in the big kitchen, which, because of the Aga, was warm in any weather.

'Hope they haven't upset the sheep,' said John, as they marched forth. 'I didn't see a tent.'

'It's been dumped,' said Rory, as they drew nearer. 'What an old heap.' Even so, rust and all, he'd love to drive it, roar up the track to the farm. 'I say, Dad! It's been nicked!'

He was right. John saw the ends of wire hanging down below the dash.

Rory was grinning.

'Can I start it up?' he asked, eyes alight.

'No, you can't,' his father answered curtly. 'Damn the bastard.' This meant trouble: the police, a lot of time wasted.

'I think you just hold the ends together,' Rory said. 'I'd love to have a go.'

'Very likely, but there may be fingerprints. All that. Don't touch it,' said his father.

'I wonder if it's a getaway car from a robbery,' Rory said hopefully, imagining himself in a heroic role on *Crimewatch*.

'If it is, they'll be long gone from here,' said John. 'We'd better go home and telephone the police.'

He walked all round the Cortina. It was clean inside, apart from wrappings from a pack of sandwiches. Whoever had abandoned it had backed it neatly up against the hedge. Fortunately the sheep seemed undisturbed, cropping calmly at the grass. John noticed tyre marks indicating that the car had been driven in a tight circle to face towards the gate, which had been properly secured; no sheep had escaped. It looked as though the driver anticipated driving out again, he thought, which meant that he might still be in the area. He'd point that out to the police, when they came.

But they were in no hurry. They thanked him for his call and said that they would check the car out – he'd given them the number – and be in touch. John meant to mention it to Eleanor, but she had gone to her office and was entering up her records, Sunday's task. Later, with their daughter, Emma, they were going over to his brother's, near Penrith, for a surprise fiftieth birthday party which his wife had organized. There was to be a barbecue, with all the family present. John wondered if his brother, a solicitor, had found out about the secret plans. He had a lot to do before they left, and the police would, no doubt, have come and gone by then.

They hadn't.

Carol could not contain her rage at what she saw as Frances's betrayal. How could she set up such a scheme, plotting it in secret, then leave with no farewell? Of course, she couldn't face Carol after such treachery. What hurt most was that Maggie knew about the trip, though even she couldn't say exactly where the cottage was.

It would all go wrong. Carol foresaw disaster. Frances would crash her car on the way up, or would quarrel with this Barbara, or the cottage would be a hovel, unfit for human habitation. In her fury, Carol wished for most of these catastrophes to befall Frances: then she could have the satisfaction of pointing out that, had she been consulted, none of them would have occurred.

'If you were set on the Lake District, I would have gone with you,' she would say. 'Though the weather there is so unreliable that the south of France would have been a better choice.'

Carol had made a career of becoming indispensable to someone. At first, it was Edward. She had planned his every hour at home, laid out his clothes, told him when it was time to leave for the office, reminded him when the car needed servicing, made his dental appointments and arranged medical checks. While they were alive, she had remembered his parents' birthdays and bought presents for them, asked him every evening all about his working day, even when he said he wanted to forget his business problems when he was at home, and, in fact, she had left him neither peace nor privacy. She was devoted to him: her whole life was dedicated to the management of his, to the extent, even, of trying to infiltrate his work, wanting to know all about the staff and their foibles, even sending anyone she knew was ill flowers or, at the least, a card. Some, but not all of this was well received, but after a time people found her nosy and interfering when she rang up commiserating on hearing of a marriage breakdown, offering to be a go-between, and on another occasion told Edward's department head of an affair she suspected between two staff members.

Edward, a mild man who abhorred dispute, never understood how he had come to marry Carol. They had met at a dinner party where he had been a last minute stand-in for another man, taken ill. The hostess, an old friend, knew that Edward, divorced but with no children, and an indifferent cook, would be happy to sing for his supper, and so he was. He was placed opposite Carol, who was subdued throughout the meal, casting glances at him from beneath her lids. He had thought her shy and, mildly interested, asked her, after dinner, what she did.

She said she was an interior decorator. Much later, he discovered that she was merely an accounts clerk in a large furnishing firm. She hadn't lied, exactly; she had simply embroidered the truth. She had come to the party with one of the male guests but made it plain that they were not, officially, a couple. Her father, she told Edward, had been killed in the war; so he was, but not by enemy action. Drunk, he had fallen down some stairs in the blackout and had broken his neck. Edward heard the true version of events from a surviving uncle at Carol's mother's funeral. By this time, they had been married for several years and he was already feeling swamped by her possessive, all-protective love. If they'd had children, things might have worked out better, he had thought: she would become obsessed with them, not him. She'd been young enough to become pregnant, but it never happened. She did not seem to mind. It was something they did not discuss.

When Edward was offered a job in the Middle East, he jumped at it, accepting before consulting Carol, and at her comment that she could not possibly live in such a climate, he had hidden his relief and said that that was just so sad. They'd have to be apart for months at a time, but he would be very well paid, she could have the country cottage which she craved, and he'd return for frequent visits. At first, dutifully, he had done that, always to find that Carol was tied up with commitments which were essential to some other person's welfare. She had to take a neighbour shopping, help a friend choose new curtains – without Carol's taste and expertise an error would be made – or visit a garden centre to choose plants, an expedition which, if postponed, would mean they would be bought too late for planting.

After a while, he came home only when he had to, to sort out business affairs. Carol cherished Willow Cottage; it was so beautifully maintained that he feared to dent a cushion with his shape. As for sex, early on they had had separate rooms; she slept badly, she declared, and did not want to wake him with her restlessness. He had soon ceased to tap upon her door. Now he had a long-time mistress, a Belgian woman working for a mining company. They conducted their affair with some discretion because of local conventions, but each had a flat in the same building. Both were happy with this state of things. Edward did not seek the messiness of a second divorce; there was no need to humiliate Carol, and she provided a reason for avoiding anything else more permanent.

As he was due home on Monday, it would have suited Carol to be away with Frances when he arrived at his usual short notice. Then he'd realize how much his comfort, during these brief spells, depended on her. Without Frances as an excuse for being out of the house, she'd have to fix other unbreakable engagements to keep them apart as much as possible.

Carol went to matins every week, not from religious conviction but to demonstrate her good intent and to keep in touch with what was going on. This Sunday, the weather was fine, so she walked, and went home by way of Ivy Lodge. No one had asked her in for sherry after the service; if Frances had been at home, she would have invited herself. Passing Maggie's house, she tried the bell. Maggie had not been in church; she was a poor attender, having doubts. There was no response. Maggie, in fact, had seen her approach and was hiding out of sight. She knew she would receive a scolding from Carol, the next time they met, for going out leaving the windows open, inviting burglary, but dodging her now made it worth the penalty. She waited a while before going near a window, so she did not see Carol cross to Ivy Lodge, where she walked all round the house looking for a weak point where she might enter. She did not find one.

At the back of the house, near the kitchen door, stood the dustbins: two of them. Carol hesitated; then she lifted the lid off one. Within a tightly tied black plastic bag, Frances's rubbish waited for collection. Poking through it was a distasteful prospect; still, for her friend's own good, Carol must do it. Barbara or no, Carol should be aware of where Frances was. In the bins there might be evidence.

She did not have to search far, for the last refuse collection had been made on Thursday and between then and her Saturday departure, Frances had not had much to throw away. Carol quite quickly found the crumpled letter – not even torn in half – from E. Lampeter, Cross Farm. How like Frances to leave it behind when it might be needed as proof of her booking. Carol extracted it; it was only scuffed, not dirty. She smoothed it out and put it in her handbag. Then she went home, where after some reflection she composed a note for Edward, telling him she had gone to rescue a friend in need and would return as soon as possible. He always took a taxi from the airport – she couldn't be expected to hang about there, waiting for him. There were stores in the freezer; he could manage.

She might be home soon after his arrival, depending on how determined Barbara turned out to be about stopping her from joining them on their holiday. It would suit Carol very well to remain away while Edward was at home.

Next, she sorted out some clothes, enough for a full fortnight, intending to leave early the next morning, giving Frances time to regret her unkindness and discover her mistake.

*

At Daffodil Cottage, Frances and Luke had spent a long time talking.

It had grown chilly, and after another visit to the bathroom, Frances had asked if she might get beneath the duvet. He had permitted it. When she said she wanted to brush her teeth, he had allowed her to have her sponge bag, taking it from her case himself.

There was a pair of nail scissors in the sponge bag.

He left the bathroom door ajar, as he had done before, but just as she was about to rummage for the scissors, he called to her to hurry up. He wished to use the toilet himself, he said.

There'd be another chance. She had to leave it now.

Luke tied her up again, and after his own bathroom visit, he went downstairs, returning with more sandwiches – ham, this time, with some for her; he'd discovered the sliced ham she'd bought that afternoon. He'd found the wine, too, and he brought up one of the bottles of burgundy.

He'd forgotten the corkscrew, and Frances saw his sudden look of anger. She knew it was frustration.

'There'll be one in the kitchen, I'm sure,' she said quickly. 'And some glasses,' she added.

'Oh. Yes, I'll look,' he said, and she heard him patter down the stairs again. How careful she must be to humour him: any attempt to escape would have to be timed to perfection, for in rage, she knew already, he would not hesitate to hurt her. Her cheek was tender, where he had hit her, earlier.

When he returned, he had pulled the cork, and there were two tumblers in his hand, fingers over their rims. She steeled herself not to notice.

'There's champagne downstairs,' he said. 'We'll have that when your friend comes.'

He untied her hands, so that she could eat, and put a filled glass of wine beside her. Frances swallowed some and at once felt better. She was hungry, she realized, and eating would keep up her strength. Silently, they both consumed their meal, and Luke refilled his glass with wine.

'Why don't you go now, Luke?' she said, when he had drunk it. 'I'm tied up. I can't get help. I don't think Barbara will get here tonight. You can take my car and my money. What more do you want?'

He did not seem to notice that she had used his name, and as he did not protest, she must have guessed correctly there.

'A rest,' he said. 'A little country visit. Just till things die down.'

'What things?'

'Just things.'

'Are you in some sort of trouble?' Of course he was: he'd done something wrong, carried out a robbery, at least.

'Made a run for it, didn't I?' he said, and smirked. 'From the nick,' he added. 'It was dead easy.'

'Oh!' This news did shake Frances. What had been his crime? Perhaps it was better not to know.

'I can't take it, see,' he said. 'Being shut up like that – it sends me wild, not being able to get outside and smell the air, see.'

'Yes.' Frances saw, all right. No wonder he had been down in the garden, gazing out across the fields.

'I haven't killed anyone. Nothing like that,' he said. It was better not to think about the man he had hurt, who had lost the sight of an eye; he shouldn't have resisted, then he wouldn't have been harmed. The judge had called Luke a disgraceful, wicked man who must receive an appropriate sentence for his shocking crime: it would be years before he had any hope of moving to an open prison, if it ever happened. Desperate, he'd faked a stomach ache severe enough to have him sent to a hospital outside the prison, one where he could have an operation; appendicitis was suspected. But Luke had drunk salt and water, enough of it to make himself very sick and cause a greenish pallor. He had looked ill. He'd almost frightened himself. He'd been prepared, if necessary, to undergo the operation, then sneak out when he was on the mend. He'd soon recover, well enough to flee. But he'd seized his chance when, doubled up, he was allowed, alone, into the toilet. Sneaking out, unseen, he'd snatched a white coat he saw hanging by an open door and had hurried to the lift, reaching the busy vestibule before he was missed. He'd had no money, but he'd jumped on to a passing bus, shedding the white coat on the way. He'd left the bus before he had to pay; it was one which still had a conductor. Later, prowling through the streets, he'd snatched a handbag, running off at top speed, his nausea miraculously gone. The owner of the bag had just cashed her social security cheque; there was enough to buy a ticket on a Green Line into the country. Then, at a filling station, he picked up the lorry. Even after today's shopping, he had some money left.

'How long had you been in prison?' Frances asked him.

His tension eased by the wine, Luke told her about his various sentences, from the short early ones to the last, though he did not describe what he had done this time. Frances listened intently, simply prompting him at intervals. What a story! How did such a person stand a chance of rehabilitation, mismanaged as he had been from his childhood? And after this fresh escapade, he would receive another sentence. What would become of him? And could she believe him when he said he'd done nothing violent? He'd avoided her eye when he told her that. Seven years seemed a long time for what he said was a minor burglary.

As they talked, the wine had an effect on both of them, and each had had a long and tiring day. Warm beneath the duvet, still fully dressed apart from her shoes, Frances felt her eyelids growing heavy and she fought against encroaching sleep. Though a prisoner, she was no longer afraid of Luke, and she wanted to remain alert, so that she could outwit him. But exhaustion and the wine overcame her, and she slept. Luke, aware that she had dropped off, fetched the other duvet and a pillow; that Barbara woman wasn't likely to come until the morning now. He lay down on the floor across the closed door of the bedroom. Frances couldn't leave without waking him, even if she could untie her bonds, which was impossible.

Both of them, worn out, slept soundly until dawn.

Frances was the first to wake. The early morning light flickered past the drawn curtains; Luke had pulled them across the windows the night before. She was stiff, forced to sleep in a cramped position, arms and ankles tied, throughout the night. Raising her head, she glanced across to where Luke lay, breathing heavily, almost snoring.

What had happened was incredible. Here she was, imprisoned by an escaped convict, a young man who seemed more interested in his domestic comfort than fleeing with her money and her car to a safer place than this. Surely he could lose himself in some large city? Or in the wilds, which he seemed likely to prefer? The police must be scouring the country for him. Wouldn't his photograph be in every paper? Maybe not, if what he'd done was not too serious. And why should they look in this area? He could hole up in the cottage for the two weeks of her rental, undisturbed. There was enough food in the house for several days, and he could soon buy more, tying her up while he went off in her car. She'd cashed a hundred pounds before she left, and had only bought the few things at the service station shop. She'd used her Visa card when she bought the groceries, and her tea and piece of chocolate cake had cost under three pounds.

If he went out, that would be her chance, but she must get hold of the scissors first and hide them.

Because he was young, and had had a fair amount to drink the night before, Luke slept on, while Frances flexed her muscles in her arms and legs to fight off cramp and stiffness, and, to keep herself from panicking, she began to think back to other holidays, Crete and Rome with Jim, and their Canadian tour two years ago, their Provence trip with Maggie and Denis, where, successfully, they shared a villa. Then she tried to remember poetry she had learnt by heart at school: Wordsworth's *Daffodils*, of course, and Shelley's *Ode to a Skylark*, bits of Keats and Coleridge, and Shakespeare. All her memories were incomplete, except for *Come Away, Come Away, Death*, which she seemed able to recall perfectly. Doing so upset her: was it an omen? Would she die here? She did not want to die yet; there were still things she might accomplish, and surely one or other of her children would eventually breed? It would be sad to die not knowing of a grandchild, and it would be a pity if Jim's wit and humour had no chance of being reproduced.

She was thinking about names for infants when there was a stirring and some groans as Luke awoke.

They'd had breakfast.

This morning, in response to a plea, he'd let her have a bath and put on some clean clothes.

At first he'd refused.

'Why?' she'd asked, quite crossly. 'There's hot water, and I've got my things here, in my case. You can stay outside the door so that I can't get away. At my age, I'm not likely to try jumping out of the window, and you'd soon catch me if I did. It can't hurt you, and I'll feel much more comfortable.'

It seemed unreasonable to disagree. Luke found her better company when she was in a good mood, and there was nothing to be gained by harassing her. She knew he had all the power.

'What if your friend arrives while you're in the bath?' he asked.

'She won't, this early,' Frances said. 'But she might phone, with a message. You could talk to her, pretend to be a neighbour, like last night. You were going to do that then.'

It made sense. Anyway, if she did arrive, he would soon deal with her before Frances could call out and warn her. She'd have to be let in.

Frances, at her leisure in the bathroom, the door closed this morning, easily extracted her scissors now. They were straight, not curved, and she spiked the tips into a piece of soap, a little bit, prised off the block of Imperial Leather Mrs Lampeter had supplied. Then she wrapped toilet paper round the ends and tucked them under her arm, points downward, inside her bra, which she padded with more paper to protect her. She had been wearing a short sleeved shirt the day before and now she put a fresh one on – pink, to cheer her up.

He tied her up again, hands in front of her this time, and taped her mouth while he had a shower. This frightened her. He was reasserting his control, but while he was occupied in the bathroom she managed to extract the scissors and push them underneath the mattress. She could have pulled off the tape across her mouth and might have managed to untie her ankles, for he hadn't lashed her body to the bed and she had a lot of movement, but it might take too long and she must play for safety.

She wondered if he had ever tied anyone up before. He tied tight knots, that was true; but though linked together, she could use her hands.

He wasn't very long in the bathroom. He'd got a stubble now, and he looked in her sponge bag for a razor, but there wasn't one. He hadn't thought of buying one the day before. He found a nail file, and he took that out in case she thought of using it as a weapon, though it would be a feeble one. Back in the bedroom, he used the file, rasping it against his fingernails. He left her gag on. He needed time to think. What she'd suggested – that he move on, taking her car and cash, made sense. She'd got no jewellery, which was a pity, just a wedding ring. Still, she was on holiday and it was best to leave good stuff at home; you never knew who you might run into on a holiday. There was that friend, though; she'd have more stuff.

After a while the silence got to him, and he ripped off the tape, roughly, so that she winced. Her skin felt sore.

'Sorry,' he said, and added, 'how about we phone a neighbour of that friend of yours and ask about her?'

'I don't know any of their names,' said Frances promptly. 'I wouldn't know who to ring.'

'Oh,' he said. 'I see.'

He freed her legs then, and told her to go downstairs. In the sitting-room, he made her sit in a wing armchair whose back he turned to the window, then tied her ankles to its legs. After that, he turned on the television and they sat through endless children's programmes. There were worse ways to pass the time, Frances supposed. There was one rather good film which she even managed to enjoy.

When it ended, he got up abruptly, went out to the kitchen and returned carrying a sharp knife.

He stooped to untie her, the knife held in his mouth. After she was free, he waved it at her.

'Bathroom now,' he said. 'And you cook our dinner after that. There's a chicken. We'll have it.'

He flourished the knife, somewhat threateningly, waving her up the stairs – he'd slipped out into the garden himself and administered his urine to a lavatera growing just outside the kitchen – whistling impatiently.

Frances was glad to move, and the kitchen door was open, letting in warm summer air. It was a lovely day. He picked up a kitchen stool and sat upon it, by the door, holding the knife and watching her.

'No tricks,' he said. Now his voice was grim. He had not mentioned Barbara for hours.

She didn't risk defiance. A good meal might improve his temper, and it would revive her; besides, she was glad to have something to do. While she prepared it, scrubbing new potatoes, slicing runner beans which, left out overnight, had gone a little limp, her thoughts turned to Carol. Frances had deliberately left the holiday address enticingly displayed among the rubbish, easily discovered if Carol thought of looking there, as Frances was certain that she would. Finding it, she might set off in pursuit. That was where the element of chance concerning Carol's own fate came in: if she was annoyed enough, or inquisitive enough, or both, to follow her up north, Frances had meant to lure her into a dangerous situation and create a fatal accident – falling from a rocky pinnacle would be the easiest. Whether it came about or not depended upon Carol's own actions. If she stayed away, it wouldn't happen.

But Carol wouldn't fall for it. She'd be so angry that she would never speak to Frances again, nor set foot in Ivy Lodge, which would solve the problem. Why, in even contemplating murder, Frances was far more evil than this sad young man now forgetting to watch her guardedly, gazing down the garden, longing to be out there.

Their lunch was excellent. She made baked apples for their pudding, and there was cream.

'That's better than the custard you get inside,' said Luke. He had set the table for her, laying down his weapon while he did so but picking it up again before she could snatch it and stick it into him. She couldn't do it, though: carving the bird – he handed her the carving knife and fork and said he had no idea of how to do it – she had another chance, and could not take it. Besides, he hadn't threatened her with death, only with a loss of liberty. She almost liked him; certainly, she pitied him. She didn't think he'd hit her again, not now.

'You can cook, all right,' he told her, belching.

They played Rummy in the afternoon. Frances had seen boxes of games and packs of cards on a shelf and suggested that they try something from among them. She rejected Scrabble; he was unlikely to be good at it, and she resolved that he had better be the winner in at least one contest.

'It's good you don't smoke,' he said. 'It's bad inside. Everyone does, nearly. Not much else to do, I suppose.'

'But you don't.'

'No. But my cellmate does. The smell's disgusting,' he replied.

'Do you read?' she asked him.

'Yeah – a bit. Travel and that,' he said. 'And crime books.'

Intellectually, Frances knew he must have committed some quite serious offence to be detained for any length of time. These days, a reproof seemed to be the usual punishment, or a few hours of community service, whatever that entailed. But what was gained by confining Luke in conditions which were, to him, unbearable? Manual labour on a building site or on a farm would surely be a better way of dealing with him. He'd lost his liberty, which was just; did he deserve torture, too? Jim had been mildly claustrophobic. Occasionally, in a stuffy room or some art gallery, or even in the underground, he had felt oppressed. Such experiences were brief and he could endure them because they could be ended, but he said that he was not the ideal companion to be stuck with in a jammed lift. Fortunately, it had never happened to him.

She wanted to talk to Luke about what he had done

and how he felt about it now, but she did not dare to jeopardize their fragile harmony.

Make friends with your captor: that was what you were advised to do in such a situation, and, to a point, she had succeeded.

He soon tired of playing games and turned his attention to *Grandstand*, on television. In the evening – they had sandwiches for supper, and more wine – there was a detective film which Luke gazed at, rapt; he clearly found it fascinating. The plot seemed far-fetched to Frances, but the Cornish setting was spectacular and beautiful; there were no urban shots.

'I've been to Cornwall,' he volunteered, refilling his wine glass. He wished there was some beer.

'Have you, Luke?' She used his name quite freely now. It would help identify him, when this strange incident was over, though by this time his fingerprints must be all over the house and they would be on record.

He told her about the holiday scheme he had been sent on.

'It was great. I wanted to stay down there, but I had to go back to my mum. After that I was in care – I told you about it,' he said.

'Yes. You had a hard time,' she said. 'Didn't you think of going back there later, when you were old enough to please yourself?'

'Yeah – but by then I'd got mates I hung out with. When I was sixteen it was just one thing after another.'

Trouble, he meant.

'Why don't you leave now, Luke?' she tried the idea again. 'It will soon be dark and no one will see you go. You could drive for miles and lose yourself.'

'I'll do it, but not yet,' he said. 'I like it here with you, and there's your friend, remember. If I leave you tied up and she comes soon after I've left, I'm dead.'

'I don't think she'll come now,' said Frances, and was forced to add, 'though it's strange she's sent no message.' This was no time to confess to her deception; he'd be furious.

'Yes,' he agreed. 'Maybe she's got killed,' he added. 'In some smash.' He sounded almost gleeful.

'I hope not,' Frances said, reprovingly, but who was she to take so virtuous a stance, considering what she had planned for Carol?

Luke had flipped channels and found another programme that attracted him. Frances watched it too. He hadn't tied her up again, and they sat there like a normal pair. Several moths, attracted by the lamplight and the flickering screen, flew in through the open window, but neither of them minded the creatures blundering about. When it began to get chilly, Frances asked him if he minded closing it, and he drew the curtains, then fetched himself more wine.

From outside, the cottage looked serene. Glancing across the valley, later on, Eleanor saw lights glowing and felt tranquil. So far there'd been no complaints, though Jasmine Cottage, nearer to the farm, was still empty; its tenants had telephoned to say that they had been delayed and would arrive the next day.

Luke tied Frances up once more when they went to bed.

'Sorry,' he ground out, 'but I don't trust no one.'

He was right not to trust her, Frances reflected.

'I understand,' she said, accepting it, tautening her wrist muscles so that the cords would not bite too tightly.

He slept across the doorway once again, drinking another glass of wine before he lay down. Soon, rather drunk, he slept.

She could get the scissors out now, and try to free herself, but she couldn't leave the room, because the door opened inwards and he blocked the way. How long could this go on? Would his spark of violence reignite? When he left, he might even take her with him as a hostage. In the dark, fear rose in her again, and she banished it by deciding that she must take some action to save herself. She managed to retrieve the scissors, and freeing her legs was relatively straightforward, though sawing to and fro across the cord took some effort. Undoing her wrists took longer, requiring more contortions, but when she managed it, she was elated. She did not hide the scissors again but held on to them tightly. They might be needed as a weapon; she could stab him in the arm, injure him enough to make him lose his equilibrium, bleed, be frightened. She would do it if she had to.

He had drunk a lot that evening. Now, he began snoring heavily. Frances tried to sleep but told herself she must waken at his slightest move; then she'd be ready. She had slipped her pumps on; barefoot flight would be impossible. Surely, after all that drink, his bladder would be bursting and he'd need the bathroom before she did?

She was right. She heard him moving while it was still dark, and Frances wasted no time as he blundered on to the landing, cursing as he stubbed his toe. She almost fell over his huge white trainers, neatly placed beside the door, as she made her move. She had pulled a pillow under the duvet to look like a figure in the bed, and, tiptoeing, she crept softly down the stairs. One of them creaked, but the steady flow of Luke's urine masked the sound. He did not flush the cistern: was that thoughtfulness, seeking not to disturb her, or mere habit? She heard him lumber back and shut the bedroom door, and the thump of his body slumping down. She waited, motionless, for several minutes. Then, heart pounding, she drew back the curtains in the sitting-room and flashed the lights on and off, three short bursts and three long ones, then three more short. She repeated it several times, SOS in Morse. Was there anyone to see her signal? If they did, would they interpret it?

After a while, sure that he must really be asleep by

now, she went to use the telephone, only to find the instrument had vanished. Luke, mistrustful, had unplugged it.

Crafty Luke! He'd probably thrown it in the garden. It was no use wasting time looking for it. Well, her car was still outside. She'd take that. Her handbag was in the sitting-room. She searched inside it for the keys, but they had gone. Frances thrust the bag under a cushion on the sofa and went to the front door. Jasmine Cottage was the nearest house. She let herself quietly out, closing the door behind her to delay him if he heard and followed her. Then, heart thudding, she set off on foot, up the road.

Luke was woken by the front door bell. Heavy-headed, hung over, he wondered for a moment where he was: this was not his smelly cell, for pale light was shining through flowered curtains. Then he remembered, and reached for the knife which he had placed beside him underneath his duvet, and went downstairs. He'd left his shoes off and briefly thought of going back for them, but, as the doorbell pealed again, he carried on to answer it, and he heard a woman shouting.

'Frances,' she was calling. 'Let me in, Frances. What are you doing here? Have you lost your mind?'

Her words did not make sense, but this must be the missing Barbara. Luke rubbed his hand across his stubbled chin, opened the door, and beamed at her.

'Hi, Barbara. What kept you so long?' he enquired, reached out a long, sinewy arm, and drew her in, holding the knife against her throat.

Carol almost fainted.

Unable to sleep, excited by her scheme, and anxious to be well away before there was any chance of Edward's arrival, she had decided to leave for Kendal during the night. There would be very little traffic to delay her, and she would arrive in time for breakfast. Frances, once she recovered from her surprise and had managed to apologize for disappearing, would be most happy to see her. Carol would be gracious to the unknown Barbara and would eventually be persuaded to remain with them for the fortnight. The cottage was probably small; Frances and Barbara could double up and Carol would enjoy a bedroom to herself. She had it all worked out, driving through the darkness.

Several times her thoughts had turned to Edward. Meeting him was increasingly difficult, though they never quarrelled and he was always civil, but whenever he came home she feared he might reveal a wish to separate officially, even divorce. If that were to happen, though he might be generous, her status in the village would be diminished. She might be forced to move, if the house had to be sold. People would say she had been unable to keep her man, and her income would be cut. By sponging on the gullible, she had put by a tidy sum in stocks and shares, prudently invested on advice from a reliable consultant, but she wanted more. If she must be officially alone, it could be only as a widow, respectable, of course, like Frances and now Maggie, and apparently grieving. On his last visit, Edward had tentatively raised the subject of their future, but she had managed to divert him and he had left without returning to it. How would separation benefit him? Marriage was a protection from the predatory, and she did not mind if he slept around, as long as he didn't press his attentions upon her. She had never enjoyed them.

Frances was very slow in answering the door, as Carol called her name.

She was very small, much smaller than her friend. That made it much easier to control her, and Luke barely needed to twist her arm as he pushed her up the stairs. Carol started whimpering.

'Shut up,' he ordered, thrusting her through an open doorway into a room where the pale early morning light was filtered through drawn curtains. 'Here's Barbara at last,' Luke said, loudly now. 'Taken her time, hasn't she? Better get her to tell us what held her up so long.'

He felt huge relief. Now he could tie up the pair of them, in separate rooms out of reach of one another, lashing them to the bedsteads so that neither had a chance of freeing herself and then her friend. They'd be found eventually, when someone came to check out the house.

But Frances wasn't answering.

Luke reached out to the light switch, using the hand that held the knife to snap it on, calling out again.

'Here's Barbara. Wake up,' he cried, pushing Carol over to the bed, staring at the humped up duvet, realizing as he did so what had happened. 'Bitch! Cow! Whore!' he almost screamed and slashed at the bed in fury, seeing the cut strands of cord as he swept the duvet to one side. Cursing, using words Carol did not think she had heard before, he flung her face down in Frances's place. 'Don't you dare move,' he said, kneeling on her back as he had knelt on Frances. He tied her roughly with the bits of rope already there, then used the knife to slash a pillow case into strips to hold her more securely, lashing her arms together, then tying more strips across her mouth, forcing it open, so that her tongue was held down. Carol, now, was almost fainting in her terror.

Luke had no time to lose. He had no idea how long Frances had been gone, but she'd soon find help. It was a good thing he'd thought of getting rid of the telephone; he'd put it in the kitchen waste bin.

He'd been stupid not to take her keys and money earlier. Now he couldn't find her bag and he dared not stop to search for it. Outside, beside Frances's Metro, stood a silver grey Honda, the engine warm, the keys still in the dash. He leaped into it and drove off, roaring out of the village.

In the early hours of that Monday morning, Rory Lampeter, who had done himself a bit too well at his uncle's party, which had lasted throughout the rest of the day, well into the evening, had felt rather sick. He'd helped his father with the milking – the cows had grown restless, waiting for them – and had had some supper, but even his youthful constitution had rebelled. He'd spent some time in the bathroom, dealing with it, then, returning to his bedroom, looked out across the valley. The Cortina had still been in the field, the night before; now, near the cottages, he saw a light turn on and off. Watching, it flashed again, three short blinks, then three longer ones, and three more short. The pattern was repeated several times. He frowned, turning back towards his bed. How strange. Crawling into bed again, he felt puzzled, trying to remember what such timing meant: surely it was some sort of code? Still feeling fuddled, he pulled the duvet over his face, almost asleep; then, suddenly, he understood. Those were distress signals. SOS. Rory, galvanized, leaped out of bed again, pulling on jeans and a sweater, finding his shoes, and went downstairs. He wouldn't wake his father; it might have been some kid fooling. He'd find out first whether anything was wrong.

So early in the day, the air was cool and fresh, sweet-smelling. He opened the back door and sniffed it, feeling better now. Could the signal be in some way connected to the abandoned car? Maybe it was the car's headlights he had seen, though he didn't think the flashes came from quite the same spot. He'd like to try the car. His father wasn't there to stop him now. He'd take a look, after he'd spied out the land.

Rory loped across the fields, a thin, fair-haired boy, tall for his age, intent only on a minor investigation, not convinced that the lights he had seen had any real significance.

There was no one in the Cortina. By the time they had returned from his uncle's house, the police had been out to see it, but the Lampeters had heard no more. Meanwhile, unknown to them, the police had discovered that it had been stolen from a service area on Saturday; the owner had been notified of its discovery, and had not yet made arrangements to collect it. From the police point of view, as it was causing no obstruction, there was no urgency. No connection had been made between it and the escape, in Greater London, of a convict.

Rory was just crossing the stile leading into the four-acre field when he heard shrill cries, and looking towards the road, he saw, in the grey light of dawn, a woman in a pink blouse waving her arms and calling to him, hurrying along.

Frances's legs were stiff and were refusing to carry her at any speed. She'd run to Jasmine Cottage only to find it was empty, but it took her several precious minutes to conclude that there was no one there. Terrified that Luke would discover her escape, she hurried along the road towards Cross Farm, quite a pull uphill. Gazing towards it as she hastened on, she had seen Rory's distant shape when he climbed the stile.

He seemed to reach her very quickly after that. She saw that he was just a boy, and for an instant feared he might be some sort of accomplice of Luke's, but she gasped out that she had been held prisoner in the cottage.

'His name's Luke,' she said. 'He's still there. He may think I'm still asleep.'

'It's all right,' said Rory. 'Let's get in the car and I'll drive you to the farm. You're safe with me,' he added, grandly. 'He won't catch you now.'

Masterful, he led her to the Cortina, fifty yards away, and helped her into the passenger seat.

'You're safe now,' he repeated.

'You believe me, don't you?' Frances was out of breath. 'I'm telling you what happened.'

Rory could see the bruise on her cheek, and her wrists were red and raw. He felt awed amazement, and a wave of pure excitement. Wow! What an adventure!

'Yes,' he said. 'I saw your signal, but I didn't understand at first. I'm sorry. Now I must open the gate. We mustn't let the sheep out.' Luckily they were at the far end of the field and had not taken heed of what was going on, but he knew how fast they could flow towards him and into the road, if they had a mind to it.

Frances was calmer when he returned to the car.

'Probably he's still asleep,' she said.

'Let's hope so,' Rory answered, bending to the dangling wires.

The engine fired, and Rory, who often drove a tractor and the Land Rover about the farm, made short work of getting the Cortina into the lane. There he braked, hopped out, and shut the gate again, just as a tide of sheep came scampering to see what was going on. He drove on up the road, changing gear smoothly, putting on speed.

His parents did not grasp Frances's story as rapidly as he had done, and they required far more explanation. John Lampeter kept asking him why he had moved the Cortina.

'That guy Luke might have used it to get away in,' he answered smugly, a theory with which the police constable who eventually arrived seemed to agree.

The Lampeters were busy tending Frances when Carol, who did not pass the farm, parked outside the cottage. Since it looked so quiet, the upstairs curtains still drawn when it was surveyed from a distance through some field glasses, the police decided that no move should be made until more officers had arrived. Two were armed, though Frances had said that Luke had no gun, only a kitchen knife. It was best to be prepared, said the police inspector who had now taken charge. The man might wake up at any minute, find her gone, and go berserk.

Frances's car stood where she had left it; there was no hint that Luke was not alone. It was still early when the police at last broke in, but Carol had been a prisoner for more than an hour before her rescue.

They drove back to Lower Ferringham in Frances's Metro. She had found the keys in a mug on the kitchen dresser in the cottage. She must have put them there from habit, on Saturday; she always put them in a mug at home.

After the police had fingerprinted the cottage – they soon identified the fugitive, and connected him with the stolen Cortina – Eleanor Lampeter and Rory set about spring cleaning it and putting in fresh bedding.

'You won't want to stay here,' Eleanor told Frances. 'Of course you must have your money back. But you can't go home yet. Your friend isn't up to it.'

Carol was in bed in the farmhouse spare bedroom. She'd kept asking about Barbara and what had happened to her, until sedated by the doctor.

It seemed best to go home. Carol had no car, and she must certainly go back as soon as she was fit. Frances had lost nothing except her watch; her car and cash were untouched, her handbag still beneath a cushion on the sofa.

Carol had revealed that Edward was due home, but she had refused to get in touch with him.

'But he'll come and fetch you, surely?' Eleanor had said. She was afraid, now, that her business might be adversely affected by this episode.

'There's no need for that,' Frances intervened, demurely. 'After you've slept this off, Carol, I'll take you back. Let's hope your car is found soon.'

Now the tables were turned, with a vengeance; Carol was dependent upon her for transport. Her suitcase and her bag were in the Honda, and the police had kept the clothes she had been wearing because they could provide scientific proof that Luke had assaulted her – for it was assault, and more. Threads and other traces would be found on him. Swamped in a pair of Frances's slacks, the legs rolled up and a belt notched in around her waist, lost in a vast sweater, Carol cowered in the front seat of the Metro. She'd been fast asleep when Frances, after a cheerful evening with the Lampeters, had slipped into the second bed in their spare room, and had not stirred till morning. The Lampeters, while wanting to be kind, nevertheless were anxious to speed these two uncomfortable guests upon their way, though Rory longed to hear more details about Frances's hours spent with Luke. She wasn't a bit young, and she'd been a prisoner for two nights and a day; he thought her quite a heroine. The other woman had gone all to pieces and she'd not been tied up long.

'Why did you follow me?' Frances asked at last, as they headed south. She did not ask how Carol had traced her; both of them knew the answer.

'I knew you'd need me,' Carol said. 'You hurt me very much, going off like that without a word, when I'd done so much for you.'

'I didn't need you,' Frances said. 'No one's indispensable, Carol. You tried to be.' She let her words sink in; they were cruel, but she should have said them weeks ago.

'There was no Barbara, was there?' Carol had worked it out now. 'You told Maggie all about her. It was lies.'

'I invented her,' Frances admitted. 'I didn't want Maggie or anyone else worrying about me. You'd done a good job of making out I couldn't manage on my own, but I can.'

Carol couldn't, though: she needed to latch on to people. But Frances would miss Maggie dreadfully; that was a parting she could do without. 'There are plenty of organizations who would welcome your help, Carol,' she went on. 'But working with them, you couldn't pick your targets.'

Targets? What did she mean? Carol did not understand her.

They drove on in silence, past the service area where Frances had spoken to the woman in the Renault. It seemed like weeks ago, instead of days. The police had told them, the night before, about the Cortina being stolen from the parking area. Luke had bought sandwiches in the shop; the wrapping was still in the car. Frances never learned that he had overheard her conversation with the stranger.

Frances hoped that Luke would get away. That was awful of her, especially as she knew, now, about the man that he had injured, but he'd so hated being shut up. Put him in a wild, open area, with some worthwhile work to do, and he'd turn out all right. Yet he'd hit her, and he'd threatened Carol with that knife. But then, she'd been seriously planning to kill Carol.

'The insurance will pay up, of course,' she said. 'For your clothes, and the car. Edward will help you sort it out. It's lucky he's at home.'

'Don't abandon me, Frances,' Carol implored her, as they drove into Lower Ferringham. 'In times of trouble, a person needs their friends.'

'You've got your husband,' Frances reminded her. 'I'm going to be very busy now.'

'Doing what?'

What would happen next, Frances was wondering: would Carol's car be found, and so lead the police to Luke? Could he somehow manage to get out of the country? Would he know how to get hold of false papers and a passport? He'd have links to other criminals who might help him. There were so many questions left unanswered, including whether or not she had really meant to murder Carol.

'I'm going to write a novel,' Frances said. A mystery novel, it would be, and she would call it *On the Run*.

Margaret Yorke

Margaret Yorke was born in Surrey, but lived in Dublin until 1937 before moving back to England. During the war she served in the Women's Royal Naval Service as a driver. She lived briefly in Yorkshire and then the Midlands, and now lives in Buckinghamshire.

She worked in the libraries of two Oxford colleges – the first woman ever to work in Christ Church library. She was also a bookseller in London.

In 1982 she won the Swedish Academy of Detection Award for the best crime novel in translation. Her books are translated and published in sixteen countries, including the United States and the Czech Republic. She is a past chairman of the Crime Writers' Association, whose Golden Handcuffs award in recognition of her contribution to crime writing over many years she received in 1993.